It was all going according to plan. Laura had been chosen to entice Lord Blair Deveril because she looked so much like the young wife he had loved and tragically lost. Now Lord Deveril gazed at her through eyes blurred by brandy and commanded, "Come here, Celina."

Slowly she went to him, expecting that at any moment he'd realize she wasn't Celina. But instead he caught her hand and drew her closer. "I've been waiting for you, my love. Why have you been away so long?"

She raised her mouth instinctively to meet his, and their lips came together. She could taste cognac, fiery and intoxicating, and she found herself wanting his kiss, needing it. Her arms moved about him, as her lips softened and parted.

He drew his head back, his eyes dark in the candlelight. "Fie on you, madam, would you have me take you here, in the library?" he said softly smiling.

"Yes," she said, yielding to a passion that was not part of any plan but that rose within her with the force of fate. . . .

Shades of the Past

Sandra Heath

A SIGNET BOOK

SIGNET
Published by the Penguin Group
Penguin Books USA Inc., 375 Hudson Street,
New York, New York 10014, U.S.A.
Penguin Books Ltd, 27 Wrights Lane,
London W8 5TZ, England
Penguin Books Australia Ltd, Ringwood,
Victoria, Australia
Penguin Books Canada Ltd, 10 Alcorn Avenue,
Toronto, Ontario, Canada M4V 3B2
Penguin Books (N.Z.) Ltd, 182–190 Wairau Road,
Auckland 10, New Zealand

Penguin Books Ltd, Registered Offices:
Harmondsworth, Middlesex, England

First published by Signet, an imprint of Dutton Signet,
a division of Penguin Books USA Inc.

First Printing, June, 1996
10 9 8 7 6 5 4 3 2 1

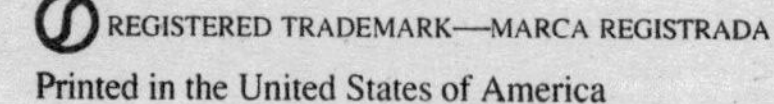

Printed in the United States of America

One

Being two-timed in love is never a pleasant experience, and it hurt a lot when twenty-eight-year-old actress Laura Reynolds learned that was what Kyle McKenna was doing to her.

Supposedly her leading man in life as well as in the TV soap in which they both played minor roles, Kyle wasn't the faithful partner he seemed, as she discovered when she came home early one night and caught him in their bed with someone else. It was a moment that changed her life. Suddenly she had to get as far away from New York as possible, and since she'd always been interested in the British stage, she decided to spend some time in England. She'd just had money left to her by her only aunt, so she simply packed up and left.

In London she shared a Berkeley Square apartment with three other actresses, one of whom, Jenny Fitzgerald, became her close friend. They went to auditions together, and managed to get taken on at the Hannover theater, which had occupied its corner site since 1816, the year after Waterloo.

The theater was in dire need of restoration. Funds were necessary, and to raise them it was decided to restage the original first night. The project was set to be a gala occasion attended by royalty, and for Laura and Jenny, members of the chorus, it was very exciting indeed.

The great night arrived, and everyone was in period costumes copied exactly from the originals. Laura didn't know it, but before the evening was over, she'd have embarked upon a much more incredible adventure in time than the mere recreation of an old theater production.

Waiting for the curtain to rise, she had no inkling of what was to come. She fiddled with her costume, a thigh-length muslin gown, and then adjusted the tall plume fixed in her long chestnut hair. Her sea-green eyes were apprehensive, because she was as prone to stage fright now as she had been on her very first night ever. It never got any better.

Jenny was at her side. Dark-eyed and striking, she was engaged to a talented young chef named Alun Meredith, who was in charge of the kitchens at her parents' fashionable Cotswold hotel, where she and Laura were to go on vacation when the gala was over.

Laura still sensed nothing as her step through time commenced. Outside the theater the past began to merge with the present, and as the modern crowds thronged the wet January night to see the royal limousine arrive, a beautiful May evening in 1816 became thinly visible! Beyond the clamor of now, the quieter tones of yesterday could be heard—the clatter of hooves upon cobbles, the calls of a flower girl on the corner, and the soft flick of a coachman's whip as he tooled a gleaming private carriage toward the brand-new Hannover.

The two gentlemen inside, Steven Woodville and Sir Miles Lowestoft, would be late, but they had a box and so weren't concerned, especially Steven, who'd had to be dragged from a gaming hell. He was thirty-two years old, blond, not particularly good looking, and cursed with frail health since having been invalided out of Wellington's Peninsular army. His black evening coat and white silk breeches were plain but well cut, and there was a simple gold pin on his neckcloth knot. A top hat shaded his tired eyes from the setting sun, and he slouched on his seat in a most inelegant manner. His best attribute was an amiable nature, which unfortunately made him easy prey to Sir Miles Lowestoft, whose good qualities were nonexistent.

But Steven had many problems, not the least of which was a clandestine liaison, begun at Weymouth last summer with Marianna Deveril, the seventeen-year-old heiress sister of a close friend. Marianna had always been intended for the future Earl of Sivintree, but it was Steven to whom she'd secretly given her heart—and a great deal more! Soon it would be her eighteenth birthday, and a ball was to be held at Deveril Park, her home in the Cotswolds. Steven had accepted an invitation to stay on as a house guest afterward, even though he knew it was tempting providence, and that if her brother and guardian, Sir Blair Deveril, ever found out, pistols at dawn would almost certainly result.

Miles Lowestoft was the last person Steven should have confided in, but he had, and was about to reap the consequences. Miles was a sly fox of a man, with amber eyes and sandy hair that gave him a vulpine appearance to match his character. Like Steven, he wore formal black, with an abundance of lace at his throat and cuffs, and there was a quizzing glass dangling elegantly from a hand where a very distinctive black unicorn signet ring shone in the evening sunlight.

Steven's lack of enthusiasm for the theater bubbled over. "I resent being hauled away from cards just to go to a first night," he grumbled.

"I could understand if you were on a winning streak, but you haven't won a single hand all day."

"I *abhor* the theater."

"My dear fellow, I'm not taking you to see the production, I'm taking you to view a particularly exquisite redheaded figurante."

Steven was irritated. "A chorus actress? You've forced me to come with you in order to watch some talentless wench with too much bosom?"

"This one is far from talentless."

"I wonder if that's what your wife would say?" Steven mused.

"Saint Estelle the Martyr would pray forgiveness for a

week if she even clapped eyes upon an actress," Miles replied acidly. He abhorred the devout, slightly unbalanced heiress he'd married and then banished to his Scottish estate. He'd married her for her money, but on the recent death of her father he'd found out he couldn't lay hands upon as much as he hoped. A large sum was mysteriously missing, and no one knew where it was.

The carriage halted at the Hannover, and as the two men alighted, neither noticed another carriage drawing up along the street behind them. The woman inside was swathed in black mourning gauze, and a veil concealed her from any casual glance, but the black unicorn ring on her finger identified her as Miles's unloved wife, Estelle, who was supposed to be north of the border.

Her tortured gaze scoured the theater facade. Who was her rival this time? A cheap little actress? A sinful fallen creature whose favors could be purchased for a few coins? Jealous tears shimmered in the shaded eyes.

In the theater, the box keeper conducted Steven and Miles to their box directly above the stage. The sound of laughter filled the crowded auditorium as the audience enjoyed the antics of the clowns cavorting on the stage.

Steven groaned inwardly. Oh, no, not clowns! His cup overflowed. He leaned back in his seat and gazed around. The smell of fresh paint, barely dry plaster, and new wood was intensified by the heat from the patent luster lamps.

Miles was looking around too, and noted a stout, sour-faced gentleman in a box opposite. He nudged Steven. "I see the Earl of Sivintree honors the premises with his presence," he murmured.

Dismayed, Steven looked at the other box. Lord Sivintree was Marianna's prospective father-in-law. "God, how I loathe that man and his chinless wonder of a son," he breathed.

"Oh, I wouldn't describe Alex as a chinless wonder exactly, more a vacant space. All the Handworths are fools, with the exception of the old boy, of course. He's as nasty a piece of work as you'll find anywhere in the ranks of England's nobility, Miles replied."

The clowns finished and the chorus came on stage. There were several redheads, but one was particularly beautiful. Steven's gaze moved over her. She was slender-waisted, with a curvaceous figure, magnificent long legs, and bright chestnut curls that might have inspired Titian himself.

Miles glanced at him. "I see you've espied her," he murmured.

"Who is she?"

"Her name is Laura Reynolds, and I first noticed her at Drury Lane," Miles breathed softly, his gaze lingering on the figure on the stage.

"Well, I can see why you're interested," Steven conceded.

"Having her isn't my prime purpose," Miles replied.

Steven was surprised. "No?"

"What does the name Celina convey to you?" Miles asked, in an apparent change of subject.

Steven became very still, for the only Celina he knew of was Blair Deveril's late wife, whom he'd never met because the marriage had taken place while he was in Spain with the army, and she had died before he was discharged. "I take it you're referring to Blair's wife?" he asked after a moment.

"You may take my word for it that Laura Reynolds might be Celina reborn," Miles replied softly.

"What's this about, Miles?" Steven asked warily.

"I have a score to settle with Deveril, and you're going to help me settle it," Miles replied softly.

Steven was startled. "Because he caught you with that ace up your sleeve in Weymouth last year?"

"There was no ace!" Miles snapped.

Steven prudently fell silent.

Miles went on. "As it happens, Deveril's false accusation is only part of it; more important by far is the diamond necklace."

Steven looked blankly at him. "What diamond necklace?"

"The family heirloom my father wagered and lost to Deveril's father ten years ago."

"This is the first I've heard of it."

A nerve flickered by Miles's mouth as he went on. "On his deathbed, my father said Deveril cheated, and since then I've been determined to get the necklace back. I don't particularly care how I do it."

Steven wasn't sure what to say. He'd always wondered what was at the root of the ill feeling between Blair and Miles, and many possibilities had suggested themselves—including a quarrel over Celina—but never a dispute over diamonds.

Miles drew a long breath. "You and sweet Laura Reynolds are going to help me retrieve what's mine. I want the real necklace exchanged for a paste copy I've had made."

Steven suddenly felt noticeably cooler, even though the theater was hot. "And how, exactly, do you propose we do this?" he asked quietly, his voice barely audible above the noise of the show.

"Before I explain fully, let me point out that there's more to it than just the necklace. I want Deveril's heart broken. Laura Reynolds's resemblance to Celina is nothing short of miraculous, and she's going to cause him exquisite emotional pain."

His chilling malice made Steven draw back. "Look, Miles, leave me out of this. You and the actress proceed without me."

"You'll do as I wish, dear boy," Miles replied softly.

"*No!*" The single exclamation was uttered so loudly that people in nearby boxes craned their necks. Steven colored, and looked angrily at Miles. "No, I won't do it," he said more evenly.

"Then I'll call all your IOU's in at once," was the ruthless reply.

"Damn you," Steven whispered.

"Most would say I'm damned already, but that's beside the point. You're going to do what I want, Steven. It's very simple. In return for your IOU's, you're to take Laura Reynolds with you to Marianna Deveril's eighteenth birthday ball next week."

Steven was appalled. "Take an actress with me to a society ball? You must be mad!"

His voice had risen again, and Miles quieted him furiously. "Keep your voice down, I don't want the world to know my business!"

Steven whispered. "I can't simply *take* her! What am I supposed to say? That she's my long-lost sister? They'll really swallow *that*!"

"It's all arranged, dear boy. They expect her to be with you."

Steven blinked. "Expect?" he repeated.

"It's easy enough. You see, I know your aunt, Lady Tangwood, was going to be Marianna's chaperone for her first Season this summer. I also know Lady Tangwood's ill health has caused her to withdraw from this arrangement and retreat to her estate in Yorkshire. The explanatory letter she sent to Deveril Park before she left, er, fell in my hands."

Miles paused, then smiled again. "One of my many talents is an uncanny ability to copy handwriting. A replacement letter, complete with Lady Tangwood's seal, was duly delivered into Deveril's hands. Its contents were quite simple. Lady Tangwood apologized most profusely for letting them down, but recommended instead a certain Mrs. Reynolds, a widow who, although young and beautiful, is a model of decorum and is everything deemed desirable in a chaperone."

Steven was shaken. "You—you've already written all this?"

"I have, and Deveril has agreed to consider the proposition. He replied to Lady Tangwood that he wishes you to bring Mrs. Reynolds with you next week for her suitability to be assessed. This letter too was, er, intercepted."

Steven's resolve hardened. "I won't do as you ask."

A flinty light shone in Miles's eyes. "Very well, but be warned, I'll not only call in all your IOU's, but see Deveril is apprised of the goings on with his sister. Even supposing you survive the resultant duel, debtor's prison isn't the most salubrious of surroundings, or so I'm told, and with your health as spent as it is at the moment, I fear you'll soon succumb to some pernicious ague or other. Be sensible, man; I'm presenting you with the means of retrieving your IOU's. Remember now, I hold all the trumps."

Steven ran his fingers agitatedly through his hair. "I wish to God I'd never told you anything about Marianna," he breathed.

"I'm sure you do, but it's a little late now."

Steven felt utterly sick. Miles did indeed hold the trumps. He had both the IOU's and the power to tell Blair and the rest of society what had gone on with Marianna. One thing was certain, call Miles's bluff on this, and Steven Woodville's obituary would soon appear in *The Times*, whether through failing health finally destroyed in prison, or a dawn meeting with Blair!

He strove to extricate himself. "You're mad if you imagine a minor actress can ape the lady sufficiently to be Marianna Deveril's chaperone!"

"Laura Reynolds is no ordinary actress; she's really very good, not a whore, like so many of her kind. She comes from a surprisingly well-bred background of Norfolk gentry, and can conduct herself in society. Her family have debts, and she came to London to be Lady Dalrymple's companion, but discovered more could be earned treading the boards." Miles gave a cool smile. "I've made it my business to purchase Reynolds's debts, as well as the family home in Norwich, so if Laura wishes to protect them, she must do as I ask. Their debts will then be wiped out, and their home safe."

Steven was bitter. "I wish I'd never have fallen in with you!"

"But you did, and now you're in my power, so I suggest you bow to my wishes."

Visions of prison and Marianna's ruin flashed before Steven's eyes. "You leave me no choice," he said, hating himself, and Miles.

Miles gave a coldly triumphant smile that reached through the centuries to touch the future Laura Reynolds as she waited nervously in the wings for the gala evening to commence.

Two

Feeling the smile's malevolence, Laura shivered and went to the peephole just as the opening bars of the national anthem sounded the royal arrival.

She saw the box above the stage directly opposite her, and the two gentlemen seated in it wearing clothes that were fashionable during the Regency. One of them was smiling directly at her, almost as if he knew she was there.

Something about him made her shiver again, and she drew hastily back. Then something struck her. "That's odd . . . "

Jenny was still beside her. "What is?" she asked.

"There are two men dressed in Regency clothes in the stage box opposite, but I thought the box wasn't to be used because it was unsafe."

"That's right."

"Then how come they're there?"

Jenny laughed. "Maybe they're theater ghosts!"

Laura looked through the peephole again. "They're very solid ghosts. They must be part of the company; why else would they be dressed up like that?"

Jenny put her eye to the peephole, but the box was empty, and she straightened. "You're definitely seeing things."

Laura stared at her. "But—"

"Look, I may be Irish, but I don't see the little people. There's no one there, Laura."

Unable to believe her, Laura looked again. This time she couldn't see anyone either.

"I—I don't understand it. I *definitely* saw two men, and what's more, one of them could see me."

"Through that little hole? Oh, come on!"

"Well, that's how it felt." Laura gave a sheepish grin.

Jenny grinned too, then gave a nervous laugh. "Oh, God, why's it taking so long to start? HRH must have placed her haute couture butt on the royal chair by now!" She pulled a rueful face. "The nerves never get better, do they? I'll be glad to leave all this and settle down to running the hotel when Mum and Dad retire and Alun and I take over."

"Tell me, is it true what they say about chefs? Big hat, big everything else?" Laura inquired a little wickedly.

Jenny raised an artful eyebrow. "Wouldn't *you* like to know?"

"I'm looking forward to our vacation," Laura said then, thinking of the picturesque country house hotel she'd as yet only seen in photographs.

"All that free Michelin rosette food," Jenny observed dryly.

"Why else do you think I'm coming along?"

"And here's me thinking you liked me for myself!"

"You? Hell no, I've just been putting up with you in order to get to the gourmet trough," Laura replied with a wicked grin.

Jenny laughed, and then looked at her. "Are you *sure* you don't want to come to the Dorchester party tonight? Everyone else will be there."

"I'm not in the mood. I'd prefer a hot drink and a good book."

"How incredibly boring!" Jenny declared, and then her breath caught as there was a sudden hush in the auditorium. She looked around at the rest of the waiting chorus. "That's the pregnant silence. Get ready girls!"

They all formed a line, then the orchestra began to play, and at their cue they danced onto the stage to ecstatic opening applause. But as Laura went through her routine, she couldn't help glancing frequently toward the empty box. She had the oddest feeling the two mysterious gentlemen were still there.

Before the night was over, she was destined to see them again, and the experience would be frighteningly real.

It happened when everyone had gone on to the celebratory party, and the theater was quiet. Laura had taken her time about changing, and thought she was alone in the building except for the stage doorman.

She wore a simple turquoise woolen dress, her hair was tied back, and her face was shiny from removing her make-up. She was just getting her coat when she heard voices from the nearby green room.

Puzzled, she looked out into the passage, where a single unshaded ceiling lamp lit the props piled against one wall. What appeared to be candlelight shone from the green room's open doorway, and there was laughter and chatter, for all the world as if a post-performance party were in progress. But everyone had gone on to the Dorchester!

She slipped along to see what was happening. The room was lit by wall candles she'd never noticed before, and there were sofas and chairs covered with rich crimson velvet. Actors and actresses in theatrical costume stood around talking, but there was something odd about them—their makeup seemed more exaggerated than it should be, and their clothes were more quaint.

She suddenly realized she didn't know anyone. There wasn't a single familiar face. Except perhaps . . . Suddenly she found herself staring at the two men who'd been in the stage box.

Miles sensed her arrival, and turned. "Ah, there you are, Laura, my dear."

Strange sensations began to pass through her, then something really weird happened. It was as if she'd become two women, her feisty modern self who was curious about the odd goings-on around her, and a much more constrained Laura from the past, who'd fallen into the grip of this unpleasant man.

Knowledge poured through her, and in an instant she knew who Miles was, and all about his plot against Sir Blair Deveril. A maelstrom of conflicting feelings swirled inside her for a few seconds, before her modern self faded almost completely and she became mainly the Laura from the past, bound to do Sir Miles Lowestoft's bidding if she wished to protect her parents and siblings. But modern Laura lingered deep inside, like a secret observer.

Miles beckoned, and she obeyed, but as she stepped over the threshold, she felt a long skirt brushing around her ankles. A *long* skirt? She glanced down, and saw her modern turquoise dress had become a primrose lawn gown, high-waisted, short-sleeved, and clinging, as fashions were during the Regency. Then she realized her hair felt different too; it was swept up into a complicated Grecian knot on top of her head, with a frame of little curls around her face.

She walked to Miles, and as their hands touched an unpleasant sensation tingled through her, like faint contact with distant lightning. Instinctively she snatched her hand away.

Miles chided her coolly. "There's no need to be uncivil, my dear; remember how easy it would be for me to destroy all you hold precious."

"How could I forget?" Well, at least her voice was the same, if robbed of its New York accent.

"Then be advised to bear it in mind. Now, I wish you to meet Steven Woodville, who is to escort you to Deveril Park." He drew her hand over his arm and led her toward his companion.

Steven inclined his head to her, and she saw in his eyes that he was being pressured as much as she was.

Miles ushered her forward a little more. "What d'you think, Steven? Will she pass muster?"

Steven's glance swept unwillingly over her. "Well, since

I have no idea what Celina Deveril looked like, I'm not really in any position to judge," he muttered.

"Don't be so tetchy, dear boy; all I'm asking is what you think of her." Miles didn't wait for a response, but went on. "I chose the gown, of course. I thought it epitomized the character she's to adopt. The rest of her new clothes are in the same vein, a collection of elegant, tasteful garments that are just a year or so out of date, just as one would expect of a widow now out of mourning and obliged to support herself after settling her husband's debts." Miles smiled, and then put a hand to her chin, stroking her skin with his thumb. "Do what's necessary to regain the necklace for me, my dear, and I promise your family will be safe; but remember, I want Deveril's spirit crushed in the process. I want him to love you, then lose you. He must suffer!"

She tried to pull away, but his grip tightened on her chin.

"Steal his heart, my dear," he said again, "but steel yours against him."

He pinched her chin so tears sprang to her eyes, then returned his attention to Steven. "It's all arranged. She's been well coached, she has the fake necklace, and a convincing wardrobe. As soon as the diamonds are in my hands, I'll honor my side of this, er, agreement with you both."

Laura looked quickly at him. "What if it goes wrong and, through no fault of mine, Sir Blair doesn't engage me as his sister's chaperone?"

"Just see Deveril *does* appoint you, my dear. Now you may go."

She turned relievedly, but he suddenly seized her wrist in a grip like a vise. "Don't let me down, Miss Reynolds," he hissed. "The breaking of Deveril's heart is as important to me as regaining the necklace, and I expect you to use every feminine wile. If it means gracing his bed, you'll do it. Is that clear?"

"Yes," she whispered.

He released her, and she gathered her skirts to hurry

from the room. As she recrossed the threshold, everything went suddenly quiet. She was alone, and in her modern clothes again.

Her heart pounded as she turned to stare at the empty room. How could she have imagined something so clearly, even down to the clammy touch of Miles's hand?

"Still 'ere, miss?" called a voice along the passage.

She whirled around. It was Fred Bates, the stage doorman, a tough former cab driver who guarded his domain like a bulldog. He gave a toothy grin. "Gawd luv us, miss, you're all of a flap! Did I frighten you?"

"I—I guess you did. I thought I heard someone in the green room and came to see."

"They've all gone long since. Maybe it was one of the theater ghosts," he said seriously, coming over to her. "The 'Annover's got two, you know, a gray lady and a one-eyed cat."

She managed a smile. "I'll be sure to keep a look-out."

"They're supposed to be lucky, so you do that, miss."

She smiled again. "Well, I guess I'll go home now. Good night, Fred."

"Good night, miss."

She suddenly felt the need to quit the theater as quickly as possible. A gray lady and a one-eyed cat? She'd just seen a few more theater ghosts than *that*!

She hurried back to the dressing room, snatched her coat and other things, then left, hardly noticing the January wind and rain as she stood on the sidewalk to call a cab. Nor did she notice the lingering intrusion of the past in the form of Lady Lowestoft's carriage.

Estelle saw her, though. Not the Laura of the future, but Regency Laura, her hood raised as she took leave of Miles and Steven at the theater entrance. It amused Miles to delay her by drawing her fingers to his lips in false gallantry, but to Estelle it seemed the gesture of a man in love.

Lord Sivintree's carriage drove past, and the earl glanced out, observing the scene by the theater door, but he paid scant attention. The moment Miles released her hand, Laura seized her chance to get away. She hurried across to the line of hackney coaches drawn up in the center of the cobbled street.

Estelle lifted her veil for a moment. There was anguish in her too-bright hazel eyes, and her hand shook as she pressed her unicorn ring to her trembling lips. Then she lowered the veil again and ordered her coachman to follow the hackney coach, but the hired vehicle had already disappeared in the crush of traffic at the end of the Haymarket.

Tendrils of the past still reached out beguilingly to modern Laura as she got out of the cab in Berkeley Square, but she was determined to explain her experience away rationally. The whole company had been working very hard getting ready for tonight's gala, and she'd just overdone it a little. Ghosts didn't exist, nor time travel, but an overactive imagination certainly did!

"You need that vacation in the Cotswolds, Laura, my girl," she muttered as she let herself into the apartment.

The exquisitely furnished Art Deco rooms were deserted; Jenny wouldn't get back until dawn, and the two other girls were skiing in Gstaad.

Well, she wasn't going to think about strange goings-on anymore. Taking a deep, determined breath, she put the whole business from her mind, undressed, and took a shower. Luxuriating in the splash of warm water over her body, she closed her eyes and raised her face to the spray, remembering times when she and Kyle had showered together. How handsome he'd been, with his golden curls and vivid blue eyes. And that smile . . .

She could almost feel him with her now, his strong body pressed to hers, his knowing fingers teasing her nipples with caresses that filled her with desire. She remembered how she'd soaped her hands and run them all over him. *All* over him! Erotic thoughts drifted deliciously into her head as she slid her soapy hands sensuously over her wet skin.

She trembled as the seductive memories became so real she could almost feel his erection, as hard as rock, pressing urgently between her legs.

With a sigh, she turned the shower to a lower temperature. "Cool down, Laura, it's only cocoa for you tonight," she murmured.

She finished the shower and dried herself, wishing she didn't yearn for so many aspects of her affair with Kyle. It was the simple things, like waking up beside him in the morning, or cuddling up to watch a movie on TV. Yes, there *had* been good times, but Kyle McKenna was a shallow cheat. True love—deep, emotional, and complete—was something he'd never encountered, and wasn't interested in. She, on the other hand, yearned for such a love, and thought she'd found it with him. She *would* find it one day, though, and she wouldn't let it slip through her fingers.

She went to make herself the promised cup of cocoa, and was about to go to bed when she noticed the telephone answer machine blinking. It was a message for Jenny from Alun. The lilting Welsh voice was rushed.

"Jen, sweetheart, it's Alun. I have to nip over to Dijon for a week or so—business, I'm afraid—so unless you can get down here to the hotel earlier than planned, we won't see each other until I get back. Try, there's a love. I know you won't get this message until after your big night at the Hannover, so I'll just say I hope it all went magnificently. See you very soon, I hope. Oh, and tell Laura I've created a mocca dessert just for her, because I know what a sweet tooth she has. I'm going to call it Meringues Laura. Anyway, bye, sweetheart, sleep tight."

Laura smiled, and turned to go to her bedroom, but then something made her glance toward the mirror over the drawing room mantelpiece. What she saw reflected in it wasn't the dazzling Art Deco room she stood in, but a candlelit Georgian bedroom with a bed that was sumptuously hung with Chinese rose silk and gold-fringed crimson velvet.

She stared, then crossed to the mirror. The alien room remained, as she slowly put her cup of cocoa on the mantelshelf, next to a Lalique figurine. At any moment she expected to find the reflection as it should be, but even though she blinked deliberately, she still saw the Georgian bedroom.

Instinct told her she was seeing the house as it had been in 1816. There were half-packed trunks standing against one of the walls, and the dressing table was almost bare. Whoever lived in the house was clearly about to leave. Had they sold up? Where were they going? Come to that, who the heck were they? This wasn't like the green room; instead of being part of things she was just an observer. What was the quotation? *For now we see through a glass, darkly; but then face to face . . .*

Face to face. Her lips parted as she suddenly realized a man was asleep on the bed. He was dark-haired and breathtakingly handsome, and she guessed he was about thirty-four or five years old. He was also naked, his body pale, supple, strong, and perfect in the light from the candle. There were soft hairs on his chest, and in a thin line down his flat abdomen to his groin, where they thickened into a forest around the swelling of his dormant masculinity, which lay long, vulnerable, and soft as velvet against the top of his thigh.

Mesmerized by powerful sensations of sexual attraction, she gazed into the mirror. A little more knowledge came to her, and she knew that this was Sir Blair Deveril, the man her Regency counterpart was to deceive and seduce, and she had to concede that far from being an ordeal, the thought of making love with him was enticing beyond belief.

Feeling a little like a voyeur, she looked at his face again. It was rugged, but at the same time almost beautiful. His lashes were long and dark, his nose straight and his lips finely formed. His hair was ruffled and thick, and worn just a little longer than she knew was really the fashion in Regency times. It was hair through which she longed to run her fingers . . .

There was a movement in the reflected doorway, and she looked toward it. Then her breath caught as she saw . . . Herself! At least, not herself exactly, but her Regency counterpart, and what was more, that Regency counterpart could see her looking in the mirror!

But then the nineteenth-century Laura looked toward the bed, and the sleeping man. She slipped out of her gown and went to lie down with him, leaning over to caress his skin and then put her lips to his thigh. He didn't stir, and her fingers moved gently and caressingly between his legs.

An erotic craving shivered through modern Laura as she watched. She held her breath as her other self grew more bold, moving her lips up his thigh toward his slumbering virility, so soft and inviting. She kissed it, running her lips and tongue along its length and then taking the end into her mouth.

He stirred then, his hands moving to lovingly stroke her hair as she besieged his manhood. There was nothing soft and slumbering about him now, he was hard and needful, steel encased in warm velvet. His body arched with pleasure as she took him to the very edge of ecstasy. Then he suddenly rolled her on to her back and straddled her, pinning her arms back and smiling down into her eyes as he penetrated her.

Watching from the loneliness of the future, Laura had to close her eyes because she was trembling so much. She felt as if hers was the body that lay so eagerly beneath him on that long-gone bed. She wished it were her, for it would be good to be possessed by Sir Blair Deveril . . .

She opened her eyes again, but to her dismay the images in the mirror had disappeared. There was only the Art Deco room, and her own reflection.

What was going on? Why was she seeing these things, feeling these things . . . ? A dreadful possibility struck her. Was it the onset of a breakdown? She *had* been under a strain since the breakup with Kyle, but was it enough to cause something like this?

Leaving the cocoa untouched on the mantelshelf, she went to the window and looked out at the rain-drenched January night. Berkeley Square was busy, a garish modern scene of wet traffic, city noise, and streetlights. She found herself wishing she and Jenny were already in the Cotswolds, as far away as possible from the pressures of London.

It was then she remembered something that made her lips part on a startled gasp. It had slipped her mind until now because Jenny always referred to her parents' hotel as simply "the hotel," but out of the blue the real name came winging back. The Deveril House Hotel!

Three

Laura decided not to say anything to Jenny. It was all so wild and far-fetched, she felt a little like someone who'd seen a UFO—deciding it was wise to keep quiet than be thought crazy. She'd had a close encounter of the weird kind, and chose to keep it to herself.

She was curious about it all, though. Was it entirely the product of her imagination, or did some of it have a basis in truth? Did any of the people actually exist? The fact that the hotel bore the name Deveril suggested the latter might be the case. Unless, of course, it was her subconscious. At the back of her mind she had known the name of the hotel, and her brain had done the rest. It was tenuous reasoning, but the best she could come up with to explain away the apparently inexplicable.

Jenny didn't prove any help concerning the origins of the hotel's name, or indeed of its general history. It seemed the Fitzgeralds had bought the house from a reclusive rock star, who in turn had bought it from an equally reclusive spinster. Beyond that, Jenny knew nothing. She'd spent little time there because of her stage career, and the only piece of interesting information she could come up with was that the nearest village was called Great Deveril. She thought her parents might know more, and when in response to Alun's message she set off a day or so ahead of Laura, who had auditions to attend, she promised to find out all she could.

That was how things stood the morning Laura drove out of London for the Cotswolds. It felt good to be setting out on vacation. Her auditions had gone reasonably well, but she wasn't unduly concerned because financially she was well provided for. There hadn't been any more close encounters, and she was beginning to relax about the ones she'd had, regarding them as a fleeting blip on her otherwise clear screen.

In spite of the cold, overcast weather, she intended to do a little sightseeing on the way, and left the freeway at Reading to use back roads to Cirencester, a market town about five miles from the hotel.

She drove into the square at about two in the afternoon, and parked outside a central hotel called the King's Head. It was market day, and the street was thronged with people and canvas-topped stalls. Everyone was hunched against the biting cold, so she turned her coat collar up before getting out of the warm car.

The moment she stepped onto the sidewalk, she experienced another close encounter. The sun seemed to suddenly come out, almost as if someone had switched on a giant electric light, and the temperature rose perceptibly, changing from winter cold to balmy summer warmth in the space of little more than a heartbeat. The clamor of the modern market and traffic was silenced to the more muted sounds of the past.

She froze in dismay. Not again! Please, not again! But as she looked nervously around her, she saw the Cirencester of 1816, where the King's Head was a posting house. She was part of events again, and wore a blue and white floral gown made of thin cotton, and a little blue velvet spencer. Her hair was piled up beneath a wide-brimmed blue hat, with several long ringlets falling to her left shoulder.

She and Steven Woodville had just alighted from his carriage, and as he instructed the coachman, she felt modern Laura fading swiftly away into the background. Steven was about to reserve her a room at the inn, for although he was to be a house guest at Deveril Park, she was merely expected to attend the ball, to which they'd drive that evening.

He wore a braided brown coat and cream trousers, and his top hat was tipped back on his head. He looked disheveled and out of sorts, and the closer they came to Deveril Park, the worse he felt. He'd been looking forward to his reunion with Marianna, but his unwilling involvement with Miles's plot had spoiled everything. He didn't want to do anything that might harm Marianna's love for him, and this present deceit could do just that.

Another private carriage approached from the London direction, and it caught Laura's attention because she was sure it had been at the Oxford inn where she and Steven had halted earlier. In fact, the more she thought about it, the more convinced she was that it had also been at the Tyburn turnpike when they'd left London. She watched it pass. Its blinds were down, but she caught a brief glimpse of a woman's hand and a signet ring.

Steven returned, but then she remembered she'd left her parasol on the carriage seat, and turned to retrieve it. The summer sunshine vanished, and the cold January afternoon and modern market returned. She stood there dazed. One moment she'd been in 1816, the next she was in her own time again. It was disorientating, and a little frightening too. Suddenly she lost all interest in sightseeing, and got back into her car to drive quickly out of the town.

Jenny had given her written directions to the hotel, and by using a road map as well, Laura soon found the route to Great Deveril village. But the lanes were winding, and after a while one pretty stone village looked very much like another. It wasn't long before Jenny's careful instructions lost all meaning because there wasn't a crossroad where Laura thought one should be, just a fork. Then when she was faced with a hump-backed bridge she'd been over ten minutes earlier, she realized she was going around in circles.

Uttering a very unladylike four-letter word, she stopped the car a few yards before the bridge, by a gate into a ploughed field. The short winter afternoon was beginning to close in, and the beautiful scenery had started to turn a little dark and mysterious. The road was in one of the many tree-filled valleys that snaked through the hills, and the bridge spanned a wide stream.

About half a mile away behind trees on top of a hill she could just make out the roofs of a village, and got out of the car to consult the map. Ash keys rattled in a tree overhanging the road, and she could hear pheasants calling raucously in the distance. The stream chattered noisily beneath the bridge, and there was such a chill in the air that she shivered.

The nearest buildings belonged to what appeared to be a large farm on the hillside below the village. It was almost hidden by a canopy of evergreens, and the gabled farmhouse was built of the glowing golden stone for which the area was so famous, but unless she trudged through muddy fields, it seemed inaccessible.

Leaving the safety of her car was out of the question, so with a sigh she looked around again. There was an isolated church on a crest about two miles away in the other direction. Surely that was a landmark of sorts? She studied the map again, and after a moment found what seemed to be the same church. If it was, the village above the farm should be Great Deveril, and the farm not a farm at all, but the hotel!

She pored over the map, and saw there should be a turning beyond the bridge. Let's take a look, she thought, then hesitated as she noticed that according to the map there was a tunnel further along the valley, running through the hill beneath the farm and village into the next valley.

What sort of tunnel could it be? A double set of blue dotted lines approached the tunnel, and the legend indicated such lines to mean a disused canal. Was the tunnel for a canal? Her interest aroused, she leaned on the gate to see if anything was visible from where she stood. In the blinking of an eye she was bathed in warm sunshine again. January became May, present became past.

It was such a shock she drew hastily back, and the moment she did so there was just the dreariness of January again. Her heartbeats quickened excitedly. Another close encounter so soon? Slowly she leaned forward, and again found herself gazing at a sunny day in May. She glanced down at her clothes. They hadn't changed, and she knew this brush with the past would be like the one with the mirror—something she'd observe without participating.

She looked at the view again. The passing centuries had seen a great change in the scenery. In 1816 the fields were a gracious park, and the hilltop village was more clearly visible because its screen of trees had yet to grow. Most of the houses and cottages were much smaller than in years to come, when they'd be gradually extended and improved, but there was one glaring exception to the rule. The building she thought was the hotel had somehow become a great country house surrounded by formal gardens, and was at least two-thirds larger than its modern substitute.

She heard dogs barking, and glanced toward the sound. About a hundred yards away she saw a man in Regency clothes riding toward her, with three springer spaniels bounding at his horse's heels. It was Sir Blair Deveril, and he'd just crossed the stream by another stone bridge that was to have vanished by modern times.

Embarrassed color rushed into Laura's cheeks as she remembered the last time she'd seen him. But he was far from naked now, for he wore a pine green coat and pale gray breeches, and a top hat which he removed as he reined in his large bay mount about ten yards away from her.

The spaniels gave no sign of seeing her, and he certainly didn't seem to know she was there as he turned in the saddle to gaze toward the house. Then he removed a glove to glance at his wedding ring. Distress twisted his face, and he swiftly drew the glove on again, as if to blot out the pain of loss. Laura could tell how much grief he still endured two long years after losing his beloved Celina.

He gathered the reins again, turned his horse toward the stream, and rode down to where the water widened into a secluded pool sheltered by elderberry bushes that were heavy with blossom. The spaniels preceded him to the shady grass, and lay down so automatically she knew he went there frequently. She could only just see him as he dismounted and stood on the bank for a moment before beginning to undress to take a swim.

A shiver of guilty anticipation passed through Laura. He was going to make a voyeur of her a second time, and she was going to watch as brazenly as she had before, because if ever a man looked good naked, that man was Sir Blair Deveril.

She saw him through a framework of summer leaves, his pale skin dappled with moving shadows that seemed almost to caress him. The horse nudged him, and he smiled, turning to put his arms briefly about its glossy neck. There was something deliciously erotic about his nakedness against the animal, especially as she could see all of him now. She knew she shouldn't look, but she couldn't help herself. He was absolutely perfect, and his virility excited her. Yearning stirred through her veins, warming her skin and darkening her eyes. It would be perilously easy to surrender to this man, to submit to whatever sexual whim he pleased . . .

He turned toward the water and dove in, cutting into the water without a splash, and at the same moment an only too modern Gloucestershire voice shouted angrily behind her. " 'Ere! You got cloth ears or sommat?"

She straightened with a gasp, and immediately found herself in the cold January dusk again. The headlamps of a tractor shone across her car, which partially blocked the road, and the irate farmer had clearly been calling her for some time.

He tipped his hat back on his balding head, and gave her a long-suffering look. "I don't mean to get funny, miss, but if you don't shift your car, so 'elp me I'll shove it in the ditch!"

She glanced back over the gate, but there were just ploughed fields. "I—I'm so sorry, I just didn't hear you. I wonder if you can help me? I'm afraid I've gotten lost."

He realized she was American. "A winter tourist, eh? We don't get too many of them."

"Not exactly. I'm looking for the Deveril House Hotel."

He grinned and pointed past her toward the house on the hill.

She smiled too. "I thought it might be, but I wasn't sure. So that's Great Deveril beyond it?"

"Yes. I'm afraid it's all too easy to get lost in these lanes. I can still manage it myself late on a Saturday night!" he gave a throaty laugh.

He probably meant it, she thought. "How do I get there?"

"The best way's over the bridge, and then turn right a little way along. It's very narrow and there isn't a signpost, but it'll take you to the Great Deveril road. You'll come to a T-junction, turn right, and in a hundred yards you'll come to the hotel lodge. There's a great big sign and two darned huge yew trees that overhang the whole road, and this time on a January afternoon it's all lit up too, so you can't miss it."

She gave a smile of relief. "Thank you."

He touched his hat. "Now then, lessen you've got some more daydreaming to do, I really would like to get home this side of tomorrow."

"Yes, of course. I'm truly sorry for blocking the way like this."

He nodded, and she returned hurriedly to her car. As she drove over the bridge, she couldn't help glancing toward the hill and the building she now knew was the hotel. She almost expected it to have turned into a mansion again, but it hadn't.

Dusk was turning rapidly to darkness as she reached the T-junction and turned toward the yews overhanging the road. Just as she was about to negotiate the corner into the hotel drive, the car headlamps picked out a road sign a little further on. It said, *To Deveril Tunnel.*

She thought no more of it as she drove slowly down the steep rhododendron-lined drive. Suddenly the rhododendrons gave way to an avenue of clipped holly trees, and the grounds opened up before her. The floodlit hotel complex appeared, sheltered in the lee of the tall evergreens. Barns and other outbuildings had been converted into sports and leisure facilities, and only the stables still served their original purpose. It had a very exclusive air, and there were luxury cars in the parking lot.

A uniformed doorman came to take care of her car and luggage, and Jenny immediately hurried out to hug her. "You're here at last! Whatever happened to you?"

"Well, thanks to your rotten directions, I managed to get lost!"

"My rotten directions? Your rotten driving, more like," Jenny replied, linking her arm. "Come on inside and have some tea. You must need it after coming so far on a day like this. Tell me, how did the auditions go?"

They went up the steps into the hotel's spacious lobby. There was a log fire, and its warmth was welcome after the chill outside. The walls had carved oak paneling, and the stone floor was laid with a specially woven carpet patterned with a heraldic design. An archway to the left gave on to a beautifully furnished lounge, and from a door on the right came the discreet chink of cutlery as the dining room was made ready for the evening.

A wide staircase led up beside the reception area, and Laura couldn't help thinking it destroyed the symmetry of the hall, as if the architect hadn't been interested in internal balance. The receptionist, a perfectly manicured forty-year-old in a blue jacket and skirt, was spraying a bowl of snowdrops with a water atomizer.

Laura looked around approvingly. "I think I'll condescend to stay," she murmured.

Jenny smiled. "Well, we *might* have you," she replied.

"Is Alun coming back soon to prepare my Meringues Laura?"

"I hope so. It's not the same here without him."

"Ah, what it is to be in love," Laura murmured, inspecting the carving around the stone fireplace. It included the same heraldic design she'd noticed on the carpet, a shield divided into a crescent moon on one side and a sheaf of bulrushes on the other. "Whose is the coat-of-arms?" she asked curiously.

"Mm? Oh, I don't really know. Someone told my mother it was a play on the names of the fellow and his wife who used to live here, but I wouldn't know. The same device appears all through the house, and in a wild flight of fancy, Mother chose to have the carpets woven to match."

Laura glanced at the carpet. A play on names? A cool finger touched her as she gazed at the crescent moon. Diana was the moon goddess, and another of her names was Selene. Or Celina! As for the sheaf of bulrushes, she remembered from somewhere that the Scottish word *blair* meant open land or marsh, and marshes usually equalled reeds and rushes! She smiled at such flimsy reasoning

Jenny linked her arm again. "Come on, then, let's have a nice cup of tea. My parents are longing to meet you."

It was then that Laura saw the engraving of the very mansion she'd seen from the gate, right down to the last window and flowerbed. All that was missing was Sir Blair Deveril riding across the park . . .

Jenny saw what she was looking at. "Ah, yes. You asked about Deveril Park. Well, that's it. My father found the picture in a Cheltenham antique shop a few weeks ago. It seems we're in Deveril Park right now, what's left of it, anyway."

Laura nodded, for what other explanation was there? She'd just seen the original house from the gate, and the hotel entrance hall was far too big for a house of the present size, to say nothing of the staircase clearly being a recent addition. "What happened to all that?" She nodded at the engraving.

"My father was told it probably burned down, but no one's really sure. The records for the first half of the nineteenth century are missing, and somewhere around that time the house was reduced from a mansion to a farmhouse. I suppose some really in-depth research would bring the facts to light, but none has ever been done."

"There's no information at all?"

Jenny shook her head. "Quite a mystery. The lost mansion, eh?"

"Yes."

Jenny looked at the engraving. "You can't see from this, because it was done before the canal was started, but there's a tunnel through the hill beneath the house. It's three miles from end to end, and was once the longest tunnel in the world—it still is the third longest, and it's going to be restored soon. Anyway, for heaven's sake let's get to that tea!"

Laura glanced a final time at the engraving, especially at the stream and the elderberry-shaded pool. Right now she felt Sir Blair Deveril as tangibly as if he stood at her shoulder. It wasn't an unpleasant sensation.

Four

Jenny's father was a very large, unexpectedly reticent Dubliner with a taste for Sibelius, and her mother was a tiny, outgoing Glaswegian who adored jazz, but they went well together, and couldn't have made Laura feel more at home. Their private apartment was next to the kitchens at the rear of the hotel, and as Laura accepted a cup of tea, she noticed the coat-of-arms on the stone mantelshelf.

She smiled at Mrs. Fitzgerald. "I understand that device is to be found all over the house," she said, nodding toward the carving.

"Yes, my dear. It's quite fascinating, isn't it? Someone said it was a play on first names, but I wouldn't really know."

"Really? Who told you?" Laura was keen to find out all she could.

Jenny's father smiled. "It was probably Gulliver Harcourt, since he appears to be the font of all wisdom in Great Deveril."

"Who's Gulliver Harcourt?" Laura asked.

"The area's resident know-it-all," Jenny supplied a little acidly.

Her mother frowned. "Don't be unkind, dear."

"Well, he may be virtually confined to that electric wheelchair of his, but he manages to be everywhere like a rash."

Her father laughed. "I know what you mean," he agreed.

His wife was cross with them. "Poor old Gulliver's just lonely, that's all, and he goes out to meet people. But you're right about one thing, he *was* the one who told me about the names." She looked at the carving. "I've tried to think what names they could be, but I can't come up with anything, except perhaps something hippie like Moonbeam and Water Spirit." She laughed.

"Celina and Blair," Laura murmured.

Jenny's mother didn't hear. "It was also Gulliver who told me the house was once much bigger. We didn't believe him until we found the engraving. Goodness, is that the time?" She looked at her husband. "Come on, we'd better get on with things. Jenny, you look after Laura. You know which suite she's to have, so take her there in a while, then you can both enjoy a leisurely dinner. The entire menu's yours to choose from."

A little later, Jenny showed Laura to the beautiful second floor rooms set aside for her. They were situated at the end of a corridor, with views to the front of the building, and were clearly among the best the hotel had to offer. Furnished in soft shades of blue and cream, they were fitted with every accessory, and were a warm and luxurious haven from the dismal January evening, which in this part of the house could be heard blustering beyond the double-glazed windows.

The bedroom boasted an antique four-poster with slender pillars and powder-blue brocade hangings, but thankfully had a sumptuous modern mattress for any guest exhausted after trying the hotel's vast range of leisure facilities. The marble bathroom had gold fittings, and a whirlpool bath Laura would have killed for in the Berkeley Square apartment.

A painting above the marble mantelshelf in the suite's living room showed the local countryside in more clement weather. It was a watercolor of a woodland scene, with an unmistakably Cotswolds landscape in the background, and had been painted when bluebells carpeted the ground. Leafy shadows dappled a track that led toward the lightning-blasted oak tree that dominated the scene, and it had all been so skillfully painted she could almost smell the flowers. She didn't doubt it was a scene from somewhere in the immediate neighborhood, for she was sure that the church spire on the hill in the background was the landmark she'd spotted earlier from the gate.

The watercolor soon slipped from her mind as she took a quick dip in the whirlpool bath, and then put on a gray woolen dress to join Jenny for dinner. After a meal that more than lived up to expectations, the two friends enjoyed a glass of Cointreau in front of the fire in the Fitzgeralds' private apartment.

Jenny leaned her head back. "This is the life, eh?"

"It'll do," Laura replied with masterly understatement.

"Do you miss the States?" Jenny asked suddenly.

"Well, I would, except the States equals Kyle McKenna."

"I thought you were over him."

"Oh, I guess I am. I'm just still mad as hell that I was such a fool. He's a remake of Casanova, but it took me a year to realize it!"

"The one it matters to most is always the last to find out."

After a moment Laura grinned. "The sex was great, though. Until Kyle, I had no idea I was so carnal. I guess I should thank him for teaching me a thing or two in that direction."

Jenny gave a disbelieving snort. "Away with you, Laura Reynolds. You're a natural-born daughter of sinful passion, and *you* probably taught *him*!" She looked at Laura. "From the photo you showed me, he seems very good looking."

"Not as good looking as—" Laura broke off, for she'd almost compared Kyle with Blair Deveril!

Jenny raised a sly eyebrow. "Go on. Not as good looking as . . . ?"

"Oh, no one in particular."

"Out with it, Miss Reynolds. Right now you're not thinking of Kyle, are you?"

Whether it was the Cointreau or the atmosphere, Laura was suddenly tempted to tell Jenny about all the odd things that had occurred. She wanted to brave the flying saucer factor and confide, but the phone rang.

Jenny got up to answer it, and almost immediately her face went pale. "Oh, God! When? How bad is he?"

Laura sat up in concern.

After a moment Jenny replaced the receiver, and there were tears in her eyes as she turned. "It's Alun. He's been hurt in a car crash. That was the hospital in Dijon. I have to go to him."

"Yes, of course. I—I'll find your parents." Laura hurried out.

Jenny's father insisted on accompanying her, and rang the airport to book immediate flights, while her mother did what she could to comfort her distressed daughter. Laura felt a little in the way, and took the first chance to speak to Mrs. Fitzgerald. "Look, you don't want me hanging around now. I'll return to London first thing in the morning."

"Oh, no, my dear, I won't hear of it. You were invited here, and here you'll stay. Besides, I'll be more than glad of your company."

"If you're quite sure?"

"Absolutely certain, my dear, although, of course, you'll be on your own a great deal. If that bothers you, and you'd *rather* return . . . ?"

"I wouldn't mind staying," Laura said quickly, a little ashamed of herself because she knew Blair Deveril was uppermost in her thoughts.

"Then stay you shall."

So that was that. Within an hour of the phone call, Jenny and her father had set off for the airport, and Mrs. Fitzgerald had returned to her duties at the hotel.

When Laura went to bed that night, she curled up in the bed, listening to the January wind moaning outside. She could hear rain dashing against the glass. And music and voices. Music and voices? Slowly she sat up. There were definitely a large number of people somewhere close by, and an orchestra playing what sounded like a minuet. It could be a TV, except her suite was at the end of the corridor and she knew the one next to it was empty. So where were the sounds coming from?

Puzzled, she threw the bedclothes back and got up. When she looked out into the passage there was silence, but when she closed the door again, the voices and music returned. Maybe it was something from the ground floor. She crossed to the nearest window and leaned out into the rain, but the sounds faded into oblivion once more.

More puzzled than ever, she returned to the bedroom, where the sounds were loudest. It was like there was a reception or something going on in an adjacent room, but she knew there couldn't be. Gradually she realized the sounds came from beyond the tall arched double doors in the wall by her bed. The tall arched what? She stared, for there hadn't been doors there earlier, and besides, there was just fresh air the other side of that wall because it was at the end of the house!

A tingle of expectation began to seep into her veins. Was this another close encounter? Could she go through those doors into the past? Even if she couldn't physically go through them, could she perhaps take a peek? She hesitated, but then thought of Sir Blair Deveril. She wanted to speak to him, know him, touch him. Maybe he was beyond those doors right now. Open them and see, Laura Reynolds, she told herself. Go on, take a chance.

She walked toward the wall, and with each step the voices and music grew louder. Her hands trembled as she reached out, then her fingers closed firmly over the handles. The moment she touched them, the doors swung back to reveal a dazzling but crowded ballroom, and she wasn't merely an observer this time, but a participant. She was among the line of guests who'd just ascended a grand staircase to wait for their names to be announced by the master-of-ceremonies at Marianna Deveril's birthday ball.

Chandeliers glittered and wall candles flickered as guests in early nineteenth-century clothes assembled for the occasion. She glimpsed herself in a gilt-framed wall mirror, and gasped, for she was Regency Laura again, elegant and beautiful in a delightful magnolia silk ballgown. Her arms were sheathed in long white gloves, and a fan and sequinned reticule dangled from her wrist. Her hair was pinned up, with several ringlets falling from a plaited knot, and there was a wedding ring beneath her left glove, for she'd embarked upon her role as the widowed Mrs. Reynolds. Several people in the queue had already been taken aback by her resemblance to Celina Deveril, for quizzing glasses had been raised, and fans concealed whispering lips.

Steven spoke beside her, his voice only just audible above the noise of the ball. "Oh, God, how I wish I'd never clapped eyes on Miles Lowestoft, let alone confided in him! I despise myself for being at his mercy." He ran a nervous finger around his fancy neckcloth.

"We're *both* at his mercy," she reminded him.

"I know. Forgive me for indulging my self-pity."

She looked at him. "What if Sir Blair doesn't find me suitable?"

"He will."

"I wish I felt as confident," she murmured, glancing around. She noticed large ice blocks placed among ferns on special stands to take heat from the air as it melted, but the night was still so hot the ballroom windows had been thrown open to the starry May sky. She wondered how they got so much ice in summer, but then their names were announced.

"Mr. Steven Woodville, and Mrs. Reynolds."

Eyes turned toward them, and there was an immediate stir as people saw a woman who appeared to be the ghost of the late Lady Deveril.

Steven's hand moved over hers on his sleeve. "Let's to it, I suppose," he murmured, summoning a bland smile to his lips as they went down the shallow flight of steps into the ballroom.

For a moment she felt panicky, and glanced nervously back over her shoulder. What if she couldn't return to her own time? What if she were forced to stay here in the past forever? But as Steven escorted her further into the ballroom, she quelled the fear by reminding herself that so far she'd been able to return easily enough. There was no reason to think she couldn't this time as well, so she walked on with Steven, but with each step she became aware of attracting more and more interest. She could hear the rustle of whispers, and several times was sure she actually heard Celina's name.

The minuet was still in progress, and suddenly Steven's hand tightened over hers as he nodded toward the crowded floor. "There's Marianna. The brunette in the gold satin gown. She can't have heard us being announced, or she'd be looking this way. Her partner is Alex Handworth, the numskull she's to marry."

Laura glanced where he indicated. Marianna Deveril's darkly elfin beauty was set off perfectly by her golden gown. Her long-lashed brown eyes were large and expressive, and her short hair was cut *à la victime*. She seemed such a picture of innocence it was difficult to believe she'd so far fallen by the wayside last summer as to surrender her all to Steven.

Her future husband was an angular young man with straight brown hair, a receding chin, and a questing nose. He hardly glanced at her as they danced, and when the minuet came to an end, he immediately went to join a group of friends—not that Marianna appeared to mind, on the contrary in fact.

Steven whispered suddenly. "That's Blair going over to her now."

Laura saw again the devastatingly handsome man she'd spied upon so reprehensibly. Seeing him with others made her realize he was taller than she thought, and as he smiled at his sister, she was aware of the air of melancholy and danger that surrounded him. He made Byronic heroes spring to mind, and—if such a thing were possible—he improved at third glance!

Regency Laura, knowledgeable in such things, assessed his clothes. His superb black velvet evening coat had to be the work of one of Bond Street's finest tailors, and the elegance of his neckcloth must have taken his valet an age to achieve. His grace of manner would have set him apart even at London's Carlton House or the Royal Pavilion, Brighton, and there wasn't a man present who came even close to him for looks or clothes. Yet as he raised his sister's hand to his lips, he seemed unaware of the fascination he exerted over the many ladies glancing in his direction.

He turned to offer Marianna his arm, and for the first time his gaze fell upon Laura. He faltered, and his brown eyes widened with shock. His reaction was so marked his sister looked inquiringly at him. He indicated the new arrivals, and Marianna's swift joy on seeing Steven was swiftly replaced with astonishment because of Laura.

Blair's gaze was unwavering, and Laura felt its steady intensity as surely as if they were the only two people in the ballroom. She could sense his confusion, and in that moment knew once and for all exactly how much she resembled his wife. Only someone who was an almost perfect likeness of Celina Deveril could arouse such a stunned reaction in her grieving husband.

The ball continued, but many interested eyes were upon the silent drama between the host and the startling newcomer. It was a scene to make Miles hug himself with glee. Blair, the man he despised so much, had been visibly stunned by his first glimpse of "Mrs. Reynolds."

At last Blair and Marianna began to walk toward them, and Laura's heartbeats quickened with each step. She couldn't look away, and was spellbound by the force in his eyes. It was a force that reached out to her as if she were the only other person there.

They halted, and Steven inclined his head. "Blair."

Blair's glance flickered to him. "It's been too long since we last met, Steven."

"Er, yes." Steven looked at Marianna, whose dark brown eyes rested on him with barely concealed longing. He managed a bow. "Miss Deveril," he murmured, marveling that this adorable creature loved him as he loved her.

"Mr. Woodville," she murmured, glancing at Laura.

Steven hastened to do the honors. "Allow me to present Mrs. Reynolds, the lady my aunt recommends."

Laura curtsied. "Sir Blair. Miss Deveril."

Blair's reluctance was noticeable, but he took her hand and raised it fleetingly to his lips. "Mrs. Reynolds," he said softly.

Images of him naked passed before her eyes, and she felt hot color rushing into her cheeks. She couldn't meet his gaze, and resorted to her fan in a vain attempt to appear collected.

Marianna turned to her brother. "Mrs. Reynolds is inordinately like Celina, is she not?" she observed candidly.

The directness startled Laura. It seemed that while Marianna Deveril could hold her tongue when it came to herself, she was also capable of a devastating candor that showed scant regard for the feelings of others, even her brother.

For a moment Blair couldn't hide the pain in his eyes as he nodded. "Yes, she is."

Steven played his allotted part to the full. "Oh, Lord, Blair, I—I had no idea . . . " he said uncomfortably, hating himself all the time.

"Why should you? You didn't know Celina," Blair replied.

"Yes, but even so . . ."

"Think no more of it."

Laura disliked herself too as she glanced inquiringly from one to the other. "Celina?" she repeated innocently, as if the name were new to her.

Blair looked away, but with all the callowness of her years, Marianna remained painfully forthright. "Celina was my brother's wife, Mrs. Reynolds. She died in a riding accident about two years ago."

There was silence for a moment, and then Blair turned to Steven and coolly changed the subject. "How is that felon Lowestoft? I'm told you're often in his company now."

"Well, not often exactly, but I know him," Steven admitted, caught a little off guard by the sudden reference to Miles.

"Have a care, for he can't be trusted," Blair warned.

Steven gave an uneasy grin. "He, er, speaks highly of you, too," he replied with mock humor.

"I'm sure he does."

Marianna smiled at Laura, and then turned to her brother with mercurial decision. "Blair, I think Lady Tangwood is right, Mrs. Reynolds is everything you could wish for in a chaperone for me," she declared.

But his response wasn't encouraging. "Marianna, now is hardly the time or the place to discuss it," he said reprovingly.

Laura was acutely embarrassed. His unwillingness was only too clearly due to her resemblance to his late wife. Had Miles made a monumental miscalculation? Would Blair reject her precisely *because* she looked like Celina? Her secret feelings were mixed. Part of her longed for Miles's plan to fail, but part of her wanted to get closer to the fascinating Sir Blair Deveril.

Marianna seemed to sense her brother's real reason as well. "Oh, Blair, it isn't fair, you know. It's hardly Mrs. Reynolds's fault that—"

"That's enough, Marianna.

"But it's my birthday, Blair, so you must grant me one wish."

He drew a long breath. "I'll compromise. If Mrs. Reynolds presents herself here at noon tomorrow, I'll interview her properly. Will that do?"

Marianna hesitated, but then gave in. "Oh, I suppose so."

Laura couldn't help but be conscious of his resentment. He didn't want to have anything to do with her.

Marianna's youth didn't prevent her from knowing when to leave well enough alone, so having achieved part of what she wanted, and as a waltz was announced, she deftly changed the subject. "Mr. Woodville?" she prompted.

Steven smiled and offered her his arm, and as they stepped onto the rapidly filling floor, Blair gave Laura a faint smile. "Would you care to dance as well, Mrs. Reynolds?" he asked reluctantly.

Somehow she managed to smile and accept. "Thank you, sir."

He set her glass aside, and as his fingers closed over hers, their gloves might not have been, for it was as if their skin touched. She moved in a dream as he led her onto the floor and put a hand to her waist. The waltz began. The music was sweet and rhythmic, seductive almost, and she seemed weightless as he whirled her around the floor. The ballroom passed in a blur, and she could hear her heart beating more quickly than usual. He affected her far more than she'd been expecting, for although she already knew she found him attractive, she hadn't realized exactly how much. But she knew now. Sir Blair Deveril was more sexually stimulating than any man she'd known before.

Oh, God, she'd never experienced anything like this, never felt such a charge of electricity that her whole body seemed alive with latent emotions. The thought of making love with him was almost intoxicating. Her breasts felt taut and excited, and there was an aching deep inside her. It was desire, urgent and uncompromising, but when she looked into his dark gaze, she couldn't tell what he was feeling.

Many eyes were upon them, and she could still hear a rustle of whispers circulating beyond the music. Once or twice she was again sure she heard Celina's name, and knew everyone was thinking what Sir Miles Lowestoft wished them to think—that she might be the late Lady Deveril.

When the orchestra played the final chord and she sank into a curtsy, Blair's fingers suddenly tightened almost roughly over hers. Startled, she looked up at him. "Sir?"

"Mrs. Reynolds, I will be blunt with you. You are definitely not my choice as my sister's chaperone."

She straightened, and drew her hand away from his. "It would be hard not to realize that, sir."

He went on. "But since Lady Tangwood speaks so highly of you, and Marianna has set her heart on it, I still wish you to come here tomorrow. You have my word that I will interview you fairly."

"I'm sure you will, sir."

"Where are you staying?"

"The King's Head, Cirencester."

"I'll send my carriage." With that, he turned and walked away.

She stood there in embarrassment, aware that other guests had observed his cool manner toward her. Suddenly she felt far too much in the public gaze, and gathered her skirts to hurry in the opposite direction. But as she went out through the ballroom entrance, the adventure in time ended abruptly, and she found herself back in the darkness of her hotel bedroom. The double doors disappeared from the wall, and everything was silent, except for the dashing of the January rain on the modern window.

Five

Sleep didn't come easily to Laura after that. The night's incredible events kept going around in her head, and she was still wide awake when the hotel began the new day.

She lay staring up at the powder-blue canopy, not knowing what to make of what had been happening. Could she still pretend it was the result of an overactive imagination? Possibly. She *might* have daydreamed what happened in the green room. She *could* have recalled the scenes in the mirror and from the gate from some explicit movie or other. Her thoughts *might* have wandered in Cirencester, and she *might* have read a romantic novel with a chapter about a ball. But what about the engraving? She *couldn't* have fantasized the outside of Deveril Park before she got to the hotel.

She supposed it was possible she'd seen the engraving before, but if so it must have been some time ago, because she couldn't remember it. But even if she had seen it before, would she really subconsciously recall it in such complete detail? She thought not. A photographic memory was *not* one of her talents; in fact, she had trouble enough learning her lines, let alone absorbing every particular of an old engraving!

Her thoughts were interrupted by Mrs. Fitzgerald's discreet tap at the suite's outer door. "Are you awake, Laura dear?"

Laura sat up. "Yes, please come in," she called.

Jenny's mother came to the bedroom door. "I forgot to

ask if you wanted morning tea, so I've brought you a cup anyway. I hope that's all right?"

"It's great, thank you. Have you heard anything from Jenny?"

Mrs. Fitzgerald put the tea down, then smiled. "Yes, and it's good news. Alun's injuries aren't as bad as was first thought, and they say he'll be out of the hospital in a week."

"Oh, I'm so glad."

"The thing is, Kieran's coming home in a day or so, but Jenny wants to stay with Alun, which means you'll still have to fend for yourself."

"I don't mind, provided you don't."

"My dear, it's a pleasure, and at least the weather's being kind."

Laura glanced toward the window, and saw bright sunlight beyond the curtains.

Mrs. Fitzgerald went to the bedroom door. "Anyway, I won't disturb you anymore. Just pop down to the dining room when you're ready. We do gargantuan breakfasts, mind, so be warned. Bye for now."

Alone again, Laura picked up the tea, her thoughts returning to the night. She glanced at the wall, but there was no sign of the doors.

About an hour later, wearing jeans and a favorite sweater, she went down to breakfast. On the way she studied the engraving again.

The receptionist smiled. "Good morning, Miss Reynolds."

"Good morning." Laura glanced at her. "I don't suppose you know anything about the internal layout of the original house?"

The woman came closer. "Well, I only know a little. For instance, the present main staircase didn't exist when the house was built. There was another staircase leading up from a second hall here, where the dining room is now." She put a varnished fingernail on the engraving.

"Oh?" Laura's mind raced, for the dining room was directly below her bedroom at the end of the present building. When she'd gone back in time from her bedroom during the night, she and Steven had just come up the original staircase and were waiting in line at the entrance to the ballroom.

The receptionist went on. "I'm told the original grand staircase certainly deserved the title. It led up to a sort of huge landing, from where one got to the main rooms, including the drawing room, the library, and a ballroom. If you want to find out more about the old house, Mr. Harcourt's the one to ask. He told me everything I've just told you."

Laura decided she would, for Gulliver Harcourt appeared to be the local oracle. "Is there a plan of the original house?" she asked suddenly, thinking there must be for anyone to have knowledge of the internal layout.

"I don't think so," the receptionist replied.

"Then how does Mr. Harcourt know what it was like inside?"

The woman's lips parted. "That's a point. I'm afraid I really haven't a clue. You must ask him."

Laura went into the dining room, where the chimes of an elegant long-case clock drifted pleasantly on the warm air. She selected a table by a window that enjoyed the same view as her apartment on the floor above, but it was the interior of the room that interested her. She tried to picture exactly where the original staircase had been. The wall paneling looked like it hadn't been touched since first put up, and so did the ceiling plasterwork. Was Gulliver Harcourt wrong?

After a while she looked out of the window instead. The Cotswolds scenery was bathed in sunshine, and she couldn't help thinking it was a world away from London. And another world again from the heartbreak of Kyle McKenna.

"Begging your pardon, miss, but there's a letter for you."

Startled, Laura dragged herself away from the view to stare at the New York postmark. The letter was from Kyle, and had been redirected yesterday from the London apartment, where the janitor had the hotel address. Why would Kyle write to her after their acrimonious parting? With a sigh, she opened it.

Hi, there, honey. I know your first impulse will probably be to tear this up and jump on the bits, but if you'll give me a chance to explain, maybe things could get better between us.

Get better? Hell would freeze over first, she thought.

I guess I treated you real bad, and deserve not to be given another chance, but I just can't get you out of my head. I screwed up by seeing someone on the side, but I was a fool. It wasn't until I lost you so completely that I realized what a huge mistake I'd made. God, you don't do things by half, do you? Not only did you leave New York, you left the States as well! It's taken me all this time to persuade Josie to give me your London address. I guess you can say she's a very loyal friend; she certainly all but spat in my eye when I turned up at her door.

Laura sighed, wishing Josie had held out.

Anyway, you must be wondering where all this is leading. The truth is, I miss you, honey, and I want you back, so, like they say in all the best scripts, I'm going to drop everything to follow you. I'm not needed on-set for a month now—my character's been sent to Alaska to look for his long-lost twin brother, would you believe! That makes two brothers, a half-sister, two stepsisters, and a fairy godfather since the show began! As I was saying, I have a month off, so I'm using the break to visit England and get you back. So expect me soon, and you'd better believe I won't leave until you give me another chance.

I guess what I'm saying is that I love you, Laura. I can't get you out of my system, and if you knew what an Oscar-winning performance I put in to get your address out of Josie, you'd know I was telling the truth.

I know you'll probably hate getting this letter, and that if you knew when I was coming, you'd be out of town for the day, so I'm not giving any dates. Just give me a chance to redeem myself. I adore you. Kyle.

Laura was bemused. Never in a million years had she expected anything like this. Not only an abject apology, but a wealth of groveling too!

Slowly she refolded the letter. Kyle meant what he said, he'd just turn up at her door, so she had to give the matter some thought between now and then. To begin with, did she still want him? She'd spent the past months trying to forget Kyle McKenna, and now he was pushing his way back into her life.

With a sigh, Laura pushed the letter into her jeans pocket. She wished Jenny were here, for it would be good to discuss the pros and cons of Kyle with a girlfriend. Pros and cons? There shouldn't *be* any pros!

With Freudian expressiveness, she speared a sausage with her fork. She was on vacation, and Kyle McKenna could go to the devil right now. Besides, last night she'd been with a man so attractive he left Kyle in the shade! A man she'd like to see again, in spite of his coldness when they'd parted after the waltz. In the space of a heartbeat she decided to return to the gate after breakfast. Just in case there might be another adventure . . .

As she drove out of the hotel grounds a little later, she had to slam on the brakes to avoid an elderly man in a motorized wheelchair who turned into the drive right in front of her. She hadn't seen him because of the perimeter wall, and his sudden appearance sent her heart into her mouth.

With an apologetic smile, he wobbled to a standstill. He had rosy cheeks, bright blue eyes, thick white eyebrows, and a bushy beard that covered the lower half of his face, so she couldn't help thinking of Santa Claus, except the wheelchair wasn't exactly a sleigh.

She leaned out. "Oh, God, I'm so sorry, I just didn't see you!"

"It was my fault, I should have looked first."

"Are you sure you're okay?"

"There's no harm done."

As he went on along the hotel drive, his wheelchair

motor whirring busily, she realized he must be Gulliver Harcourt. Oh, well, now wasn't the time to talk. She'd leave it for later.

She got to the gate a few minutes later, and parked the car well out of the way of tractors. Everything looked much better in sunlight. The stream sparkled, the catkins seemed very golden against the clear blue sky, even the rattle of the ash keys seemed more pleasant. But would anything happen? Fingers crossed, she leaned on the gate.

The view didn't change; she could still see the hotel. Deeply disappointed, she started to walk away. Clearly there wasn't to be a close encounter this time, but then she hesitated. Maybe she'd give it one last try. She turned back again, and with a shock found herself in the past. The temperature had risen to May, and Deveril Park had spread grandly across its hillside. She was Regency Laura, and in the lane behind her waited the carriage and horses Blair had sent to the King's Head. She'd asked the coachman to halt while she plucked up courage for her imminent interview. She needed to compose herself because Blair had pointedly avoided her after the waltz, so she knew there was very little chance of being engaged. Her resemblance to Celina counted against her, not for.

Wondering what lay in store, she smoothed her skirts nervously, then glanced down at her clothes. She wore a rose velvet spencer over a plain white lawn gown, and her straw bonnet had wide rose ribbons. She heard men's voices by the carriage, and turned.

The lane had lost its modern paved surface, and was little more than a dirt track. The coachman was leaning over to speak to someone just out of sight. His voice was broad Gloucestershire. "I didn't reckon I'd see you just yet, Ha'penny Jack. The fair's not for another few days."

The unseen man replied. "I knows I'm early, but there's a plump widder woman I've a mind to see in the village. Name of Dolly Frampton."

"But will she want to see you, that's the question! You

traveling showmen think you're so marvelous, but you ent nothin' really. You can't neglect the likes of 'er from one year to the next, and expect 'er to welcome you with open arms when you deigns to come back. You'd best know she've been seen out and about with the butler from the big 'ouse."

Laura moved to see what someone called Ha'penny Jack was like. He proved to be a burly fellow of about thirty, with lank brown hair and a round face. There was a battered tricorn hat on his head, and his brown coat had seen better days, but it wasn't his clothing that commanded attention, it was the immense gaudily-colored box he carried on his back. It was so heavy he was bowed by its weight, and at first Laura couldn't think what on earth it was. Then she realized. if he was a traveling showman, the box was his puppet theater, and he was called Ha'penny Jack because that was what he charged.

The showman prepared to walk on, but then paused to nod back along the lane in the direction of Cirencester. "Reckon this must be the day for carriages to lurk in country byways," he observed suddenly. "I just passed another one. It must have been coming along behind you, otherwise you'd have seen it drawed up by the big elm tree two 'undred yards back. Its blinds was pulled down tight, but someone were inside, I heard 'em."

Laura's ears pricked. A carriage with lowered blinds? Could it be the one she'd noticed yesterday? Oh, surely not. She could understand noticing it at Tyburn, Oxford, and even passing the King's Head, for those places were all on the same main route to the west, but this would be different. There wasn't anything main about these lanes, and if it *were* the same carriage, she'd have to wonder if she were being followed.

The coachman glanced back along the lane, and then shrugged. "Probably some young blood on a tryst with another man's wife."

"Probably." Ha'penny Jack shifted load. "Well, I'll be on

my way afore I seizes up under this lot. You comin' to the fair?"

"Yes. Sir Blair's given everyone the day off as usual."

"See you then." The showman began to trudge away.

The coachman called after him. "Reckon you'll be an attraction at the prize ring this year, when you and the butler punches 'ell out of each other for Dolly's favors!"

Ha'penny Jack was scornful. "I'd make mincemeat out of 'im!"

"That'll be the day!"

The sound of a church bell drifted from the village, and the coachman stood up to peer over the hedge at her. "Reckon we'd best be going, madam. Sir Blair don't like to be kept waiting."

She returned. "I gather there's a fair soon?"

He nodded. "The Mercury Fair at Great Deveril, madam."

"Mercury?"

He shrugged. "Sommat to do with the god of trade and gain. His day's the twenty-fifth of May, and the fair's 'eld 'round then every year. It's a big occasion; everyone comes from miles." He gathered the reins, making no attempt to get down and open the carriage door for her. Lady Tangwood as chaperone was one thing, someone who needed to earn her living quite another.

She glanced along the lane in case she could see the carriage the traveling showman had mentioned. The lay of the land was against her, but she could see the top of the elm tree. She climbed into her seat and closed the door behind her. The whip cracked and the vehicle jolted forward.

The lanes were the same ones that existed in the future, and in bad weather couldn't be much more than mud tracks, but they were passable enough now, and it wasn't long before she recognized the lodge ahead. Just before the carriage turned through the gates, she looked to where the modern signpost to the canal tunnel would stand. There was nothing there now, but she could see the narrow lane that led down the hillside. In times to come it would be overhung with trees, but here in 1816, its banks were grassy.

The drive still swept down between rhododendrons, but when the grounds opened out, there was no holly avenue, just close-trimmed lawns beyond which stood the original mansion, its golden stone gleaming in the May sunshine. What would happen to it, she wondered? Would fire destroy all but a third?

She remained seated as the butler emerged from the house. He was in his late thirties, of medium height and stocky build, with blue eyes and thick brown brows, and was dressed in a black coat and gray breeches. His hair was concealed beneath a powdered bag wig which made him look rather severe—in fact, his whole demeanor was somewhat imposing—and Laura felt a perverse desire to laugh as she thought of him in a prize ring with Ha'penny Jack! It was hard to imagine anyone less like the traveling showman, and she couldn't help thinking Dolly Frampton must be a woman of wide taste in men.

He opened the carriage door. "If you'll follow me, madam, Sir Blair is in the lower gardens with Miss Deveril and Mr. Woodville."

She looked into his shining blue eyes, and with a start realized there was something oddly familiar about him. She felt she'd seen him somewhere before. Perhaps she'd noticed him at the ball. Yes, that must be it.

Gathering her skirts, she alighted. She heard peacocks calling on the lawns, and the summer breeze rustling the ivy on the house. The air was sweet with the scent of flowers, and horses whinnied in the nearby stables as she followed the butler toward the gardens on the other side of the house.

Her heartbeats quickened. In a matter of moments now she'd see Sir Blair Deveril again.

Six

There was no evergreen windbreak in 1816, so the view over the valley was unbroken as Laura followed the butler to the gardens. She scanned the landscape for the gate where this latest close encounter had begun, but as she looked, she saw a flash of light under the solitary elm tree a little further along the lane.

She could see the carriage Ha'penny Jack had mentioned, and it was very like the one she'd noticed yesterday. There was another flash, and she realized it came from the carriage itself. Was the sun reflecting off something? One of the lamps, perhaps? There wasn't time to wonder more because the butler led her further around the house and the view changed.

Suddenly she could see the canal. It curved from an adjoining valley like a silver ribbon, passed a waterside inn, then came directly toward the hillside before vanishing somewhere below the Deveril Park gardens. Barges moved slowly on the shining water, and more were moored along the bank. A whitewashed cottage stood close to the hill, and as she looked, a man ran into view from where she believed the tunnel portal to be. He called to a woman hanging washing in the cottage garden, and she immediately left what she was doing. More men came from the cottage and nearby barges, to gather concernedly by the cottage gate. Laura could tell something was wrong, but then the curve of the hill cut the view as the butler conducted her across a sunny terrace in front of the house, and down balustraded stone steps to the sloping flower-edged lawns.

Gardeners were scything the grass, much to the annoyance of the peacocks, whose complaining cries echoed in the warm air. Beyond the birds' noise, Laura heard laughter, then she saw Blair, Marianna, and Steven in an arbor that was overgrown with roses. They were seated on white-painted wrought iron chairs enjoying cool glasses of lemonade, and the three spaniels she'd seen from the gate were on the grass at their feet. It was an idyllic scene of which Laura could hardly believe she was part, but as Harcourt led her across the sweet-smelling lawn, she knew it was all very real.

Marianna wore a yellow and white gown and a wide-brimmed yellow silk hat with daisies around the crown, and her shawl and red velvet reticule lay on the table before her. She was seated beside Steven, who had on a green coat and fawn breeches. He glanced at his love with an open adoration that would be impossible to misinterpret if Blair chanced to look, and it told Laura the Weymouth liaison had been resumed right here at Deveril Park. The lovers were defying all the rules, and were guilty of betraying Blair's trust. Heaven help Steven if they were found out, she thought.

Her attention moved to Blair himself. He wore an informal gray coat and cream breeches, and the light breeze ruffled his dark hair and unstarched neckcloth. Suddenly he looked directly at her. His face bore no expression she could assess, except his brown eyes were perhaps a little quizzical, and his unsmiling lips gave nothing away. She was very conscious of the immediate barrier he raised. It was an invisible, impenetrable, but almost tangible shield.

She had no way of knowing what he was thinking, but for her the attraction he exerted hadn't diminished at all. Merely looking at him set her at sixes and sevens, and to look into his eyes was to know a desire that verged upon the sinful. Everything about him wreaked havoc with her common sense, and in those few moments it was very hard to remember that her nineteenth-century self had come here unwillingly to do Sir Miles Lowestoft's work. But the Laura of the future wasn't at all unwilling; in fact, she was swept along by the sheer excitement of these travels in time. And by the exhilarating feelings this man aroused. In this last she knew she and her Regency alter ego were united, for they were both strongly drawn to Sir Blair Deveril.

The butler announced her, and Blair stood. "Very well, Harcourt."

Harcourt? Of course! Laura suddenly realized why the butler had seemed so familiar—his bushy-browed blue eyes were the same as those of the man in the wheelchair. He must be Gulliver Harcourt's ancestor!

Blair inclined his head to her. "Mrs. Reynolds."

"Sir Blair."

Steven had also risen and murmured her name, but he avoided her eyes as if he knew she'd already perceived the way things were between Marianna and him.

She nodded. "Mr. Woodville. Miss Deveril."

Blair drew out one of the wrought iron chairs. "Please take a seat, Mrs. Reynolds. Would you care for some lemonade?"

"That would be most agreeable, thank you, Sir Blair."

The scent of roses was heady as they all sat down, and when ice chinked in the crystal jug, Laura was reminded of the ice in the ballroom.

Marianna smiled at her. "I trust you've recovered from the ball, Mrs. Reynolds?"

"Yes, thank you. I was truly honored to attend." Blair's gaze was still upon her, and Laura couldn't help meeting his eyes. An electric current seemed to charge the air between them until it crackled.

Marianna spoke again. "I enjoyed every moment of it; indeed, I think I shall be eighteen again soon in order to have another," she declared, her flirtatious glance briefly encompassing Steven, who had the grace to color a little.

Marianna went on, "I trust you will not find country life too dull after London, Mrs. Reynolds?"

She spoke as if it were all settled, and the forthcoming interview a mere formality, but Blair's face told a different story. Laura managed to smile at her. "Country life is always pleasing, Miss Deveril."

"Oh, I can't *wait* to go to town and have my first Season, but at the same time I'll hate to leave Deveril Park." Marianna gazed up at the house. "I love it so much here," she breathed.

Laura saw how Blair looked at his sister. His eyes seemed unaccountably sad. What was he thinking? she wondered.

Marianna gave a quick laugh. "I'm afraid I get sentimental about this place."

Laura smiled. "I can quite understand why, Miss Deveril. I'm sure I'd feel the same if I lived here."

"You don't think me foolish?"

"Of course not." Laura returned her glance to Blair, and with something of a shock found herself meeting his gaze again. The atmosphere between them was such they might have been the only people present.

Marianna's unsettling lack of diplomacy sprang to the fore again. "Oh, Blair, I hope you're going to honor your promise, for I do so like Mrs. Reynolds and wish her to be my chaperone."

He bridled slightly. "Since when have I *not* honored a promise?"

"I don't know, but you may choose to make an exception of this occasion because she's so like Celina," Marianna replied, still without seeming to realize the effect her bluntness could have.

Blair flushed angrily. "That will do, Marianna."

"Forgive me, Blair, but it has to be said."

"No, miss, it doesn't!" he snapped.

Laura exchanged a dismayed glance with Steven. If Marianna wished to sabotage everything, she was going the right way about it. Blair clearly found the resemblance to his late wife something that was very hard to deal with, and his sister's careless observations didn't help in the least.

At last Marianna realized she'd trodden on sensitive ground, and became effusively apologetic, which was almost as bad. "Oh, Blair, I—I'm terribly sorry. I didn't mean anything, truly! Oh, I feel dreadful now. Please forgive me, I just didn't think."

"You seldom do." Blair stood, and turned to Laura. "Perhaps you and I should walk together away from unwelcome interruption, Mrs. Reynolds?"

Marianna blushed. She blushed still more when she caught Steven's eye and saw the reproval written there.

Laura rose, and as she slipped her gloved hand over his sleeve, was aware that even touching him so formally was a sensuous act, like a prelude to much, much more . . .

The arbor was close to steps to the next level of the gardens, where fountains played among formal flowerbeds. The spaniels accompanied them down to where a gravel path crunched beneath their feet, and the scent of roses was replaced by the poignant fragrance of lavender. A large fountain of stone dolphins splashed in the center of the garden, and Blair led Laura toward it.

"Mrs. Reynolds, I trust you'll excuse my sister's lack of reserve. I fear she believes in saying what she thinks."

"I seem to recall that last night you were equally as forthright," she replied, thinking of his parting words after the waltz.

He didn't respond as they walked on. The sound of water was refreshing, and sunlight flashed through the cascades as he invited her to sit on the stone parapet around the fountain. The spaniels immediately sprawled at their feet, their ears twitching hopefully as he searched in his pockets, but he took out a Spanish cigar.

He glanced at Laura. "Do you mind if I smoke, Mrs. Reynolds?"

"Not at all, sir."

He searched for his luminaries, and shortly afterward a thin curl of smoke rose from the cigar. He looked at her. "You're justified in pointing out my rather ungallant conduct last night. I'm afraid I coped rather badly. I'll be frank. I hoped that this morning your resemblance to Celina might be less apparent, but you're a painful reminder of what I lost two years ago."

His sadness carved through Laura like a knife, and suddenly she loathed Sir Miles Lowestoft even more than before. Nothing excused the vicious spite behind the plot, and she hated herself for having anything to do with it, albeit under duress. She was helping shatter what was left of Blair Deveril's already broken heart, and it was despicable. For a moment she couldn't speak, but at last found her tongue. "I—I'm sorry I've aroused sad memories, Sir Blair."

"It's hardly your fault, Mrs. Reynolds. Truth to tell, everything reminds me of her anyway, especially this house, and it's become too much."

She looked quickly at him. "What do you mean?"

He smiled a little wryly. "Don't misunderstand, Mrs. Reynolds. I don't intend to put an end to myself, it's simply that Deveril Park is full of constant memories, and the only way to be free is to sell and leave. In fact, it's already a *fait accompli*, and when I sign the documents in a day or so, Deveril Park will have a new owner." He drew on the cigar and then exhaled slowly. "I've bought an estate in Ireland called Castle Liscoole, but Marianna doesn't yet know anything, so I'd appreciate it if you didn't mention it in front of her."

"I wouldn't dream of it, sir, although I think perhaps you should say something soon," she replied, recalling Marianna's declarations about the house a few minutes earlier.

"I know, but my reasoning is that her imminent betrothal to Alex Handworth will mean she will soon be too preoccupied with the wedding and her own future residence to be much concerned about what happens to Deveril Park."

"You may be right, sir, and if so then all well and good. But if you're wrong . . ."

"Being presented with a *fait accompli* is cruel?"

"Not cruel exactly, more unfortunate."

"How diplomatic you are," he said a little dryly. He was about to say more when something caught his attention in the valley. It was another flash of light from the mysterious carriage, which was visible again from this lower point on the hill. "Someone's using a telescope," he murmured.

Laura looked too. A telescope? Was that what it was?

He put the matter from his mind. "Mrs. Reynolds, I realize I'm laboring the point, but until I feel it right to break the news to Marianna, it really is important you say nothing."

"I've already given you my word, sir."

"Now I fear I've offended you."

"There's nothing at which to take offense, sir," she replied.

He fell silent, and she studied him surreptitiously. He was toying absently with his wedding ring, half removing it and then pushing it firmly back into place again. The subconscious gesture screamed of his inability to put the past behind him. He'd gone so far as to actually sell Deveril Park itself, but just as he made the bold and irrevocable move, a woman who was the living likeness of his beloved Celina came to haunt him again.

Never had he seemed more Byronic than he did at that moment. The air of enigmatic sadness surrounding him might have belonged to Childe Harold himself. It was more affecting than she could bear, and suddenly she knew she couldn't go through with the plan. She'd have to tell Miles she'd failed to be engaged, and pray he'd stay his hand where her Regency family was concerned. There was just no other choice now she knew how much Blair still suffered from Celina's death.

She got up. "Sir Blair, I think it best if we bring this embarrassing meeting to an end, don't you? I know you don't wish to employ me and only consented to this interview in order to placate Miss Deveril. And now I fully realize how like your late wife I am, I don't wish to pursue the post anyway. I suggest we avoid further awkwardness by informing Miss Deveril that although you offered me the position, I declined because the terms weren't acceptable. That way she will not accuse you."

She turned to leave, but he stopped her. "One moment, Mrs. Reynolds."

"There's nothing more to be said, Sir Blair."

"I *did* approach this interview with the firm intent to turn you away, but you're clearly a person of great sensitivity and thoughtfulness, and probably admirably suited to the task of taking my sister in hand. It would therefore please me to discuss the post with you after all."

Torn, she paused. To leave would ease her conscience, but to stay would mean being with him a little longer . . . Conscience was vanquished.

Down in the valley, beneath the shady branches of the elm tree, Estelle's carriage had still not departed. Its window had been lowered and she was observing the Deveril Park gardens through a small naval telescope once owned by her late father. The black unicorn on her signet ring caught the sunlight as she adjusted the glass to concentrate upon the two figures by the fountain at Deveril Park. They were framed against the dancing water, but only Blair's face was visible. Then Laura turned her head, and Estelle's thin hands tightened over the telescope with uncontrollable hatred.

"He told me you were dead, you little whore, and soon you'll wish you were. He's come here to be with you, but he's mine, and he always will be," she breathed.

Laura didn't sense the malice directed at her from the valley. She was too swept along by the intensity of her feelings for Blair. It was like being a moth attracted to a flame—knowing she'd be burned, but still having to flutter ever closer . . .

He dropped the cigar and ground it beneath his heel before giving her a quick smile. "Perhaps I should outline the duties expected of you. For the next month you will take charge of Marianna here at Deveril Park, then accompany us to my Berkeley Square residence for the Season."

For a moment she was again looking into the mirror at her London apartment. *For now we see through a glass, darkly; but then face to face . . .* She was face to face with him now, and the feeling was one of exquisite emotion, pure, clear, and sweet as emotion had never been before. Oh, God, she was falling over a precipice. Like Alice on her way to Wonderland.

Suddenly she knew he was experiencing some of the same feelings, because he deliberately avoided her eyes. "You'll, er, be required to oversee Marianna, and attend any function to which she is invited but to which I cannot escort her. She'll need firm direction, for her headstrong ways are bound to lead her into various faux pas. If she's to succeed as the future Countess of Sivintree, what she needs above all is a modicum of restraint, a quality she sadly lacks."

"She's very young," Laura replied, remembering her own conduct at eighteen. There had been occasions when she'd opened her mouth before thinking, which embarrassed her to recall even now.

He nodded. "Yes, she's young, and I hope her unchecked tongue is only the fault of youth, not an enduring fault of character," he said with feeling. He glanced at her. "Do you think you can manage her?"

"I know how to go on in society, and I believe I know how others should be expected to go on as well. Is that not what is desired?"

"Yes, I suppose it is." He searched her eyes for a long moment, and then smiled. "The finer points remain to be discussed, but the post is yours if you wish, Mrs. Reynolds."

Her heart leapt. "Are—are you quite sure, Sir Blair?"

"Perfectly sure."

She felt the change in him. The electricity between them almost lit the air, the barrier was lowered, and the warmth in his glance allowed her in. No, it allowed the image of Celina in. She had to be honest with herself. The feelings aroused in him now really belonged to his dead wife.

But Laura knew she was beginning to pay a price for persisting with a charade she knew was wrong. Today she'd eagerly sought to return to the past—in fact, she'd gone out of her way to do so—and she'd sacrificed conscience. Now her heart was Blair Deveril's for the taking. And so was her body. She felt no hidden shame as she acknowledged the truth about herself, for no matter how preposterous this whole situation, no matter how transitory and ultimately fruitless, she was falling deeply in love with this man. Nothing would ever be the same for her again. Nothing.

"I accept," she replied, her moth's wings burning around her.

"That's what I hoped you'd say. When can you commence?"

"Will tomorrow be too soon?"

"Tomorrow will be excellent. I'll send the carriage at the same time as today. And, of course, it's still at your disposal now."

The spaniels suddenly leapt to their feet, and gazed back toward the steps up to the previous garden. Blair and Laura turned to see Harcourt hastening toward them. He was out of breath, and his wig was askew as he tried to summon a little composure before speaking.

"Sir Blair, there's a problem in the tunnel. They've discovered another crack in the brick lining about a quarter of a mile from the Great Deveril portal, and it seems bad enough to be in danger of falling in!"

Laura's lips parted. So that was what had happened.

Blair ran a hand through his hair. "Plague take it! See my horse is saddled, and be quick!"

"I've already taken the liberty of issuing the instruction, sir." The butler hurried away again.

Laura looked at Blair. "Another crack? It's happened before?"

"Yes. The hill isn't limestone all the way through, but partly fuller's earth as well. It's given nothing but trouble from the outset, and prevents the canal from being profitable. Forgive me, Mrs. Reynolds, but I really must go. Please rejoin Marianna; I'm sure you and she will have much to discuss."

But Laura suddenly felt a compulsion to return to the future. This particular close encounter had become so steeped in excitement and conflicting emotions, she just wanted to slip quietly back to her own time for a while. The past was weaving a beguiling spell over what was left of her common sense, and she needed to get away from the magic of Sir Blair Deveril in order to examine thoughts and feelings that at present were running away with her.

She gave a quick smile. "Miss Deveril and I can discuss everything later, Sir Blair. For the moment I have a number of letters to write to friends and family, as well as to my lodgings in London to arrange for my remaining belongings to be sent here, so I should return to the King's Head."

"As you wish." He took her hand and drew it to his lips. For a breathless moment she was sure he smoothed her palm with his thumb, but then he released her to hurry away, the spaniels at his heels.

He paused briefly to tell Marianna and Steven what had happened, then hastened on toward the house, where a groom had already brought his horse. Laura returned to the rose arbor, and Marianna greeted news of her employment with delight. Steven was relieved to know the business of the necklace wouldn't fall solely to him, and he said as much as he escorted Laura to the carriage.

Soon she was driving away from Deveril Park again, but as the coachman began to maneuver toward the hump-backed bridge, Estelle's carriage suddenly appeared from nowhere, thundering at such breakneck speed that collision seemed inevitable. Laura's coachman started to rein in, but the oncoming vehicle didn't check its pace. Then, at the last second, it swerved and swept past with only an inch or so to spare.

In a blur Laura saw a woman's thin hand holding a blind aside, wearing the signet ring she'd noticed in Cirencester the day before, but then the other carriage had passed. It hurtled on along the lane, its team kicking up dust, and Laura's coachman managed to halt his frightened team after the bridge, right by the gate. He stood up to hurl furious abuse after the retreating vehicle, then remembered his passenger. "Are you all right, madam?"

She managed to reassure him. "Yes, I—I think so." She'd seen a signet ring like the strange woman's somewhere before. But where?

"Shall I drive on, madam?"

"I'll just get out for a moment, I—I feel a little shaken."

"Certainly, madam."

She alighted and crossed quickly to the gate. The moment she walked through it, the May warmth vanished and the much cooler air of January took its place. Deveril Park ceased to be, and in its place on the hillside was the hotel. She ran to her car and fumbled with the ignition key before taking off with wheel spin worthy of Indianapolis because she was so anxious to get away from the gate.

She drove haphazardly, following lane after lane until she began to feel more calm. Today the impossible had happened. She'd gone back in time and fallen in love with a man from Regency England! There was no point denying it. Sir Blair Deveril was suddenly everything to her. This wasn't a game, it was only too real, so the choice before her was simple. Either she tried to avoid all contact with the past, or she carried on with her eyes wide open to the unknown consequences. There was no contest. She wanted to experience the physical reality of the lovemaking she'd watched in the Berkeley Square mirror. She wanted to lie beneath him and have him look down at her with a love that matched hers.

She smiled suddenly. Yes, the choice was simple—she had to go back again if she could. Who knew, maybe she'd already had her quota of adventures? But if she hadn't . . .

Seven

To reach the hotel, Laura had to drive through Great Deveril. It was a picture-postcard Cotswold village boasting a magnificent medieval church and stone cottages with terraced gardens that in summer tumbled with flowers. It also had a famous green that had figured in many a TV costume production.

She drove slowly around the green, just to take a closer look, and noticed a lane leading steeply down between the churchyard wall and a cottage with a porch guarded by stone lions. It was called Barge Lane, which she supposed implied it led to the canal. There was one way to find out, and on impulse she turned down it.

At the bottom she emerged in a meadowed valley through which ran both the canal and a stream very like the one Blair had bathed in. Almost immediately she came to the canalside inn she'd seen from Deveril Park. It had changed very little since 1816, except to gain a restaurant extension and a parking lot by the water. In one direction she could clearly see Great Deveril and the hotel on the hill, while the other way the tree-choked valley led toward a hilly skyline pierced by the isolated church she'd used as a landmark on the map. She was sure the church was the one in the watercolor in her suite; if so, the wooded valley was where the picture had been painted.

Appropriately, the inn was called the Bargee's Arms, and was popular even in winter when there was little tourist trade. Pleasure rowing boats were moored to the bollards that had once secured barges, and the busy towpath had almost disappeared. From the inn the canal curved east across an open grassy meadow for two hundred yards before vanishing among more trees near the foot of the hotel's hill. This was the long exposed stretch she'd seen from the garden at Deveril Park, but although she looked, the trees obscured any view of the cottage or the tunnel. She found it hard to believe that this tranquil spot had been the scene of such busy waterborne commerce. But she'd seen the past, and knew.

She decided to have a coffee before walking to the tunnel, so she parked her car and got out. The chill in the valley air struck her, and she wished it really were May instead of January! Hunching her shoulders, she hurried into a low-beamed bar where a roaring fire had been lit in the inglenook. It was a typical English country pub, with horse brasses, copper pans, round tables, cushioned settles, and pictures from a bygone age, in this case old prints of canal life. There was a murmur of voices from the restaurant, and a waitress hurried past with ham salad and french fries.

The bartender was a thick-set, middle-aged man who gave her a beaming smile when he detected her American accent. "Coffee, miss? Just take a seat, and I'll bring it over."

"Thanks." She went to an empty settle next to the inglenook.

Several minutes later, after the bartender had brought the coffee, she heard a familiar whirring noise and saw Gulliver Harcourt gliding toward her in his electric wheelchair. She didn't doubt it was him, or that Blair's butler was his ancestor.

"I thought I recognized you, miss!" he said, maneuvering to a halt next to her. He had a pint of beer in his hand, and had been sitting with a group of friends at a nearby table when he noticed her.

"You get around," she said.

"Oh, my chariot can move," he replied with a grin, patting the wheelchair as if it were a trusty steed.

"It's Mr. Harcourt, isn't it?" she ventured.

He was taken aback. "You know who I am?"

"I'm staying at the hotel, and the Fitzgeralds mentioned you." Oh, and by the way, I've just met your great-great-something-or-other in 1816!

"You're a friend of the Fitzgeralds'?"

"Yes. Well, of Jenny's really."

He smiled. "May I join you?"

Right now there was nothing she'd like more than to ply him with questions. "By all means, if you think you'll be safe. I may not be behind the wheel now, but I might spill coffee all over you instead."

He chuckled. "I'll take the chance. Cheers," he said, raising his glass.

"Cheers," she responded with her cup.

"Are you staying in the area long?"

"A week or so."

"I hope you enjoy it. We've plenty to offer, though of course there'll be plenty more when the canal and tunnel are fully restored."

"I guess so. I suppose the canal was once very important?"

He shook his head. "Not as important as its owners hoped."

"The owners? I suppose that's the Deverils?"

"You know about them, eh?"

"I know the hotel was named after them."

He nodded. "They owned all the land hereabouts, and Sir James Deveril was the first major shareholder in the canal."

"I've only heard of Sir Blair Deveril."

What could only be described as a guarded look descended over Gulliver's eyes. "What do you know of Sir Blair?" he asked.

"I, er, read about him somewhere," she replied dismissively, and then went on quickly, "What happened to the family? Are they still around?"

"That I really don't know. Sir James was Sir Blair's father, and that's more or less all I know. The family's history seems to die out at the same time as their house, Deveril Park, which disappeared from the records in about 1816. The story goes there was a fire. Anyway, it suddenly reappeared a fraction its former size and under different ownership in about 1850, so either the Deverils sold up and moved on, or they just died out. Something of the sort, anyway."

"I think Sir Blair purchased some place called Castle Liscoole in Ireland," she said.

"Did he?" Gulliver studied her. "How do you know that?"

"Oh, I researched Castle Liscoole once, that's all, although don't ask me to remember details, I'm hopeless with things like that. You mentioned 1816 a moment ago, and it rings a bell. Wasn't there some trouble with the canal tunnel in that year?" She was fishing quite blatantly, and knew it.

"Yes, there was. A cave-in, actually."

"Really?"

He nodded. "It wasn't the first, or the last. The tunnel always caused problems and expense, and in the end proved the end of the canal. It was the geology of the hill, you see. Instead of being oolitic limestone all the way through, it has patches of fuller's earth that have to be shored up with brickwork to protect the tunnel. It would have been limestone all the way if the engineer had driven through in the right place, but he made an error in his calculation, and it went through one hundred yards to the north. It passes only a few feet beneath the cave under the Deveril Park cellars."

"There's a cave?" she asked with interest.

"Er, yes." Gulliver's hand seemed to tremble as he raised his glass, and she thought he'd gone a little pale. What was bothering him? She had to know. "Is something wrong, Mr. Harcourt?"

"Wrong? No, why should there be?"

"I—I don't know. You just seem a little, well, uneasy."

He gave a quick grin. "It's the awful beer they serve here," he joked. "You asked about the cave. There's a few of them hereabouts, and this one was always used to store ice at Deveril Park because it was always cold. And before you ask, the reason I know for certain what the cave was used for is because it's mentioned several times in the early canal records. Many of the later records went astray like those of the house."

Laura sat back. So *that* was how there'd been so much ice at the ball! She looked at him as something else occurred to her. "The coat-of-arms at the hotel *is* a play on names, isn't it?"

He drew a long breath. "I *think* it is, but that's all."

She waited for him to expand on the subject, but he didn't, so she ran a fingertip around her coffee cup. "I guess Sir Blair Deveril is represented by the bulrushes, and his wife Celina by the moon?" she ventured.

He lowered his glass abruptly. "You're exceptionally knowledgeable, miss," he observed.

She resorted to the excuse he'd used. "It's just a guess."

He cleared his throat. "Yes, well, that's what history's all too frequently reduced to—guesswork."

His evasive manner was both intriguing and infuriating. What was his problem?

The bartender came over to ask if she wanted more coffee.

"Yes, thank you." She pushed her cup and saucer toward him.

"Old Gulliver boring you to death, is he?"

Gulliver gave him a dark look, but Laura smiled. "Actually, I'm really interested. I was asking about the Deveril House Hotel—or at least, about the mansion it used to be."

Ron cradled the coffeepot on a napkin. "Did he tell you about my old great-grandfather?"

Gulliver snorted. "That old nitwit!"

Laura looked from one to the other. "No, he didn't."

"Well, he was a canal watchman here, and lived in a cottage right by the tunnel."

The cottage where the woman had been putting out the washing, Laura thought.

Ron went on. "Anyway, he had a skinful one night and wandered off. No one knew where he was, least of all his wife, who was a real fearsome piece. She suspected him of having a fling with a woman in the village the other end of the tunnel, so she drove over there in the pony and trap to catch him at it. The woman said she hadn't seen hide nor hair of him, so back my old great-grannie came, only to find him home. White as a sheet he was. Said he'd been up at Deveril Park as it had been way back in the past."

Laura stared at him. Deveril Park as it had been in the past? What else could it mean but that, like her, the old watchman had traveled back in time! So she wasn't the only one it had happened to! She was so shaken she couldn't speak.

Ron didn't notice her startlement. "My great-grannie wasn't having any of his yarns, especially as she soon learned he'd been seen rowing out of the canal tunnel like a bat out of hell! She said he'd been to his fancy woman after all, and dreamed up the story to hide his two-timing tracks. He swore he hadn't, but the more people heard of his tale, the more ridicule he got. In the end he gave up and admitted he'd been with the other woman."

Laura fixed her gaze on her coffee cup. The flying saucer factor, she thought. The watchman decided to let his wife think the worst. It was better to be branded a womanizer than mad!

Gulliver scowled. "The Sawyers are all full of fancy," he said sourly. "It began with that philandering scapegrace over there." He nodded toward a picture on the wall that Laura hadn't noticed before.

She saw it now, though, and almost gasped aloud, for it was an old drawing of a traveling showman so like Ha'penny Jack it had to *be* him!

She looked swiftly at Ron, but unlike Gulliver and the butler, she couldn't see any likeness at all between him and the burly showman she'd seen in 1816. She summoned a quick smile. "You—you had a traveling showman ancestor, Mr. Sawyer?"

"Yes, a chap by the name of Ha'penny Jack Sawyer, would you believe? I suppose I should be grateful he stayed around long enough after the Mercury Fair to marry and make things legal."

"Who did he marry?" she asked, thinking it must have been Dolly Frampton.

"A farmer's daughter by the name of Harriet Stanley."

"Oh." Maybe Dolly had wised up to roving Jack after all, and married Harcourt the butler! Laura looked at Gulliver, and saw how intently he avoided her eyes.

Someone on the other side of the room called for service, and Ron nodded. "Well, reckon I'm needed over there," he said, and hurried away.

Laura's thoughts were swinging in all directions at once. Not only had she met Gulliver's ancestor, but Ron Sawyer's as well! And more than that, she was sure Ron's other forebear, his canal watchman great-grandfather, had traveled back in time too!

Gulliver took the opportunity to escape from her questions. "Well, I suppose I should mind my manners and go back to my friends," he said briskly.

She was content to let him go for the time being. He clearly knew more than he was letting on, and she intended to ply him with questions again. So she smiled. "And I think I'll go see the tunnel now," she said, finishing her coffee.

"Be careful, miss. The towpath doesn't go through, and

many a sightseer's had a drenching from leaning over a bit too far to see in as far as they can. You see, the horses or donkeys were led over the hill by a path, and the barges were legged along by their crews lying down and walking against the tunnel sides or roof. Three miles took a lot of strength and stamina, I can tell you."

"So I can't go in even a little way?"

"I'm afraid not. There are gates across it because the place leaks like a sieve where springs have found their way through the brickwork, especially in winter, and there are unrepaired roof falls. Ron takes sightseers in his boat in the summer, but not this time of year."

"I just want to take a peek."

"You can do that from the entrance; just be careful."

"I will," she said, getting up. "Good-bye, Mr. Harcourt."

"Good-bye, Miss . . . ?"

"Reynolds, Laura Reynolds."

For a moment there was no mistaking the astonishment in his eyes, but then he managed to smile again. "Good-bye, Miss Reynolds," he said, and before she could say anything more, he turned his wheelchair to glide away.

She gazed after him. Her name had shaken him. Did he know about her Regency counterpart? Yes, that had to be the explanation, although how he knew, she couldn't say. Unless . . . A startling possibility struck her. Had he gone back in time too? Why not? Anything was possible in this neck of the woods, and it would certainly explain his evasive manner. More UFO factor! One thing was certain; she'd *definitely* be seeking out Mr. Gulliver Harcourt again!

She paid Ron for the coffee and went out into the pale January sunshine again, crossed the parking lot to the canal, then followed the towpath toward the tunnel. Her head still rang with all the things she'd found out at the inn. It was like reading an absorbing novel; each page she turned led her deeper and deeper into the story, and took her closer to the characters. It was addictive. She didn't just *want* to know what had happened here in 1816, she *needed* to know. She was a time travel junkie!

The wind whispered over the canal, rustling through the reeds that grew along the bank, but she gradually became aware of the chatter of the stream that also led along the valley. She could see its willow-lined channel swinging suddenly closer to the path ahead where both waterways entered the trees. Great Deveril and the hotel remained visible on the hill, but she still couldn't see the tunnel or the cottage.

As she reached the trees, she thrust her hands into her pockets, for it was much colder in the shadows. Woodpeckers filled the air with their noise, and she knew that in 1816 she'd have heard the Deveril Park peacocks. Ivy and moss grew over the little-used path, and snowdrops grew in hollows, then the gurgle of water became louder as the stream passed through a culvert beneath the canal, before flowing on along the valley in the direction of the gate.

But the canal swung sharply toward the hill, which seemed to completely bar the way ahead as suddenly she came upon all that was left of the cottage, a single wall and chimney rising gloomily beside the path. There was an ancient upturned rowing boat beside the remains of the garden gate. Once painted blue and adorned with an elegantly carved stern, it had now rotted beyond redemption. A tall Norway spruce tree grew nearby. There weren't any others around, and she guessed it had once been a Christmas tree inside the cottage. Maybe Ron Sawyer's forebear, the other time-traveler, had planted it one Twelfth Night.

She walked on, and saw the tunnel portal only about ten yards in front of her. Set into the hillside and castellated like the gateway of a medieval fortress, it was crumbling in places. The tunnel mouth yawned black and mysterious, and a few feet in she could see the gates Gulliver had mentioned.

Her pulse quickened uncomfortably as she went to place a hand upon the old stonework. A strange feeling immediately tingled through her, and the past swung close. Suddenly the wind picked up slightly, soughing through the spruce tree behind her. She gasped and turned, half expecting to see 1816 again, but there was just the cold January of the present.

She faced the portal again, and the past brushed against her face like a cobweb. The black velvet heart of the tunnel seemed to close in, as if trying to lure her inside, and water dripped constantly somewhere beyond the light at the entrance. She remembered what Gulliver had said about springs, but then felt a sudden chill draft on her face. It was accompanied by the soft sigh of drawn air, like happened in subways, except this was much more eerie.

She was about to pull back when she heard something in the distance. It was like a muffled sob from the depths of the tunnel. Was someone trapped in there? Her pulse raced, and she called out in a trembling voice. "H-hello? Is—is someone there?"

There was only the moaning of the wind.

She called again. "Hello?"

The tunnel took up her voice, repeating it over and over into infinity, but as the echo at last died away, she was sure she heard the sob again. Primitive fears surged through her, and suddenly all she wanted to do was cut and run.

She fled along the towpath again and, on reaching her car, slammed the door and locked it behind her. Then, for the second time that day, she fumbled with the ignition before taking off like something at Indianapolis.

Eight

After such an eventful few hours, Laura would have liked something alcoholic on her return to the hotel, but it was tea that awaited her, for she was waylaid by Mrs. Fitzgerald and pressed into "a brew and a wee chat."

The moment the tea was poured, Jenny's mother kicked off her shoes and lounged back exhaustedly. "Lord, what a day. Oh, before I forget, there was a call for you while you were out. It was one of your other flatmates. She said to tell you first Gstaad was wonderful, and second you've been called for a second audition. I wrote the details on the pad."

Laura picked up the pad, then her eyes brightened delightedly. The production at the Hermes theater was set to be one of the most prestigious shows in the West End, and she wouldn't just be part of the chorus!

Mrs. Fitzgerald watched her face. "Good news, mm?"

"Yes." But then Laura's smile faded. Going for a second audition would mean leaving what was happening here.

"What is it, my dear?"

"Oh, nothing."

The phone rang, and Mrs. Fitzgerald answered. "Jenny, sweetheart! How are you? How's Alun? Oh, good . . ." After chatting for several minutes, she handed the call over to Laura.

Jenny sounded as if she were in the next room, not Dijon. "Hello, Laura? I hope you're not too bored without me?"

"I'm fine. Doing a little sightseeing, as it happens." And if you only knew the sights . . . !

Mrs. Fitzgerald was called away, and Jenny immediately interrogated Laura. "Right then, suppose you tell me what's wrong?"

"Wrong? Why, nothing."

"You don't fool me. Your voice is a giveaway. Tell Auntie Jenny."

The flying saucer factor was still a powerful deterrent, so Laura lamely resorted to blaming Kyle instead. "I've heard from the two-timing rat. He got my address, and is coming over here to try to win me back."

"You're joking!"

"I wish. He says he realizes how much I mean to him, and so on."

"He's probably found just how much cash your aunt left you," Jenny replied cynically. "Or did he know before?"

"Well, no, he didn't. We parted a few days before my aunt died." Laura lowered her eyes. Her stress levels must have been sky high then. Maybe they still were, and she really *was* seeing things now. She'd finally flipped!

Jenny condemned Kyle's motives. "He's after your money, but the thing is, do you want him back?"

"I—"

There was a click, and suddenly the line went dead. Laura hung around, but the minutes passed and the phone remained silent.

Stress hallucinations or not, returning to the past was still uppermost in Laura's mind, but although she drove to the gate again, nothing happened, and in the end she returned disconsolately to the hotel. Maybe there'd be no more time travels. Still too low-spirited to go inside, she visited the stables and on impulse booked a horse for the following morning. She was asked if she'd like to accompany the local fox hunt, which was meeting at the hotel at the time of her ride, but she declined. Horse riding was one thing, hounding dumb animals quite another.

After that, she went for a short walk to while away the remainder of the afternoon daylight. Her route took her to the opposite bank of the stream from the gate, and she paused by the pool where Blair had bathed. It was open to view now, for the elderberry bushes had long since gone.

She pushed her hands into her coat pockets, and shivered in the winter cold as she gazed across the water. She had no way of knowing if her adventures were over, but if they were, she'd always have her memories. She might be standing here in the fading light of a January afternoon, but in her mind's eye she conjured that day in a long past May, when Blair had gone for a swim he thought no one else could witness.

She relived those erotic minutes. The sadness in his eyes affected her unbearably, and his head-turning good looks quickened her pulse. A frisson of excitement shivered through her as she recalled his arms around the horse's neck, then the shiver of excitement became breathless yearning when she remembered how he'd turned and she'd seen his naked masculinity. "Oh, Blair . . . " she whispered, as he dove into the water and the image faded.

She made herself go down for dinner that evening, and sat at the same table intending to return to her suite as quickly as possible. One of her favorite old movies, an unashamedly romantic weepie, was on TV in a short while. Maybe it would distract her. One thing was certain, right now she was in just the mood to blubber into her handkerchief!

The long-case clock in the dining room was striking as she got up to leave, but suddenly all the lights went out. At least, that was what she thought, until she realized it wasn't quite dark after all, more like sunset. The modern dining room had vanished, so had the guests, and although the chimes continued to ring out, they were different, and when she looked toward the sound, she saw a much taller, older clock. The close encounters weren't over! She was back in Deveril Park again!

Overjoyed, she glanced around. She was at the foot of the staircase that led to the spacious landing and the main rooms, including the ballroom, drawing room, and library. The original dining room led off to her right, its door where there'd be the window by her hotel table. There were voices in the adjacent entrance hall, and she saw a small team of footmen, under Harcourt's supervision, using stepladders to light the chandeliers. Outside it was a beautiful summer dusk, and she could hear the peacocks calling before they roasted for the night.

It was the end of her first day at Deveril Park as Marianna's chaperone. She wore an olive green taffeta evening gown with a silk shawl, and her hair was in an elegant Grecian knot. Her false wedding ring felt unpleasantly cold, reminding her of Miles.

She wasn't alone, for Steven was at her side, and they'd just returned from an after-dinner stroll in the gardens. Blair's spaniels had accompanied them, while Blair himself was down at the tunnel consulting with the canal engineer, who'd arrived post haste from London. Marianna was writing a letter in the drawing room.

The walk in the gardens hadn't gone well because Laura knew she'd spent most of it trying to make Steven see reason over Marianna, and now she resumed the argument. "I still say you're being reckless beyond belief, Steven," she said, her voice low so Harcourt and the footmen couldn't hear.

"I wish you didn't know anything about it," Steven muttered.

"Well, I *do* know. Steven, the future Lady Sivintree is most definitely out of bounds, so it's madness to continue what you began at Weymouth! You *must* stop. If it should all come out, you'll have Blair's justifiable fury to face, and he's unlikely to be understanding!"

"I don't need reminding of the dangers," he replied, running a hand slowly through his hair. He wore a corbeau-colored coat and white silk breeches, and looked tired and anxious, as well he might under the circumstances. But his pallor was also a reminder that he'd probably never enjoy robust health again. He looked earnestly at her. "What do you think Blair would say if I went to him and confessed about my feelings for Marianna?"

Her eyes widened. "I think he'd throw pieces of you to the dogs," she replied bluntly, bending to pat one of the spaniels.

Steven sighed. "You're right." He changed the subject. "Have you thought of anywhere else we might look for the necklace?"

They'd used every spare moment that day to look in all the likely places, but to no avail. She shook her head. "It's obviously kept somewhere very safe indeed, and to be honest, I don't know how we're going to find it."

Steven glanced at her. "Maybe we should simply ask Blair."

She was exasperated. "At the dinner table, maybe? How excellent this mulligatawny soup is, Sir Blair, and by the way, where are the diamonds?"

"I wasn't envisaging it quite like that. Come on, Laura, you've clearly made considerable progress with him—indeed I'd go so far as to say you've definitely aroused his interest—so what harm would there be in mentioning the necklace? No, don't look at me like that, for I was going on to say that as Celina is wearing it in the portrait in the library, I'm sure you could refer to it that way."

"So could you," she pointed out, then fell silent. Yes, she'd aroused Blair's interest, it was there in his glance—the desire, the exciting shadows, the hint of sensuality that promised so very much—but he hadn't said or done anything to take things further. The anticipation was suspense beyond belief, but deep inside she was sure his restraint was still due to Celina, whose ghost seemed to fill this house. It was Celina he saw when he looked at Laura Reynolds. The beloved shade, not the living woman.

The ticking of the long-case clock in the staircase hall seemed loud as she glanced regretfully at Steven. "I don't think it would be wise for either of us to mention Celina's portrait. She's still mistress of this house. And of its master," she added quietly.

"He wants to forget her, why else is he selling this place?"

She looked quickly at him. "You know about that?"

"He told me last night, and that he'd told you."

"What of Marianna?"

He shook his head. "He's waiting until her own plans divert her." He leaned against the newel post and returned to the matter of Celina. "Have you seen the portrait yet?"

"No, I haven't been in the library. There seem to be so many painters and plasterers that I presumed it was closed."

"You can still get to the books, and you can certainly see the portrait. It's on the wall above the fireplace, and you really should take a look. It could be a picture of you, Laura."

A reproachful female voice suddenly addressed them from the top of the staircase. "Where have you two been? I've been looking for you." It was Marianna, pretty in cerise silk, her pink ruby earrings sparkling as she came down toward them.

Steven smiled adoringly. "Forgive us, but it was such a warm evening we went for a walk in the gardens. We thought you were intent on letter-writing."

"I only managed a few paragraphs. I never intended to put pen to paper this evening, because Blair promised to play cards with me. Then that odious engineer arrived and lured him away." Marianna sighed. "Poor Blair, the canal and tunnel are a dreadful millstone, and now he's faced not only with having to temporarily close both, but costly repair bills as well."

There was a clatter from the entrance hall as the footmen finished lighting the chandeliers, and folded the stepladders to carry them away. The spaniels immediately pattered over to Harcourt, for it was their mealtime.

Marianna looked at Steven again. "Will you play cards with me? Oh, and you too, Mrs. Reynolds."

Laura smiled at the reluctance with which she'd been belatedly included. Her presence was the last thing Marianna wished.

Steven nodded. "Yes, of course we will."

Marianna sighed. "I have to make the most of my freedom while I can, for Alex and his horrid father arrive soon from Dublin."

Laura shifted uncomfortably, aware of her chaperone duties. "I don't think you should speak of the earl like that," she warned.

"Well, he *is* horrid, and Alex isn't much better."

"If you feel so strongly, perhaps you should speak to Sir Blair."

"I've tried, but he won't listen." Marianna paused. "Will you speak to him for me?" she asked suddenly.

Laura was startled. "Me?"

"Yes. He'll pay attention to you."

Color entered Laura's cheeks. "I doubt that very much. Besides, it's hardly my place to speak to him on such a subject."

"It is if I ask you. Oh, *please*, Laura. You remind him of Celina, and he always listened to her," Marianna replied with customary frankness.

Laura colored still more. "Paying attention to his late wife is rather different from accepting advice from a mere chaperone."

"Maybe, but will you help me?" Marianna pleaded.

Laura gave in. "I'll try, but I doubt it will make the slightest difference."

Satisfied, Marianna turned to Steven. "Let's to cards then," she said, and her cerise skirts rustled as she hurried back up the staircase.

Steven looked at Laura. "We've been dragooned, I believe."

"*You've* been dragooned, I'm merely a necessary adjunct," she corrected. "Besides, I'd rather take a look at Celina's portrait now the library is empty, provided I can trust you alone with Marianna. Can I?"

"Of course!" he replied indignantly.

"See that you mean it. I'll join you in a while."

He hurried up the stairs, and Laura followed more slowly, pausing at the top to select a candle from the table where a number were always kept in readiness and could be lighted from a night lamp always placed there at dusk. It wasn't quite dark yet, but she wished to examine the portrait properly.

Steven and Marianna could be heard in the drawing room as she crossed the landing and paused to look into the ballroom, so vast and empty now that it was hard to believe how many guests had thronged it for the ball.

The library was dark, and the smell of paint and fresh plaster was very strong as she went inside. Dust sheets loomed eerily in the darkness and as she closed the door behind her the candle flame shivered. Glass-fronted bookcases reflected the leaping light as she stepped carefully around a decorator's trestle to pick her way past the sacks of plaster, buckets of paint and varnish, and other paraphernalia littering the room.

Apart from the bookcase, most of the furniture had been moved to one side and protected with more sheets, but the covering on a large pedestal desk had been dragged aside. On the polished green leather surface stood a decanter of cognac and a glass.

She saw the portrait facing her from the chimney breast, and her breath caught, for everything she'd been told was true. She and Celina Deveril might be one and the same person. She went to look more closely, placing the candleholder on the mantelshelf before gazing up at the canvas. Celina was seated in the Deveril Park rose arbor, with a basket of flowers on the table and more blooms loose on her lap. She wore a low-necked white muslin evening gown that clung to her figure, and her hair tumbled in chestnut profusion over her bare shoulders. She looked charmingly informal, except for the dazzling three-string diamond choker gracing her throat.

The candlelight swayed over the exquisite brushwork, and Laura's absorption was complete. There was something uncanny about looking at someone who was so like her she might have been looking in a mirror.

There was a step in the doorway behind her. It was Blair.

Nine

Blair's hair was windswept after riding back from the tunnel, his dark blue coat was unbuttoned, and he'd loosened his neckcloth a little.

He came toward her, and Laura felt her cheeks redden at being caught so obviously studying the portrait. "I—I'm sorry, Sir Blair, I didn't mean to . . ."

"There's no need to apologize, Mrs. Reynolds. The portrait is hardly a secret, nor is the fact that you and my late wife are very alike."

He stood beside her to study the portrait. "That necklace looks as if it were fashioned for her, don't you think?" he said softly.

"It—it's a very fine piece of jewelry."

"I wish it *had* been made for her, but the truth is more mundane. I fear it was won at the card table." He reached up to touch the painted diamonds. "She loved that necklace more than anything else, and wore it at every opportunity. I vow, society must have wondered if I was a miser and it was the only piece she possessed."

"I can see you loved her very much."

"I still do," he murmured.

His words were painful to her, and she spoke of something else. "I—I trust the engineer didn't report too badly at the tunnel, Sir Blair?"

"I fear he and I are at odds. He says the damage can be ignored as nothing further will develop, but I have reservations. What if he's wrong?"

He is, a cave-in happens here in 1816, she thought, remembering what Gulliver had said. "Perhaps you should follow your own judgment, Sir Blair."

"It's better to be safe than sorry?"

"Yes."

He smiled. "Probably, but I have to consider the livelihoods of those who work on the canal. Closing the tunnel for unnecessary repairs means severing their income. It's one thing if I have no choice, quite another if I merely have vague doubts."

"It can't be easy for you."

"It's part of life's rich pageant," he murmured, and then looked at her and sighed. "Life's pageant is also what Marianna must soon face properly, Mrs. Reynolds, and I'm anxious that she should be prepared. As you know, Lord Sivintree and his son will soon arrive from Dublin, and the betrothal will take place soon afterward. May I speak candidly?"

"Yes, of course."

"As a widow, you're accustomed to how things are in this world. Rightly or wrongly, a wife is supposed to obey her husband, but I'm afraid Marianna will confront Alex Handworth on everything. To say she lacks subtlety is to make a monstrous understatement, and she's making it clear she doesn't hold her future husband in particularly high esteem. Storm clouds loom on all horizons, and I'd appreciate it if you did all in your power to impress upon her that she'll achieve far more if she toes the line. Defiance and the stamping of pretty feet don't succeed, but charm and circumspection often do."

Remembering Marianna's request, Laura held his gaze. "Forgive me for saying this, Sir Blair, but is this match the best thing for Marianna?"

"It's what my father wished."

"It isn't what Marianna wishes."

He met her gaze. "Your solicitude for my sister does you credit, Mrs. Reynolds, but you trespass upon that which does not concern you. I've employed you to attend to Marianna's introduction to society, and that is *all* I've employed you to do."

The rebuke washed icily over her, and she wished she'd held her tongue. "I'm sorry I caused offense, Sir Blair."

"I'm not offended, Mrs. Reynolds."

"I fear you are, sir, and rightly so."

A glimmer of humor touched his lips. "Mrs. Reynolds, I strongly suspect you'd have said nothing at all if my sister hadn't prompted you."

She flushed a little.

"I thought as much."

"But that doesn't mean I don't agree with her," she added frankly.

He raised an eyebrow. "Indeed?"

"At the risk of trespassing all over again, I have to say I fear Marianna is so firmly set against the match that nothing will dispel the storm clouds you mentioned a moment ago."

He was silent for a moment. "I'll bear what you say in mind, Mrs. Reynolds," he said then.

"I do hope you aren't too angry with me."

He looked into her eyes, and then suddenly put his hand to her cheek. "It's impossible to be angry with you," he said softly.

His touch seared her skin, and she came within a heartbeat of closing her eyes and moving against his fingers.

Another heartbeat passed, and he lowered his hand in some embarrassment. "Now I'm the one who trespasses," he murmured, and moved away from her. "Where is Marianna now?"

"In the drawing room playing cards with Mr. Woodville. I was about to join them when you came in."

"Don't let me keep you. I'll honor you all with my company in a short while."

Their eyes met again, then she turned to hurry away.

Blair gazed after her, and then turned to the portrait.

"Oh, Celina, why do you still do this to me?" he breathed, but the painted eyes gazed sightlessly back, and the sweet lips remained in their eternal smile.

He went to the great writing desk to pour a large measure of cognac. He drained the glass in one mouthful, and immediately poured another. Then he turned to the doorway where last he'd seen Laura, and raised the drink in salute.

"I wish I'd never met you, Mrs. Reynolds, but here's to you anyway," he muttered, then drank the second glass. A wry smile played upon his lips as he reached for the decanter again. To hell with cards; tonight he intended to drown his sorrows. And lay ghosts.

There was no sign of Blair when the three cardplayers abandoned their game at past midnight. Candle in hand, Laura crossed the landing to go to her room on the third floor, but she paused at the foot of the secondary staircase, right opposite the library, because she couldn't help noticing the faint light shining beneath the door. After a moment she went on up.

Her room was at the back of the house, in a wing that wouldn't survive to become part of the hotel. It overlooked the kitchen garden and part of the stables, and in daylight she could see the windows of what would one day be the Fitzgeralds' private apartment.

Moonlight flooded everything as she placed the candle on the bedside table and then drew the curtains. How and when would this adventure end? Would she have to bring it to a close herself by going back down the main staircase? Or would it just happen?

The olive taffeta whispered as she stepped out of it to slip into a voluminous white silk nightgown with pink ribbon ties at the throat. She got into the bed, and lay back between the lavender-scented sheets. For a moment she was afraid to close her eyes, fearing to trigger the time travel, but when at last she did so, she remained in the past. She lay there in the darkness, her thoughts of Blair and the way he'd suddenly put his hand to her cheek. What had it signified? His attraction toward her for herself? Or the temptation to touch someone who brought Celina back for a while? Common sense told her it was the latter, but oh, how she wished it were the former . . .

Sleep overtook her, but she awoke with a sudden start. Her eyes flew open, and she sat up expecting to find herself in her hotel suite, but she was still in 1816. What had disturbed her?

Flinging the bedclothes aside, she went to the door to look into the passage. Everything was dark and deserted. Many of the upper servants slept on this floor, including Harcourt, but no one else seemed to have heard anything, for all the doors remained closed. Gathering up her gown, she hurried to the secondary staircase and looked down toward the landing.

Slowly she descended, and as if to emphasize the lateness of the hour, the clock in the entrance hall began to chime three in the morning. The notes drifted gently up through the silent house as she saw the faint waver of candlelight still shining beneath the library door. Was it Blair?

As the chimes died away, it occurred to her that it might be burglars. Should she raise the alarm? No, for if it was Blair after all, he'd clearly not be pleased. Better take a look first. She tiptoed across the landing and hesitated before stealthily opening the door and peeping inside.

Blair was there, his solitary figure dimly illuminated by the almost exhausted candle she'd left on the mantelshelf all those hours before. He'd taken his coat off, and was slumped in a chair he'd drawn up at the desk. His shirt was undone to the waist, and his neckcloth lay on the desk where he'd flung it. There was no sign of the decanter and glass she'd found earlier. But then she noticed them lying broken on the hearth beneath Celina's portrait. They'd clearly been thrown there, and that was what had awoken her.

His frilled shirt was very white in the candlelight, and he

was unaware of Laura's presence as he gazed up at the portrait. She hadn't realized anything was on the desk, but he suddenly leaned forward to take the diamond necklace from the flat leather jewelry case that lay there. The precious stones glittered and flashed like white fire in the candlelight, their brilliance spilling sensuously over his fingers as he looked at the portrait again, then kissed the necklace as if it were still warm from Celina's skin.

His lips lingered on the diamonds, and Laura found she was holding her breath. Oh, to be those diamonds . . . Silent longing filled her. She wanted to go to him and stroke away his sorrow.

Suddenly he sensed her presence, and turned to look directly at her. The cognac had him in its spell, and he saw the wife he mourned so much. He smiled. "Ah, there you are, my love."

Laura was rooted to the spot. What should she do?

"Where have you been, Celina?" Still holding the necklace, he got up and came around the desk toward her.

She had to say something. "I—I didn't mean to disturb you."

"You know I'm always glad to see you," he said softly.

"But, I . . ."

"Come here." The command was uttered softly, like a caress.

Slowly she went to him, expecting that at any moment he'd realize she wasn't Celina. But he didn't, he was too far in drink.

He caught her hand to draw her closer. "I've been waiting for you, my love. Why have you been away so long?"

She couldn't answer. His fingers burned against hers, and she couldn't pull away. She didn't want to . . .

He let go of her hand to fasten the necklace around her throat. The diamonds shimmered against her skin as he slid his fingers into her hair.

She raised her mouth instinctively to meet his, and their lips came together in a long, exquisitely loving kiss. She could taste cognac, fiery and intoxicating, but though she knew she should leave, her treacherous body trapped her with desire. She wanted his kisses. Needed them. And although she knew she was stealing his love, she couldn't help herself. Shame knew no place in her actions, she felt too much for that. The spellbinding emotions he'd aroused were too much to withstand, and as those emotions ran riot through her, she surrendered body and soul to irresistible temptation.

Her arms moved about him, and she slid her fingers over his back, exulting in the sheer ecstasy of holding him. He was warm and real, his body firm, lean, and muscled. She remembered watching him on the riverbank, and desire stirred even more intensely through her. She wanted him—oh, how she wanted him . . . The diamonds glittered at her throat as her lips softened and parted beneath his. Seductive coils of sexual need twined around them both. His hands enclosed her buttocks through the soft stuff of her nightgown, and he pressed her hips to his. The dormant masculinity she'd gazed upon by the stream was now rock-hard and throbbed potently against her. She felt as if her whole body would dissolve with excitement.

He moved her erotically from side to side across his arousal, and shuddering pleasure almost robbed her of consciousness. She leaned her head back, her breath escaping in a long sigh as she gave herself up to waves of pleasure.

He drew his head back, his eyes dark in the candlelight. "Fie on you, madam, would you have me take you here?" he said softly.

"Yes," she whispered.

"Have you no modesty?"

"None at all," she replied, slowly untying the ribbons of her nightgown with trembling hands and allowing the garment to slither to the floor around her feet. Her body was smooth and inviting in the gentle light, and her taut nipples cast small shadows across the fullness of her breasts.

Then she slipped her arms around his neck, molding herself voluptuously against him as she moved her hips against him, before drawing his tongue deep into her mouth. No man could have resisted such abandonment. White-hot with passion, he pressed her against the desk, his fingers sliding knowingly over her thigh and then between her legs.

No words were needed. She pulled away to lie back on the desk as he undid his breeches. His erection sprang out, imperative and pounding, and her breath caught with incredible pleasure as he pushed the tip gently between her legs. He skillfully applied gentle pressure, arousing her almost unbearably before sliding fully inside her. She melted with the kind of gratification she'd never dreamed could exist, and gasped as he withdrew to thrust in again.

The cognac hadn't robbed him of his potency, nor had it dampened his ardor. He was virile, practiced, and above all he was making love to the woman he worshiped. It was Laura Reynolds whose body he penetrated, but it was Celina he saw in her sea-green eyes, and as his strokes became more urgent, culminating in an explosion of sensual delight, it was Celina's name he cried out as he gave up his soul.

She reached up to cling to him, and the tears on her cheeks were the first acknowledgment of guilt. She'd knowingly seduced him, but she was the one who now paid the price. He thought he'd just made love to his wife, but Celina was dead, and in the morning, when the cognac released him from its grip, he'd remember—and he'd hate Laura Reynolds.

For the moment, however, she still held him. She needed to glean every last second of these stolen moments. His virility softened slowly inside her, and after several sweet minutes of lingering kisses and caresses, he pulled away at last to straighten his clothes.

She was afraid to look into his eyes, afraid she'd see bitter realization there, but as he smiled at her, she knew he still saw his wife. "I love you so much," he whispered, drawing a fingertip across one of her nipples.

"And I love you, Blair," she replied with heartfelt honesty.

He bent to retrieve her nightgown, then helped her to slip into it again. After that, he put his hand gently to her throat, caressing her skin and the necklace with his thumb.

"You are the most perfect of women, the keeper of my soul and the jailor of my heart. To look at you is to want you, and to be without you is to . . . To be without you is to . . ." A puzzled look came over his face, and she knew he'd remembered Celina was dead.

Suddenly he didn't seem to see her anymore. A glazed look descended over his eyes and he released her. "A cognac fantasy," he whispered. "No more than a damned cognac fantasy . . ." He turned to fling himself into the chair by the desk. He leaned his head back, and closed his eyes.

She went to him, putting out a hand to touch his hair. He didn't know she was there, nor did he react when she bent to put her lips to his. Tears stung her own eyes as with trembling hands she unfastened the necklace and put it into its case. She couldn't steal it. Tonight she'd sinned enough by knowingly usurping Celina's place in his arms, luring him into sexual intimacies he'd never have permitted if sober, and she'd known full well what she was doing. She had no excuse for the shamelessness of her actions, nothing to say in her own defense, except that she loved him.

Gathering her skirts, she left the library. Her courage failed then. She couldn't face him again, not after this. So instead of returning to her room on the floor above, she went down the grand stairs, because it was the way back to the future. As she reached the bottom, suddenly everything changed, and she was in the hotel dining room again.

It was the middle of the night, so there was no one to see as she ran to the seclusion of her suite and flung herself weeping on the bed.

Ten

Laura felt ragged the next morning. She'd cried herself to sleep, and was all too soon disturbed by the sound of hooves and voices outside. At first she thought it was 1816 again, then she remembered the hunt.

Glimpses of the night darted starkly through her as she lay there, and tears began to sting her eyes again. She wished she hadn't succumbed to temptation, but shame couldn't take away the exquisite pleasure she'd felt in his arms. The intensity and fervor of his lovemaking strongly lingered even now, and her body felt warm and sated. No, not sated, for she could never have enough of him. He was a man no woman could ever tire of, and whose kisses left the recipient yearning for more.

But he was bound to remember what had happened, and for her to return to 1816 again would be to face his contempt. She'd known last night that she couldn't endure that, and her decision remained firm today. At least . . . Deep in her heart part of her wanted to see him again no matter what.

The hounds yelped excitedly outside, and she got up to look. It was sunny but frosty, and the lawns were white. The horses' breath stood out in clouds, and the riders' scarlet coats were vivid against the winter background. Mrs. Fitzgerald and several maids had been handing around trays of stirrup cup, and withdrew as a horn sounded and the hunt moved up the drive.

* * *

After taking a light breakfast in her suite, Laura dressed in jeans, a sweater, and a warm jacket, then slipped out to the stables where her horse was quickly brought. To avoid the gate, she decided to explore the woodland beyond the Bargee's Arms, and see if she could find the spot depicted in the watercolor.

After stopping at the pub to say hello to Ron Sawyer, she rode along the valley, following a frosty track between the trees. From time to time she heard the hunt in full cry in the distance, and the unsteady note of the horn, but it didn't come any nearer. Suddenly the track entered the clearing in the painting, the blasted oak was right in front of her, and on the hilltop beyond she saw the church against the cold, clear sky. The bluebells weren't in flower, and there were no leaves on the trees, but she was in the right place.

Without warning, it seemed the grayness of the winter undergrowth intensified to bright green, and a haze of bluebells began to spread over the ground. The sun was suddenly much warmer through the leaves above her head, and she could hear the joyous song of a skylark. It was May 1816 once more, and in spite of her decision not to face Blair again, she was secretly glad.

She was alone in the clearing. Her roan horse had changed to a dark bay, and the conventional saddle to a sidesaddle. She wore a gray riding habit, and her hair was piled up beneath a little black beaver hat. She was free this morning because Marianna's music tutor had come to give her weekly harpsichord lesson, and she'd ridden this way in response to a note from Miles. Steven should have been with her, but he'd left at dawn to visit a friend in Cheltenham, and she hadn't seen him since playing cards the night before. She had yet to see any sign of Blair.

She was still determined not to go ahead with Miles's plan, and didn't regret not exchanging the necklace last night when she had the chance. Right now she could have been on the point of handing over the diamonds, but instead she intended to say she and Steven hadn't been able to find the necklace, and suspected it was no longer at Deveril Park, perhaps not even in Blair's possession. As to the rest of what Miles wanted of her—that she break Blair's heart—she was going to insist her resemblance to Celina had proved a deterrent, not a lure.

Miles's note told her to come to the old oak, and she waited nervously for him to arrive. She *had* to persuade him his plan wasn't going to work, and that she and Steven should be allowed to go free. Only then could she rest easy with her conscience. As easy as she ever could after last night.

She heard hoofbeats, and her heart sank as she saw Miles riding toward her. He wore a very stylish green coat with brass buttons, and looked as if he were about to set off for the Hyde Park parade. She hid her loathing behind a bland expression as he reined in beside her.

"Where's Woodville?" he demanded without preamble.

"He left for Cheltenham before your note arrived." She met his gaze. "Before you say anything, I have to tell you we haven't been able to find the necklace; in fact, we don't even know if it's still at Deveril Park."

He dismounted slowly, then removed his top hat to rest it casually over the pommel of his saddle. Her gaze was drawn to his ring. The black unicorn! Of course. Why hadn't she remembered before? But who could the mysterious woman be? Her mind raced. Who would have a signet ring that matched his? Who else but his wife! Was Lady Lowestoft following her? Why, though? Why on earth would Miles's wife wish to . . .

Her thoughts were snatched back because her horse tossed its head agitatedly when Miles suddenly seized its bridle. "Don't think to gull me, madam, for I promise you'll regret it!"

His cold anger frightened Laura, but she kept her nerve. "I'm not trying to gull you. Steven and I have searched all over, but the only trace of the necklace is in Lady Deveril's portrait. We think it may have been sold."

"Sold?" He shook his head slowly. "Oh, no, Deveril

wouldn't do that, the necklace means too much to him. I'm sure you'd like me to think you and Woodville have been diligently combing Deveril Park from attic to cellar, but I don't believe a word of it."

"I swear it's the truth."

"No, you're lying!" he breathed, reaching up suddenly to jerk her from the saddle.

She fell among the bluebells, and her thick chestnut curls spilled over the crushed flowers as her hat rolled onto the track. In a moment, Miles was upon her, pinning her bodily to the ground with his face only inches from hers.

"Tell the truth!" he demanded angrily.

"You're hurting me!" she cried.

"I'll hurt you a great deal more unless you're honest with me!" He thrust his hips warningly against her.

She knew what he was threatening to do, and her mouth ran dry, but she didn't change her story. "I *am* being honest! We can't find the necklace!"

"It's there somewhere, and I expect you and Woodville to find it. Is that clear?"

Her eyes were huge as she nodded. "Yes," she whispered.

He moved a hand to her waist, pulling her body sensuously to his. "And what of your personal progress with Deveril?"

She felt his breath on her face, and tried not to shudder. "I—I'm not making any. He isn't interested in me."

His vulpine gaze flew to her eyes. "More lies, my dear?"

"*No!* To him I'm his sister's chaperone, a superior servant, and that's all. I think he engaged me because of the letter from Lady Tangwood."

It was plausible, and he knew it, but he didn't release her. "Try harder with him from now on. I want him brokenhearted all over again!" His voice shook with malice.

She summoned tears. "I can't *make* him want me!"

"Oh, I think you can, Laura." His glance moved down to her breasts. "Any red-blooded man would want you, and Deveril's certainly that."

"You'd have done better to select someone totally unlike

his late wife. He looks at me and sees a past he's trying to forget."

For a long moment he didn't say anything, but then to her relief he loosened his hold a little. "Then it's up to you to make it a past he wishes to relive," he breathed. "You're an actress, my dear, so use your imagination."

Her eyes still shimmered with tears. "But—"

"But nothing! I'll allow you a few days' more, but next time we meet, I expect progress with Deveril *and* the necklace, do you understand?"

"Yes," she whispered.

He got up from her and then tossed a letter down. "In the meantime, I suggest you read this. It's a little reminder of your obligations."

Slowly she sat up, her hair tumbling around her shoulders. The letter was from her "mother" in Norwich and, although addressed to her, had already been opened and read by Miles.

Norwich. May 20th, 1816.

My dearest Laura,

Please forgive me for writing to you like this, but things are very bad. Your father's debts and ownership of the house have passed to Sir Miles Lowestoft, who is threatening the very worst unless you do as he wishes. We don't know what all this is about, but if it's in your power to appease him, then I beg you to do it for our sake. Your poor father's health has been broken by the strain, and I don't know where to turn, except to you. If you love us, please do everything Sir Miles demands, no matter how much you may abhor it. We depend upon you, my dear. Please don't fail us.

Your loving Mother.

The words cut into Laura like a dagger, for although in the future her parents had died in a plane crash, here in 1816 the woman who wrote the letter really was her much-loved mother. She could see the tired face of the anxious woman at the escritoire in the ancient manor house outside Norwich, where Regency Laura had been born and brought up in such happiness. The desperate letter appealed to a cherished daughter's conscience.

Summoning all her acting skills, she met Miles's gaze. "Please believe me when I say I'll do all I possibly can. I love my family, Sir Miles, and if I can save them I will. Trust me, please." Her voice quivered, and she didn't have to try to squeeze tears into her eyes, they came anyway.

He was taken in, but still had no compunction about threatening her. "Very well, I'll trust you, my dear, but be warned I'm still more than prepared to throw your kith and kin to the wolves. And you'd better remind Woodville about his IOU's, for I wouldn't want him to become too complacent in Miss Deveril's sweet embrace."

He pulled his gloves on again, and remounted after donning his top hat. "I'll ride here at ten every morning, so if you have anything to tell me, you'll be here then. Do you understand? "

"Yes."

"If you know what's good for you, you'll bear all my warnings in mind." He gave a thin smile. "*À bientôt, ma chère*." Doffing his top hat with mock gallantry, he turned his horse and rode back along the track in the direction of the Bargee's Arms.

She pushed the letter into her pocket and then rose shakily to her feet, brushing moss and bluebells from her riding habit. She was trapped between two loyalties, one to her family, the other to Blair. Could she be true to both? She could if the necklace's hiding place remained unknown, and she convinced Miles that Blair really couldn't be seduced! She gazed after him. He'd taunted her about being an actress, well, she'd show him! She'd be the greatest tragedienne ever!

He disappeared from view, and after doing what she could with her hair, she picked up her hat and pinned it back into place. She knew she didn't look as immaculate as she had when she'd set out, but if anyone asked, she'd just say she had a slight fall. She looked along the track again, her thoughts returning to Miles. She'd leave things as they were for a few days, then wait here at ten in the morning to tell him she really couldn't make any progress at all with the necklace *or* Blair, and she'd bring Steven with her to back her story. She didn't doubt he'd help. Because of Marianna, it was in his interest too to get out of Miles's clutches if he could.

She drew herself up sharply. She mightn't be here in the past in a few days' time! She might be somewhere in the future, unable to do anything about anything! There was no way of knowing what would happen from one hour to the next, for she certainly didn't have full control over her time travels. Sometimes she could precipitate a journey, like happened the first time she'd returned to the field gate, but other times it just occurred, like last night in the hotel dining room, and here in the woods today. And so far she'd been able to choose when she returned to the future, but intuition warned her not to rely on it.

She turned to her horse, and seeing the animal's bay coat reminded her she'd set out from the hotel on a roan. What had happened to it while she was here in the past? Had she simply disappeared from its back? A case of "now you see her, now you don't"? She drew a long breath. There was so much she didn't know or understand, so much she wanted to know, but one thing was certain—finding herself back in 1816 without warning meant sooner or later she had to confront Blair. It was an ordeal she wished to get over and done with, so she remounted and followed Miles back along the track.

She emerged from the woods by the inn, and noticed a small blue rowing boat among the moored barges. By the decorative carving on its stern, she knew it was the boat that in the future would lie rotting by the ruined cottage. Then she also noticed that the barges were making ready to leave, and she realized with dismay that the tunnel had been left open after all. She prayed no one would come to any harm when the cave-in happened. Maybe Gulliver Harcourt knew. Surely he couldn't object to telling her whether or not anyone was caught in the 1816 roof fall? She'd ask when she returned to the future.

Suddenly she heard a whip crack along the track behind her, turned with a startled gasp to see the mysterious carriage bearing down on her. The coachman shouted a warning, and she just had time to maneuver her frightened horse out of the way as the carriage swung onto the road. The blinds were still lowered, but the woman was holding one aside. She wasn't wearing her veil, and Laura caught a glimpse of eyes as dark as coals, and a pale, almost ghostly face framed in mourning muslin. Was it Miles's wife?

Laura glanced uneasily back at the fresh wheelmarks on the track. Somehow she didn't think the carriage just happened to drive that way. Had her meeting with Miles been observed? If so, what might Lady Lowestoft think she'd witnessed? Remembering how Miles had pinned her to the ground, and how his lips had been so close to her face she'd felt his breath, Laura was aware that the meeting might have seemed like a tryst. She kicked her heels and rode on.

In the swaying carriage, Estelle's face was contorted with jealousy. She'd made it her business to learn Miles's travel plans, and knew he'd taken rooms at the inn on the road to Stroud town. Intercepting the anonymous note he'd sent to Deveril Park had been easy enough, stableboys could always be bribed, and so she'd been waiting secretly in the woods.

She'd watched as her husband lay down with the harlot, watched how close they'd come to slaking their lust beneath the trees. God would punish such sinfulness!

Eleven

At the Deveril Park stables, Laura handed her horse to a groom, then approached the house through the kitchen gardens. It was too much to hope Blair wouldn't remember. In those final seconds in the library he'd realized she couldn't be Celina, and from there it was an only too logical step to the truth. It was no defense to point out he'd been a willing participant; he'd been in his cups and racked with grief, but she'd been only too sober.

What did he think? Was he angry? Shocked? Bitter? Oh, God, maybe it was all three. How could he possibly want her beneath his roof anymore? Maybe he'd dismiss her! Her steps faltered as the thought occurred to her. What would happen then? Feeling sick with misgiving, she entered the house by way of the rooms that were to become the Fitzgeralds' private accommodation.

She soon heard Marianna at the harpsichord, and as she reached the foot of the main staircase Harcourt called out to her. "Ah, there you are, Mrs. Reynolds. Sir Blair wishes you to await him in the drawing room."

Her heart sank with foreboding. "Very well. Where is he now?"

"In the gardens with Mr. Vesey-Smith, his lawyer."

"Thank you, Harcourt."

"Madam."

She hurried up to her room to change into her white lawn gown, then tidied her hair. Her mouth was dry and she felt more sick than ever. There could only be one reason why Blair wished her to attend him in the drawing room, and that was to request her to leave. She had no doubt at all that this was the case, nor could she reasonably blame him, for she'd impersonated his wife in a most abandoned and unforgivable way.

She went down to the green-and-gold drawing room, directly across the landing from the ballroom. Paneled and hung with tapestries, it enjoyed a magnificent prospect over the gardens and canal, and she went to look out. The spaniels dashed across the lawns, and she looked down to see Blair strolling with an elderly gentleman in somber lawyer's garb, who nodded sagely at what was being said.

She turned back into the room. Sunlight shone upon the garniture of Chinese vases and bowls on the mantelpiece, and she noticed a number of documents scattered over a table. Everything was quiet. The minutes ticked endlessly by, and her apprehension became unbearable, but at last she heard someone coming. Hurriedly she sat down on a sofa and folded her hands neatly in her lap. At least she could *look* dignified and self-possessed, even if she didn't feel it, but then she realized two men were approaching, and her composure vanished. Was she to be dismissed in front of his lawyer?

She stared at the doorway in dismay as the two men entered, accompanied by the spaniels. Blair's dark eyes went directly toward her, and she knew he'd remembered everything. Ashamed color drenched her cheeks.

"Ah, there you are at last, Mrs. Reynolds," he murmured.

"Sir Blair."

"May I present my lawyer, Mr. Vesey-Smith? Henry, this is my sister's chaperone, Mrs. Reynolds."

Surprise marked the older man's face as he saw how like Celina she was. He glanced at Blair, then dissembled as he came over to take her hand. "I'm delighted to meet you, Mrs. Reynolds."

She was at a loss. Was it usual to effect polite introductions before summarily dismissing an unwanted employee? "Mr. Vesey-Smith," she murmured politely.

The spaniels went to lie in a patch of sunlight by one of the windows, and Blair adjourned to the table where the documents lay. He looked at the lawyer. "Come and rest your bones, Henry," he said, drawing out a chair.

As the lawyer sat down gratefully and began to place the documents in order, Blair leaned his hands on the table. "Henry, I realize it's the eleventh hour, and you've come here to finalize everything, but there's something I wish to do before I sign. I must seek a neutral opinion. That is why I've requested Mrs. Reynolds to join us."

Laura stared at him.

The lawyer was taken aback too. "Well, of course you have the right to seek as many opinions as you wish, but I must point out that Castle Liscoole is a very desirable property, and you've acquired it for a song."

"It isn't Castle Liscoole that's necessarily in question."

The lawyer was astonished. "You're reconsidering Deveril Park?"

Blair didn't answer as he selected a sheet of paper and brought it over to Laura. "Mrs. Reynolds, this is a sketch of the estate I've purchased in Ireland. What is your impression?"

Her eyes met his for a moment, but she couldn't tell anything from his manner, except that he'd definitely recalled the night's events. Confusedly, she turned her attention to the pen-and-ink drawing of a seventeenth-century country house beside a beautiful island-dotted lake. "I—I'm not sure what you want of me, Sir Blair," she said at last.

"Just tell me what you think of the property."

"Well, it's very handsomely situated," she said a little lamely.

"A worthy replacement for Deveril Park?"

"It depends on what you mean, Sir Blair. It seems a fair exchange, but its history isn't your history, is it?" She looked up into his eyes.

He gave a faint smile. "History is sometimes an unwelcome tie, and needs to be cast off."

"Then Castle Liscoole would seem suitable, but little will be achieved if the past crosses the Irish Sea with you. Please don't ask me more, for it's not my business." She wished he wouldn't toy with her like this. Why didn't he simply pronounce sentence and have done with it?

He lowered his voice to a whisper the lawyer couldn't hear. "Madam, after last night, I would have thought us sufficiently intimate for you to be much more forthcoming."

Her cheeks flamed as he returned to the table. "Henry, I've decided. I'll sign, but only on the strict understanding that I will not vacate Deveril Park until the end of the year. It will take that time to pack everything and settle all outstanding matters."

"You mentioned this stipulation before, Blair, and the purchaser is willing to wait." The lawyer selected the necessary documents, then held out an inked quill.

"Why is the prospective owner so intent upon anonymity?"

"I really don't know. An agent was employed throughout."

"His identity will soon be known when he takes up residence, so why go to these lengths now?"

The lawyer shrugged. "No doubt he has his reasons."

"Such secrecy arouses the unfortunate suspicion that all is not as it should be," Blair observed as he signed.

"The sale is perfectly legal, and, now you've signed, it's final and binding too. In anticipation of your agreement, the new owner has already placed the necessary sum in my care, so nothing more is required. Whatever happens, Deveril Park is now off your hands. In just the same way that Castle Liscoole has been *on* your hands from the moment of purchase," the lawyer added prudently as he began to heat the sealing wax.

Blair gave an ironic laugh. "I wish I'd decided upon this sooner, I could have saved myself the expense of refurbishing the library! The work's too well in hand to call a halt now."

"I'm sure the new owner will be most appreciative."

"I'm sure too," Blair said dryly.

The lawyer looked at him. "As the sale concerns only the house and park, I must ask what you intend to do about the remainder of the estate—the farms, mills, canal interest, and so on?"

"I intend to dispose of everything, and wish you to put it all in hand, but the welfare of tenants, workers, *et al,* must be taken properly into account. I'll offer the servants the choice of coming to Castle Liscoole or taking their chance with the new owner."

"You may leave it all to me, Blair." Mr. Vesey-Smith dripped some molten wax on to the first document, and as Blair pressed a seal into it, the lawyer looked sadly at him. "I'm so sorry it's all come to this, Blair. I didn't think the day would come when the Deverils left Deveril Park."

"Nor did I, but sometimes now I find myself positively despising this house and its memories." Blair's glance moved briefly to Laura.

A few minutes later Blair prepared to see the lawyer to his carriage, but turned to Laura first. "Please wait here, Mrs. Reynolds, for I still wish to speak to you."

She nodded wretchedly.

Mr. Vesey-Smith shifted a little uncomfortably. "Look, Blair, I'm quite capable of seeing myself to the door. I, er, I'll be in touch directly."

"And I'll arrange to vacate this house by the end of the year."

They shook hands, the lawyer left, and at last Blair faced Laura alone. "Now, Mrs. Reynolds, I think we have some rather private and delicate matters to discuss," he said quietly.

She rose unhappily to her feet. "Is there any need to discuss anything, sir? We're both aware of the facts."

"Are we? Mrs. Reynolds, I'm not really sure of any *facts* except that you and I made rather passionate love on the desk in the library."

"What else is relevant, sir?"

"To begin with, I'm most intrigued to know your reason for consenting to such an astonishing intimacy with a man you hardly know. My reason is only too obvious, I was far too gone in cognac to tell fact from fantasy. I yearned for Celina, and you became her. Now, you don't strike me as a woman of easy virtue, yet you not only permitted my advances, but matched them. Why?"

She raised her eyes. "We all have fantasies, Sir Blair."

"And yours is to make love on a desk with a virtual stranger?" he asked bluntly.

She didn't say anything. How could she tell him she loved him when he'd just pointed out they hardly knew each other?

"I've been honest, so please allow me the same courtesy."

"I—I know I should have turned away last night, but . . ."

"But?"

Oh, what was the point of pretending? She'd done it because she hadn't been able to resist! And shamefully wrong as it had been, she knew she'd do it again! "I was tempted," she said, meeting his gaze squarely.

"Are you saying I seduced you?"

"No, I'm only too aware it was the other way around. I did it because I wanted to, very much indeed."

"The needs of a woman used to the marriage bed?"

"No."

He looked at her again. "Then what? To simply say you were tempted isn't sufficient. You might be tempted by a ring in a jeweler's window, but I doubt you'd steal it, so what was so irresistible last night? What was it that turned lady into wanton?" Suddenly he came close and put his hand to her chin, forcing her to look at him. "Why did you let me make love to you last night?"

Confession came spilling from her lips. "You're right that we hardly know each other, but from the moment I met you, you've affected me as no other man ever has, or ever will. If there's such a thing as love at first sight, then that's what happened to me at the ball the other night. Love made a whore of me! Is *that* sufficient explanation for you?"

"Whore was not a word I used."

"It's what you think."

"No, Laura, it isn't."

He'd used her first name! She looked swiftly into his eyes. "Then what *do* you think?"

"That your explanation is more than sufficient." Incredibly, his thumb moved softly against her skin before his hand fell away. "Perhaps I should confess a little. You see, there came a point last night when I knew you weren't Celina." He laughed a little self-consciously. "I wouldn't have admitted anything if you hadn't been so painfully honest just now, but since you have been, it's only fair that I should do the same."

"What are you saying?" she whispered.

"That deep inside I knew you weren't Celina the moment we kissed."

She stared at him. "But, I thought—"

"Oh, what a tangled web we weave, When first we practice to deceive . . ." he murmured softly. "So who was the seducer last night, Laura? You? Or me?"

Her heart thundered. "It's now my turn to ask your reasons, sir," she whispered.

His lips parted to answer, but then they both heard Marianna'a sobbing cries as she hurried up the main staircase. "No, I don't believe you! Blair wouldn't do that! He *wouldn't* sell Deveril Park without telling me!"

The spaniels leapt to their feet, whining, and Blair drew sharply away. Laura's senses were at sixes and sevens, and she could have wept at being interrupted at such a vital and heartstopping moment. Another few seconds and her wildest dreams might have been realized!

Instead, he was turning toward the door. "Henry must have told Marianna!" he breathed. "Dammit, I should have reminded him to be on his guard with her!"

Laura's disappointment was so keen that for a moment she didn't care that Marianna had been acquainted with the harsh truth about Deveril Park. But almost immediately she was ashamed. Marianna loved this house, and had just learned of its sale. She was bound to be desperately upset.

The spaniels rushed over to Marianna as she halted in the doorway. She took no notice of them as she gazed accusingly at Blair. Her dark eyes brimmed with tears, and her shaking hands were pressed into the folds of her pink jaconet gown. "Tell me it's not true you've sold Deveril Park!" When he didn't reply, more tears sprang to her eyes. "How *could* you?" she breathed.

"Marianna, what difference does it really make? You'll soon be married and mistress of your own house, and . . ."

"No!" she cried. "I despise Alex with all my heart!"

"That's enough! Hysterics will avail you of nothing!"

But emotion ran riot through her now. "You don't care about me, or how I feel. Well, I won't marry Alex, because I love Steven! I've already given myself to him!"

The revelation dropped like a thunderclap. Stunned silence hung in the air, broken only by the dogs' uneasy whining. Then Marianna's breath caught as she realized the enormity of her blurted confession. The color drained from her face, and with a little cry she gathered her skirts and fled, followed by the anxious spaniels.

Laura was beset by conflicting centuries and attitudes. Her modern self could only sympathize with a headstrong young woman who loved one man but was being forced to marry another. Such sympathy placed her in opposition to Blair, who now hurried after his sister.

Laura followed, but the drama still unfolded, for as Marianna reached the top of the staircase, Steven returned from Cheltenham much earlier than expected. The spaniels rushed down to greet him as he crossed toward the staircase hall, where the unfortunate Mr. Vesey-Smith still hovered in agitated dismay. Steven bowed quickly to the lawyer.

"Sir," he said politely, for they weren't acquainted, then he bent to pat the eager dogs as they bounded around him.

Mr. Vesey-Smith inclined his head. "Sir."

Then Steven looked up with a glad smile at Marianna. "The wanderer returns, as you see! I arrived in Cheltenham only to find my friend had removed himself to Bath, and—" He saw her pale face. "What's wrong?"

"Oh, Steven!" With a sob she ran down to him.

Blair and Laura watched as Marianna flung herself weeping into her lover's arms, and the ensuing embrace robbed Blair of any hope that his willful sister had told untruths out of resentment over the house sale.

Steven's face drained of color as he realized that the secret liaison was somehow out, but he held Marianna tenderly, stroking the nape of her neck and whispering loving words as he looked guiltily up at her brother.

Mr. Vesey-Smith began to realize just how much he'd unwittingly stirred. "Blair, I—I don't know what to say. I didn't realize . . ."

"I don't hold you to blame, Henry, I'd just be obliged if no word of this went beyond these walls."

"Of course. I—I'll, er, leave then." Bowing uncomfortably, the lawyer hurried away.

Laura watched as Blair went slowly down the stairs. "What's been going on, Steven?" he asked, his tone ominously amenable.

"Blair, I—I didn't want it to happen, but—"

Blair reached them. "Go to your rooms, Marianna," he said levelly.

"No!" she cried defiantly.

"Do as you're told!" Blair snapped.

She remained rebellious. "I *won't* go, and you can't force me!"

Steven looked at her. "Do as he says, Marianna."

"But—"

"Please."

More tears shimmered in her eyes, but she obeyed, hurrying back up the staircase. The spaniels pattered with her, whining and brushing her skirts as she didn't go to her rooms, but ran into Laura's arms.

Blair was like ice as he faced his friend. "I thought I could trust you, Steven."

"You can, but Marianna and I love each other."

"I need hardly point out that she's pledged to Alex Handworth." Blair's voice shook with suppressed emotion.

"I know, but—"

"Don't give me excuses, Steven. Marianna's transgression is bad enough, but yours is unforgivable."

"Please let me explain."

"Explain what? That you've betrayed our friendship and ruined my sister? Oh, I think that's all better left unsaid, don't you?"

"I *love* Marianna, and she loves me."

"You presume somewhat, Steven. What right have *you* to express any feeling for my sister? You have no income or prospects, you're up to your worthless neck in debt, and now you've shown yourself to be a fortune hunter."

At the top of the staircase Marianna gave an anguished sob. "No, Blair! That isn't true!"

Blair turned to her. "It is, Marianna, for you may be sure he wouldn't have risked all this if it weren't for your inheritance."

Steven colored. "Her inheritance makes no difference to me, Blair."

"You're right, sir, for until she's twenty-five it depends upon my consent, and *that* I will never grant," Blair replied.

Marianna's breath caught. "You wouldn't do that!" she cried.

"But I would, as you'll discover if you put it to the test."

She stared down at him. "I hate you," she whispered.

"I'm merely looking after your interests, as is my duty."

Marianna's hands clenched. "And it serves my interests to make me marry a creature like Alex Handworth?"

"It's an excellent match, and one, may I remind you, that our father wished to—"

Marianna broke in. "I'll *never* marry Alex, nor will he want me when he realizes I'm no longer the chaste bride I should be!"

Blair turned frozen eyes upon Steven. "Is this true?"

"Would that I could deny it," Steven replied, his face ashen.

Blair's fist caught him on the chin with such force that he teetered backward and fell. Marianna screamed, and the spaniels began to bark frantically as Blair dragged Steven to his feet, then struck him again.

Marianna sobbed hysterically, and Laura cried out, "For pity's sake, don't, Blair!" She didn't realize she'd used his first name.

He hesitated, but then turned away, silencing the spaniels with a single sharp word.

Steven sprawled on the floor with a cut lip. "I—I deserve this, Blair, but I still love Marianna! It has nothing to do with her fortune, but everything to do with adoring her more than life itself!" Still dazed, he staggered to his feet.

Blair didn't look at him. "Leave this house immediately."

"For God's sake, Blair, can't we discuss this more reasonably?"

"Leave, or so help me I'll put an end to you here and now! Your belongings will be sent on."

Marianna sobbed as Steven looked helplessly up at her, then walked away. She called desperately after him. "I still love you, Steven, nothing will ever change that!" Gathering her skirts, she fled toward her apartment.

The outer doors closed behind Steven, and Blair stood with his head bowed, his whole body taut with violent emotion. Laura could feel his agony. The rules of his age left him no option except to be the tyrant, but he was also a man who knew what it was to really love. She looked sadly down at him. "Oh, Blair," she whispered, and the echoes took up the soft sound of her voice.

He turned to look up at her. "I had no choice, Laura, I *had* to do it . . ."

Her name rested on his lips like a caress, but as she gazed down into his eyes, he began to melt away. Everything became blurred and distant, and suddenly she realized she was in her hotel suite!

"Blair?" She called out desperately, as if somehow she'd be able to bring him back. But the future was all around her.

There was a knock at the door. "Laura, honey, I've tracked you down at last!" It was Kyle.

Twelve

Kyle knocked again. "Laura?"

She looked angrily toward the door. It was Blair she wanted to see, not the bed-hopping toad who'd once broken her heart!

"Laura, honey, I know you're in there because I heard you."

Unwillingly, she opened the door. He was the same as ever—golden, tanned, and confident. His designer clothes were casually perfect, and his voice pitched at a calculated note of lazy amusement that once had curled her toes with pleasure, but now grated. "Hi, honey. Guess you didn't expect to see me."

"No, I didn't expect to see you, and don't call me honey."

"Okay, but don't I at least get a welcoming kiss?"

"Well, since you're not welcome, no, you don't."

He glanced around. "Have you got someone with you? I heard you talking. Well, maybe not talking exactly. You called someone."

Yes, I called Blair, she thought. She looked at him. "I don't know what you thought you heard, but there's no one here."

He looked at her. "I'm not flavor of the month with you, am I?"

"Go to the top of the class." She turned back into the room, glancing at the watercolor before facing him. "What do you want, Kyle?"

"What kind of question's that? I've come halfway across the world to be with you again, and you ask me what I want? I want *you,* Laura."

"Well, I don't want you." Oh, how true it was. She felt nothing for him now, except perhaps irritation.

Ignoring the rebuff, he leaned back against a chair, and surveyed her. "You're looking good, Laura," he murmured with a smile.

"And you haven't changed a bit," she replied.

He changed smoothly to a different tack. "Look, sweetheart, I'm sorry for the way I treated you. I was a heel."

"Why the past tense? You were, are, and always will be a heel."

"I'm different now, really I am."

"Did hell just freeze over?"

"I guess it must have. Look, Laura, you mightn't want to believe this, but I didn't know how much you meant to me until I'd lost you. Let's try again; I promise it'll be different this time."

"Kyle, I've spent the last months forgetting you exist, so if you think I'm going to fall into your arms again, you'll be disappointed."

"Don't be like this, honey. At least give me a chance."

"Why should I?"

"Because we once meant a great deal to each other, and I think we can be like that again."

"God, you amaze me. You think all you have to do is sashay back into my life and pick up where you left off. Well, it doesn't work like that anymore. I'm over you, Kyle, and that's the way I want it to stay."

"There's someone else?"

She met his eyes squarely. "Yes."

"Who is he?" he demanded, unaccustomed to rivals.

"Well, since you don't know him, there's not much point telling you his name."

"An English guy?"

"Yes."

"So who is he?" he insisted.

"All right. Sir Blair Deveril."

He put on a Noel Coward voice. "*Sir?* Oh, how terribly, terribly impressive."

"You never could do a good English accent," she said crushingly.

He flushed. "And you clearly can't take a little teasing. What is it with this guy?"

"Don't blame Blair for anything. It's just over between you and me, and the sooner you cotton on to that small point, the better."

"But I don't want it to be over."

"And what Kyle wants, Kyle gets? Well, not this time, so tough."

"I didn't expect you to throw yourself joyfully back into my manly embrace, but nor did I expect you to spit in my eye."

She remembered what Jenny said about his being after her money, and the irony of the situation struck her. Back in 1816, Blair accused Steven of being a fortune hunter; now, here in modern times, she suspected Kyle of the very same thing. "Why the interest in me, Kyle? Am I the most lucrative prospect you have right now?"

"Lucrative? I don't know what you mean." But he avoided her eyes.

"No? Well, I guess it doesn't matter anyway; you see, if you've come after me for my money, you're too late, I've squandered the lot. The only reason I can stay at a place like this is because I know the owners."

His jaw dropped. "You're kidding."

"I wish I were." She smiled brightly. "Still, your globe-trotting must mean your bank balance is healthy enough for us both, mm?"

He straightened. "My purse is always like Mother Hubbard's cupboard, you know that."

"Yes, I do. Nice try, Kyle, but you've fallen on your designer butt."

"You're a hard woman, Laura Reynolds."

"Not before time, where you're concerned."

He shrugged, but then gave her a boyish smile. "How about one last shower together, for auld lang syne?"

"Get lost, Kyle." She went toward the door.

"Well, it was worth a try," he replied philosophically.

She paused. "There's just one thing I'd like to know."

"Ask away."

"Were you told I was here in my rooms, or did you just come up on the off chance I'd be in?" She knew it was a strange question, but needed an answer. Today's time travel had commenced in the woods, but ended in the hotel. What had happened here in the future while she'd been in the past? If someone had seen her come up to her rooms, then it meant she had remained visible.

He was bemused. "What do you want to know that for?"

"Just tell me, please."

"I asked the receptionist, she said she saw you return from your ride and come straight up here. Okay?"

She opened the door and stood aside for him to pass. "Have a nice day," she murmured.

"Gee, thanks." He didn't look back as he walked away.

She closed the door, and leaned against it for a moment. He was already out of her thoughts, for she was too taken up with knowing she didn't disappear during her time adventures. She apparently carried on as normal while part of her managed to go back to 1816. It was like she divided in two somehow, but was only aware of what happened to one "twin." She didn't know how else to describe it.

She heard a car drive off furiously, and knew it was Kyle, who drove like that at the best of times, let alone when he was annoyed. "Good riddance," she murmured, feeling absolutely nothing for him. He might as well have never existed.

She flung herself on a sofa, put her hands behind her head, and gazed up at the ceiling. So much had happened today. From being racked with conscience about what had taken place in the library, she'd been swept toward unbelievable hope by Blair's confession that he'd known what was happening. If only Marianna hadn't called out when she did. And if only there was someone to talk to about all this! She desperately wanted to confide in someone, but there wasn't anyone. Except perhaps Gulliver, who she was sure knew much more than he was letting on. She was pretty certain Ron Sawyer's great-grandfather had traveled in time at least once, and that Gulliver knew it—perhaps because he too had had such an adventure. It was worth tackling him again, and there was no time like the present, especially as she also wanted to ask him if anyone got hurt in the 1816 tunnel fall. Getting up, she reached for her shoulder bag and a coat, and hurried out.

She was told Gulliver lived at Lion Cottage, on the corner of Great Deveril green, and a quarter of an hour after her impulsive decision, she parked her car alongside the churchyard wall. The cottage was the one she'd noticed when she'd driven down Barge Lane to the canal, and took its name from the fierce stone lions supporting the porch. The air was bitterly cold in spite of the sunshine, and the bare sycamores swayed against the sky.

She knocked at the cottage door, and after a moment was answered by a plump middle-aged woman in a comfortable floral dress. Was she Gulliver's wife? Somehow Laura hadn't imagined him being married.

The woman smiled. "Yes? How may I help you?"

"Is Mr. Harcourt in? My name's Laura Reynolds."

Gulliver's voice echoed along the whitewashed passage. "Tell her to come in, Dolly."

That was the name of the merry widow whose favors were vied for by Ha'penny Jack and Harcourt the butler, Laura thought with interest. What had she been called? Dolly Framwell? No, Dolly Frampton, that was it.

The woman smiled and stood aside for Laura to go in. Gulliver's electric wheelchair stood in a corner off the passage, and he was in the parlor, a jumbled room where piles of books and papers cluttered every conceivable surface. He occupied a chintz-covered armchair by the fireplace, and a pair of walking sticks rested against his knee.

"Ah, we meet again, Miss Reynolds. Please take a seat, if you can find one free."

Dolly tutted and went to remove some books from a nearby sofa. "I don't know why you waste your money getting me in three days a week, Gulliver. I can't clean most of the place because you won't let me move this lot!"

"Don't you want the job, Dolly Frampton?" he demanded with mock severity.

Laura's lips parted. Dolly Frampton! Exactly the same name! Surely the woman *had* to be the merry widow's descendant!

Dolly frowned at Gulliver. "You know I want the job."

"And I'm happy with the arrangement, so don't fuss."

Laura studied him. His tone was grouchy but his eyes kind, she thought. He was fond of her. Maybe as fond as his ancestor had been of hers.

Dolly sighed. "Don't pretend you've forgotten I'm a Renwick now."

"How could anyone forget you married that old misery?"

"That's no way to talk in front of company," Dolly chided, and then smiled at Laura. "Would you like some coffee, Miss Reynolds?"

Gulliver answered. "Yes, she would, and remember she's an American, so expects good coffee."

"I only make good coffee," Dolly replied tartly, and went out.

Laura sat down and fiddled with her car keys as she glanced out of the window at the long walled garden behind the cottage.

Gulliver looked at her. "I expected you to call, Miss Reynolds," he said.

"You did?"

"Well, your interest in Deveril Park and the tunnel could only be described as marked."

"And so was your reluctance to answer my questions," she replied candidly.

He raised an eyebrow. "The direct approach?"

"I see no point in beating about the bush. I think you know more than you're letting on."

"Well, if you imagine I have some dark reason for withholding information, you're wrong. I'm sorry to disappoint you, but the only reason I'm reluctant to talk about Deveril Park and the tunnel is that researching them led to my being confined to a wheelchair for these past twenty years."

She was startled. "What happened?"

Dolly returned with a tray of coffee, which she placed on a free corner of a table by Laura. "I'll let you pour, my dear; Gulliver's liable to spill it." She looked at him. "Will there be anything else?"

"No, that's all, Dolly. Thank you."

"I'll see you tomorrow then. Good-bye. Good-bye, Miss Reynolds."

Laura smiled at her. "Good-bye, Mrs. Frampton, I—I mean Mrs. Renwick, it was nice meeting you."

The woman smiled and then bustled out. The front door closed behind her, and as the sound echoed along the passage, Gulliver sighed. "There she goes, back to that miserable old codger of a husband."

Laura put her keys down and began to pour the coffee. "I'll take it you don't care for Mr. Renwick?"

"He's a mean-hearted, selfish, bad-tempered, dim-witted old sod," Gulliver replied. "Still, I suppose it's not my place to criticize; I gave up that right twenty years ago . . ."

"By not proposing first?" she ventured shrewdly as she gave him a cup of coffee.

"Something of the sort." He pressed his lips together, then smiled a little ruefully. "The tunnel must bear the blame for that too, I fear."

"The tunnel? I don't understand."

"Well, as I said just now, researching Deveril Park and the tunnel was why I ended up in a wheelchair. I couldn't ask Dolly to spend the rest of her life with an invalid. I wouldn't change my mind, so she married Jim Renwick instead."

"What happened? Was there an accident?"

"Yes. I was interested to see some shoring up ordered by Sir James Deveril back at the turn of the nineteenth century, so I rowed in to look. I went smack into a new roof fall no one knew about, damaged my spine, and I've been like this ever since."

She didn't know whether to mention the 1816 fall after that, but decided she would. "Mr. Harcourt, was anyone hurt in the cave-in of 1816?"

"Not as far as I know."

Well, that was something, she thought, then found herself asking him a very pointed question indeed. "Why were you so startled when you learned my name?"

He laughed. "Startled? I don't know what you mean, my dear."

"Come on, I think you know as well as I do that there was a Laura Reynolds at Deveril Park in 1816; that's why you were so rattled when you heard who I was."

"I still don't know what you're talking about," he insisted.

"Oh, yes, you do. I think you also know there was a Harcourt who was Sir Blair Deveril's butler, a Dolly Frampton who was a widow in the village, and a traveling showman called Ha'penny Jack, Ron Sawyer's ancestor, who was the butler's rival for Dolly's favors."

"My dear, there have been Harcourts, Framptons, and Sawyers hereabouts for centuries." His tone was light, but his eyes were guarded.

"Mr. Harcourt, why won't you come clean? It's driving me crazy that I can't discuss all this with anyone, and here you are, knowing all about it, but refusing to talk."

"Please don't presume to tell me what I do and don't know, Miss Reynolds," he replied quietly.

"I'm sorry, but if you'd just be straight with me—"

"There's nothing to be straight about," he interrupted.

She put her coffee aside frustratedly. "There *is*, I know there is! There's something strange going on around here, and I'm certain you know all about it. What about Ron Sawyer's great-grandfather, the canal watchman? All that business about going back to Deveril Park as it was? I know, and I think you do too, that he traveled back in time. I've been doing the same thing, going back to 1816 and becoming the other Laura Reynolds!"

Gulliver's cup slipped from his fingers, and shattered on the floor. She bent to retrieve the pieces, but he shook his head. "Leave it."

"But—"

"Leave it, Miss Reynolds, and then please leave this house."

She straightened with a few pieces of china in her hands. "I'm sorry if I've upset you, but I think you know what I'm talking about. Maybe you've traveled in time too."

A nerve flickered at his temple. "Close the door on your way out," he said quietly.

"At least tell me where you saw the floor plan of the old house."

"There isn't one."

"But you told the hotel receptionist—"

"I asked you to leave, Miss Reynolds. Be so good as to do so."

She stared helplessly at him. "Please, Mr. Harcourt."

"Good-bye, Miss Reynolds."

She put the broken crockery on the tray, picked up the car keys, and left the cottage.

But as she emerged from the porch, the scene on the village green brought her to a startled standstill. The Mercury Fair was setting up beneath sycamores that were suddenly in full leaf. There were people, wagons, booths, and animals everywhere, and the noise was tremendous, from hammering and shouting, to music and dogs barking. She saw acrobats, tightrope walkers, minstrels, puppeteers, a prizefighting ring, and a fortune-teller's booth. Men were assembling a wooden roundabout with leather horses and little carriages, and gypsies led strings of ponies to a far corner of the green, where horse sales would be held.

Laura realized the car keys had become reins in her hands. She was in her riding habit, and her horse was drinking from a water trough by the door of Lion Cottage. Excitement sharpened through her. Would she see Blair in a moment?

But as she turned, the person she saw was Ha'penny Jack. The showman was peering angrily through one of the windows of Lion Cottage. It was the parlor window, and there, on a settle enjoying tea and smiles, were Harcourt the butler and Dolly Frampton. At least, she presumed it was Dolly, for the woman bore a distinct family resemblance to Dolly Renwick.

Hoofbeats approached, and she heard the familiar barking of the spaniels. She turned gladly, and saw Blair riding toward her, but her gladness on seeing him again was tinged with guilt, for if he should discover why she'd ridden to the village, he'd be very angry indeed. And rightly so.

Thirteen

The reason Laura felt so guilty was the note in her pocket. It was from Marianna to Steven at the King's Head, and was to be given to the Cirencester stagecoach that would shortly pass through the village. As Blair rode toward her, his cranberry coat bright in the sunshine, she wished she hadn't gotten involved, but arranged matches and unwilling brides were anathema to the Laura of the future.

The atmosphere at the house had been tense since Steven was thrown out, especially as Marianna refused to give any promise of obedience when the Handworths arrived in a few days' time. Laura knew how difficult Blair's position was, but she felt justice was on the side of the lovers, and so had agreed to carry the letter.

Blair reined in beside her. Sartorially he was as stylish and perfect as ever, but the shadows in his eyes told her of the strain he found the situation with Marianna. He smiled at her. "You came to see the fair?"

"Yes," she lied, almost wishing he hadn't smiled. She didn't deserve it. It wasn't simply that she was on Marianna's errand; her whole existence here in the past was based on deceit and treachery. It was Blair she looked at, but Miles Lowestoft's cunning face she saw . . .

"We need to talk, Laura," he said softly, his voice almost lost in the noise of the fair.

Warm color touched her cheeks. "Yes, I know."

"You made your confession, but Marianna interrupted before I could finish mine." He held her gaze. "When we made love in the library, I knew you weren't Celina. The cognac made little difference, except perhaps to brush aside my inhibitions. Sober I wouldn't have behaved as I did, but in my cups I gave in to the desire I'd felt for you since the night of the ball."

She lowered her eyes. "For me? Or for Celina?"

"For you, Laura." He dismounted and took her hand, raising the palm gently to his lips. "I don't look at you and see my late wife, nor do I see someone who is merely in my employ, I see the woman who has made me live again. Before you I hadn't made love in two years, but you aroused me from that numb existence. You've changed me, and it doesn't matter that we hardly know each other. All that matters is how we feel."

For a quivering moment she thought he would kiss her right there in the green in front of the entire village, but instead he said, "Shall we ride together?"

"If you wish."

He lifted her onto the side saddle, then remounted and turned his horse toward Barge Lane. "We have time to ride along the valley before the weather changes," he said, nodding toward the horizon, where storm clouds were beginning to loom.

With the spaniels loping before them, they left the noise of the fair and rode down into the valley. If they'd looked back they'd have seen Estelle's carriage drive slowly around from behind a cottage across the green, and halt at the top of the steep lane. Estelle quivered with loathing as she watched them. The redheaded harlot would soon pay for her sins!

Laura and Blair rode on. The hedgerows cast cool shadows, and the clip-clop of the horses' hooves made a pleasant sound. Honeysuckle and wild roses filled the air with fragrance, and skylarks tumbled joyously in the blue sky overhead. It was perfect and no words were needed as they made their way to the Bargee's Arms, where they left the road to follow the towpath toward the tunnel. At the culvert they followed the stream along the valley below Deveril Park. There was something magical about the sound of the horses, the warmth of the sunshine, and, above all, about the undercurrents of emotion passing between the two riders. Laura felt as if this time, place, and man, were her destiny.

The gate appeared ahead, and as they reached the pool with its fringe of elderberry bushes, Blair reined in and dismounted. "This is one of my favorite places," he said, tying both horses to a branch, then reaching up to help her alight.

The scent of elderberry blossom was seductive, and the heavy cream flowers swayed as the light breeze quickened slightly, presaging the approaching change in the weather. The spaniels lay down in the shade as Blair led her into the shelter of the bushes, where no one could see. She reached up to unpin her hat, and her hair fell heavily over her shoulders. Blair looked away suddenly, and she knew he was thinking of Celina.

"It *is* my likeness to Celina that makes me of interest to you, isn't it?" she said resignedly.

"No, but the way your hair fell then did remind me of her." He saw she needed reassurance. "Shall I tell you the truth about Celina? She was sweet and submissive, and I adored her, but she wasn't an angel. If she wanted something really badly, nothing would stand in her way. She wanted me, and broke many rules to have me."

Laura was taken aback, for somehow she couldn't imagine the flawless Celina doing anything she shouldn't.

He removed his gloves and broke off some elderberry flowers, separating them between his fingers. "It wasn't until after the marriage that I found out what she did in order to wear my ring, and by then it was too late. Oh, don't misunderstand, I didn't regret marrying her, far from it, but I couldn't approve of her actions."

Laura was filled with curiosity. What on earth had Celina done? Clearly it had shocked him, but not enough to harm his love.

But he couldn't bring himself to explain further just yet, so he smiled. "All I want to say is that although you look like Celina, that's as far as the resemblance goes. She didn't have your passion, and would never have instigated lovemaking. As to surrendering on a library desk . . . !" He smiled a little more, and shook his head.

"Maybe she would, if the situation had arisen."

"Never. I loved and accepted her as she was, but she had no fire, whereas you . . . You, Laura, are a vibrant flame." Fragments of blossom clung to his fingers as he touched her face.

There was seduction in his voice, and she closed her eyes. "Have you brought me here to make love to me?" she whispered.

"It's what I want to do more than anything in the world."

"It's what I want too," she breathed, feeling weak as his hand moved sensuously in her warm hair.

He pulled her close, and their lips came together in a kiss whose currents ran through their veins like molten gold. Her body ached with desire, and she had no thought of resisting. She succumbed to the erotic spell he cast over her. This man was everything, and as he began to unbutton her clothes, she was beckoned on by the promise of sexual delights beyond her dreams.

It was cool as they lay naked on the grass, but their kisses threatened to scorch their flesh. His lips were tantalizing as he took one of her nipples into his mouth, sliding his tongue over it until a myriad dizzying sensations of pleasure danced through her entire body. Her hands roamed over him, stroking, caressing, and exploring. She felt the broadness of his back, the slenderness of his waist, and the compactness of his firm buttocks. Her fingertips crept into the forest of hair at his groin, and enclosed the length of his erection. She closed her eyes as he pressed into her hand, and as she stroked him she was rewarded by his groan of pleasure. His mouth urgently sought her in another kiss.

Her eyes remained closed, but the sunlight dazzled her.

She was vaguely aware of the grass, of the sweet scent of elderberry, and of the clear water flowing close by, but they were all on the edge of her senses, for Blair dominated her consciousness. Her heart beat just for him, her body ached for him, and her spirit yearned to be with him for eternity. As he moved on top of her to invade the inner sanctum of her soul, she knew she'd defy fate, heaven, hell, even the grim reaper, in order to be with him.

She cried out with joy as he sank deep into her, iron hard with arousal. His thrusts were slow at first, to expertly build pleasure. Every inch of him took her closer to complete ecstasy. Then his own need intensified, and as he became more swift and urgent, their hearts beat in unison. He paused at the final moment to prolong the exquisite gratification, but then release carried them away on wave after wave of delight. The pleasure died away slowly as they clung to each other on the grass. They were still joined, and her parted lips moved against his shoulder. His skin was warm and damp, and she breathed in the perfume of his body.

He bent his head to kiss her lips, then he rolled aside and lay gazing up at the sky. "If time were to stop now, I would not complain," he murmured.

Oh, yes, let this moment go on forever . . . But time might snatch her away at any moment, and fling her into the future existence she no longer wanted. She sat up, pushing her tangled hair back from her face. Her pink-tipped breasts were pert in the slightly cool breeze from the stream as she plucked a blade of grass and twirled it thoughtfully between her fingers.

He got up suddenly, his body smooth and perfect in the sunlight before he dove into the water. He cut into the surface with barely a sound, and the ripple reflections glanced off his skin as he glided underwater for a moment before coming up again and turning to smile at her.

She went to join him. The coldness of the water made her breath catch, and she felt weeds brushing against her as she lowered herself to the shoulders. He swam over to her, catching her close to kiss her, and as the water flowed exhilaratingly around them both, he cupped her breasts in his hands and teased her nipples. More kisses followed, and soon she felt his long shaft rising against her as urgently as it had so short a while before. Their passion was so fierce that one act of love had barely touched it, and as he pressed her to the bank they were both oblivious to everything but their need for each other.

The water's chill was almost caressing as he made her his again there in the pool. The gratification was as intense, and he knew so well how to give pleasure that she floated on a tide of sensuality. She thought briefly of Celina. Poor Celina, never to have known this side of him. Never to have experienced the ecstasy Laura Reynolds knew now . . .

They remained in an embrace afterward, until the sound of voices warned them someone was nearby. They broke apart in the water to see two gamekeepers walking along the far bank, with no idea anyone was in the pool. The spaniels had gotten up interestedly, and Blair hissed at them. "Sit!" The dogs lay down again, but remained alert as they watched the other bank. Laura was relieved the elderberries afforded such seclusion. The gamekeepers walked on without knowing what they'd so nearly interrupted, and of one accord she and Blair left the water to put their clothes on.

The air was cooler now, and the clouds that had earlier been a promise on the horizon had spread to make the sunlight watery. They dressed quickly, and she was glad her hair was only wet at the tips. Without a comb it was difficult to manage the heavy curls, but she achieved a reasonable knot, and pinned her hat on again. Then she sat on the grass, watching Blair as he tied his neckcloth. Thoughts of Marianna and Steven suddenly entered her head. "Blair, may I presume a little?"

"I suspect I will not like what you're about to say."

"It concerns Marianna and Steven."

"Laura, if you're going to plead on their behalf—"

"They really are in love, you know, and if you try to make her marry someone else, she'll never forgive you. Is that what you really want?"

"You know it isn't, but I can't possibly agree to let her become Mrs. Steven Woodville. The fellow's penniless and has left a trail of IOU's over London ever since he reached his majority. Marianna may love him, but I suspect he's only interested in her inheritance, and I'm damned if I'm going to let her marry an adventurer like that!"

"Marianna's expectations don't make any difference; he'd love her if she were as penniless as he is."

"Which is what she will be if he marries her—at least, she will be until she's twenty-five, which for him is a very long time."

"You'd really stop her inheriting until then?"

"Yes."

"That's very harsh."

"I'm left no choice if she persists in this totally unsuitable liaison."

"Are you saying Steven has no redeeming features? I can't believe you really mean that. He was your friend, which would hardly have happened if you didn't like or respect him."

"What difference does it make whether or not I like him? It's his qualities as a husband that are in question, and on that score he fails."

"Because of his financial position?"

"Yes."

"Only because of that?"

He hesitated. "Yes, I suppose so."

"So if he were a wealthy man, you'd consider his suit?"

He drew a long breath. "Yes."

"Which means the Handworth match isn't your final word on Marianna's future."

He looked at her. "You're a sly woman, Laura Reynolds."

"Me, sir?"

"You, madam." He smiled a little.

"She really doesn't want to marry Alex Handworth," Laura pressed.

"I know. Very well, I'll release her from the match, but I won't agree to Steven Woodville. Although how I'm going to explain my decision to the Handworths, I really don't know."

Laura was startled by his sudden capitulation. "You—you'll release her?" she repeated.

"Don't sound so surprised, for I *am* open to reason, you know."

Laura smiled. "Marianna will be so happy when you tell her."

"Will she? I doubt it, for her sole purpose is to get to the altar with Woodville, and that's as far away as ever."

"She'll be content for the time being."

The sun vanished behind the clouds, and the breeze became noticeably cooler as the first drops of rain began to fall. Blair pulled Laura to her feet and lifted her onto her horse. No one had seen them enter the little elderberry glade, and no one saw them leave again either.

Fourteen

It was raining quite heavily by the time Blair and Laura handed their mounts to two grooms and hurried into the house, but then something happened to destroy the idyllic happiness of the past hour.

Laura had forgotten Marianna's letter, but suddenly it fell to the floor. Blair immediately put his foot on it. "Why do you have a letter from Marianna to Steven Woodville?" he asked quietly.

A chasm suddenly yawned between them, and she felt so dreadful she couldn't think of anything to say.

"Your silence speaks volumes," he said, picking the letter up.

"Blair, I—"

"What does it contain?" he interrupted.

"I—I don't know," she replied truthfully.

"I find that hard to believe." He broke the letter open, and read the few lines scribbled there. Then he thrust it into her hand. "I suggest you read it, to refresh your memory."

She scanned the brief lines, and her heart fell.

My darling Steven, I will be waiting for you as planned. Don't worry if I'm late, for I will definitely come, and I'll soon be your wife. I love you with all my heart. Your adoring Marianna.

Blair put his hand to her chin, forcing her to look at him. "They clearly plan elopement, and you have been aiding and abetting them! What a fool you've made of me, to be sure. Well, you won't do it again, for I wish you to leave Deveril Park. Is that clear? I want you gone from here within the hour!"

He turned on his heel and as he walked away, a rumble of thunder stole across the lowering skies outside. He'd nearly reached the staircase when he saw the butler.

"Ah, Harcourt, inform Miss Marianna I wish to see her in the drawing room without delay."

"Sir." The butler hurried away.

Blair turned to Laura. "On reflection, I think you should be present at this interview," he said.

"But—"

"Consider it your final obligation whilst in my employ." With a contemptuous bow, he went to the staircase, and after a moment she followed.

Outside, the rain fell even more heavily, and another growl of thunder rolled over the heavens. It was fitting weather for the desolation she felt inside. She'd placed herself in conflict with Blair over something to which he'd already partly come around, and she'd done it for a young woman who'd used her sympathy to confirm plans for elopement! She never dreamed Marianna and Steven intended such a thing, but naively thought they'd rely on reason and persuasion to further their cause.

Blair didn't say anything as they waited in the drawing room, and it seemed she could hear the unhappy thudding of her heart. His face was that of a stranger. The barrier he'd erected that first night at the ball had reappeared, and it was as if that wonderful hour by the stream had never happened. She gazed wretchedly toward the skies outside. A distant flash of lightning lit the clouds, and then more thunder rumbled toward the horizon, but inside the atmosphere was as silent and bitterly cold as she imagined it would be in the ice cave beneath the house.

Light steps approached, and Marianna came in. She wore a primrose muslin gown, and there was a lime green silk shawl around her shoulders. Her face was pale, and her eyes bore signs of recent crying. She halted just inside the door, and raised her head defiantly. "You wish to see me?"

"I do, miss. What's the meaning of this?" He thrust the letter toward her.

Her lips parted and her eyes flew accusingly to Laura, who looked just as accusingly back.

Blair shook his head. "Oh, no, Marianna, don't think to blame your agent, for she didn't pen this missive, you did. Her crime as far as you're concerned is that this piece of paper chose a singularly inappropriate moment to fall from her pocket." He held his sister's gaze. "When and where is Steven expecting to meet you?"

Her lips pressed mutinously together.

"I asked you a question, Marianna."

"I'm not going to tell you," she replied.

"Don't defy me, miss!"

"I'll never tell you."

"Very well, I'll find him at the King's Head."

"No! Please, no!"

"He knows what to expect, he's not a fool. I can't allow this to pass without taking the only honorable action."

"A duel? Oh, no! Please, Blair!" Marianna cried tearfully.

"There's nothing more to say. Now go to your rooms."

With a stifled sob, she turned and fled.

In spite of her resentment at being used, Laura wanted to go after her to comfort her, but as she stepped toward the door, Blair's angry voice halted her. "Oh, no, madam, your duties here are over."

Swallowing back tears, she faced him. "At least let me comfort her a little. Your anger may be justified, but she's eighteen, deeply in love with Steven, and you've just told her you intend to call him out!"

"I'm a monster, am I not?" he flung back bitterly. "For endeavoring to protect my sister from a womanizing opportunist who's pursuing her in order to escape the duns, in your eyes *I'm* branded the wrongdoer! Well, perhaps that's more an indication of your lamentable standards than any failing on my part!"

"Think what you will of me, but at least allow that Marianna is in great distress and needs the sort of comfort that at the moment you're far too angry to give. Let me go to her."

"So that you may carry further messages? I think not."

"You have my word that I will not do anything."

"Very well, but you are still dismissed. As soon as Marianna is calmer, I expect you to quit this house."

She hesitated, and then looked imploringly at him. "I'm deeply sorry about the letter. I really didn't know what it contained, but that doesn't excuse my actions. I wish I hadn't done it, because I know it's changed the way you think of me, but nothing can change the way I feel toward you. I still love you."

"Your feelings are of no interest to me, madam."

His coldness was absolute, and without another word she left the drawing room.

But as she crossed the landing to go to Marianna's apartment, time intervened yet again. Deveril Park disappeared, and was replaced by her hotel suite.

Everything seemed to be spinning, and she had to steady herself by holding on to a chair. Her riding habit had gone, and she was wearing her modern clothes again, and except for the missing hours, it was as if she'd just left Gulliver's cottage and driven straight back here. Rain dashed against the window, and she glanced out to see the weather had changed here in the future as well. The sunshine had gone, and there were clouds—just as there were in her heart.

The force of Blair's anger and contempt was still all around her, tormenting and mocking like a nightmare, and a sob rose in her throat. "Blair, oh, Blair . . ."

Light footsteps approached, bringing an echo of Marianna, but then she recognized Mrs. Fitzgerald's tap at the door. "Laura, my dear?"

"Yes?" Laura hastily composed herself.

Jenny's mother came in. "There was a message from one

of your flatmates when you were out. The audition people are a tad annoyed you haven't been in touch, and I'm afraid that unless you turn up tomorrow, you can kiss the part good-bye."

Right now Laura couldn't have cared less about the audition.

"Are you all right, my dear?" Mrs. Fitzgerald looked at her in concern.

"Yes, quite all right, thank you. To be honest, I don't think I'm interested in the audition anymore."

"But I thought the show was set to be one of *the* productions this year." Mrs. Fitzgerald's eyes cleared. "It's that fellow, isn't it?" she declared.

"Kyle? No, it's nothing to do with him."

"Well, I've given you the message, what you do about it is your business." Jenny's mother turned to leave, but then glanced at the window as more rain spattered the glass. "What a change for the worse," she observed.

"Yes." Laura looked out as well, and suddenly thought of the ice cave again. "Mrs. Fitzgerald, I was told there's a cave under the hotel. Is that right?"

"Why, yes, but you can't get into it, I'm afraid. It was bricked up in Victorian times, maybe even earlier."

"Would you mind showing me?"

"Not at all, but it's not very interesting, just a blocked off doorway in the corner of the cellars. I'll take you now if you like."

The steps to the cellars lay close to the kitchens at the back of the hotel, and the air seemed muffled as Laura followed Jenny's mother down into the poorly lit darkness. They passed beneath the dining room, where footsteps could be heard overhead as the maids set the tables for the evening meal.

The door into the ice cave lay at the very end of a passage. It was easy to make out because it was filled with bricks, and the rest of the cellar wall was stone. Mrs.

Fitzgerald looked at it, and then glanced at her. "Well, I did say it wasn't very interesting."

"It's odd to think there's a cave on the other side, isn't it? Not very nice, actually," Laura added as a sudden shiver passed over her.

A draft of air crept from somewhere. It was sharp and cold, and carried with it a soft sound, like the ghostly sob she'd heard at the tunnel portal. A chill finger ran down her spine, and then she heard the sob again, only this time it was accompanied by a distorted, far-off voice. *Help us, please . . .*

She gasped, and Jenny's mother looked at her in surprise. "What is it, my dear?"

"Did—didn't you hear? It was a voice, someone calling for help!"

Mrs. Fitzgerald's jaw dropped. "A voice? No, I didn't hear anything."

They both listened again, but there was nothing. Jenny's mother smiled reassuringly. "I expect it's just this old place. It's always creaking and making noises."

But as one they turned and hurried away from the old bricked-up doorway. They almost ran up the steps into the brightness and warmth of the hotel, and Mrs. Fitzgerald immediately closed the cellar door behind them. Then she gave a self-conscious laugh. "Goodness, you've quite given me the shivers!"

"I've given myself them as well," Laura admitted ruefully, glancing back toward the cellar door.

"Remind me never to watch a horror movie with you."

Laura smiled. "I'll try." She paused. "I don't suppose it's possible to get into the cave somehow, is it?"

"Haven't you had enough of a fright?"

"I guess not."

Mrs. Fitzgerald shrugged philosophically. "Well, you can't get in from the hotel without knocking down the brickwork, but there may be a way from the canal tunnel. You see, the tunnel's directly below the cave, but it shouldn't have been. I gather the engineer made a mistake in his calculations. Anyway, part of the cave floor gave way when they drove through, and it had to be sealed up. Maybe the old brickwork has fallen away. That's all I can think of. But I wouldn't recommend going into the tunnel, my dear, it's a horrible place, and quite unsafe with all the roof falls. Ron Sawyer does boat trips into it in the summer when there hasn't been too much rain, and he says it's still like Niagara with all the springs bursting through even then."

"Do you think he'd take me in if I asked real nice?"

She puzzled Mrs. Fitzgerald. "Why are you so interested, my dear? The cave *can't* be a pleasant place, and I *know* the tunnel isn't."

"I'm just curious, that's all." Laura didn't really know why she was making such a thing about it, but she couldn't help herself. Something about the cave was getting to her suddenly.

Jenny's mother shrugged. "Well, I can give Ron a call, if you like?" she offered.

"Would you?"

"Consider it done." Mrs. Fitzgerald hastened away.

Laura looked at the cellar door again. For a moment it seemed she could still hear the uncanny voice. *Help us, please . . .* The primitive unease returned, and without further ado she hurried after Jenny's mother.

Fifteen

Ron agreed to take Laura into the tunnel the next morning, so she passed the rest of the day as best she could.

That night she lay awake listening to the rain, and trying to will the ballroom doors into existence, but the hours ticked fruitlessly past, and at last she tried to sleep. Sleep wouldn't come, though, and eventually she decided to try a glass of hot milk, which usually worked. Rather than ring for one, she thought she'd go down to the kitchens and get one herself, so she put on her robe and went to the door, but as she touched the handle, it seemed to dissolve.

Suddenly she was in her Regency nightgown on the landing at Deveril Park, and the only light was the flicker of the candle in Blair's hand as he came up the staircase toward her.

The cranberry of his coat was vivid in the candle glow, his neckcloth hung loose, and shadows moved over the walls, flashing on his wedding ring as he saw the white of her nightgown. His eyes darkened as she stood in his path. "You can no longer trap me with tenderness, madam."

"Please talk to me, Blair," she begged.

"There's nothing to say," he replied coldly.

"Forgive me for agreeing to take Marianna's letter."

"You expect too much." There was no softening in his eyes.

"I expect nothing; I beg everything."

"Glib words."

"Sincere words," she countered. "Please don't think I'd

have carried that letter if I'd realized they meant to elope. I thought they'd try to persuade you to their point of view, nothing more."

"And that makes it all right? Laura Reynolds didn't look further than her meddling nose, and so must be forgiven her transgressions?"

"I admit I meddled, but my motives—"

"Were insupportable," he interrupted coldly.

"Would *you* agree to marry someone you loathed simply because someone else said so?"

"That's different."

"Why? Because you're a man and at liberty to choose?"

He drew a long breath. "That's the way of this world, Laura."

"If you were in Marianna's place, you'd see things differently."

"I'm sure I would, but I'm *not* in her place. It's my duty to see her future is secure. Steven Woodville can't provide security. It may have escaped your notice that a husband is supposed to keep his wife, not the other way around," he said acidly.

"What if he were wealthy, married Marianna, and *then* lost everything? Would you still say they couldn't use her inheritance?"

"That's hardly the same thing."

"Maybe not, but the end result is exactly the same—Marianna would be supporting Steven."

"How clever you are at turning an argument in your own favor."

"I've turned nothing, sir, I've merely pointed out an incontrovertible fact. You'd clearly find it acceptable for Marianna to provide for Steven if he *became* penniless, but not if he's penniless now."

"I see I'm being charged with double standards."

"No, just with standards which do not seem to apply to royalty. Princess Charlotte, who will one day be queen, has this very month married Prince Leopold of Coburg, whose prospects and financial status hardly stand up to comparison with hers. What do you say to that, sir?"

"Nothing, for it's an example with which I cannot argue."

"Why can't Steven be Marianna's Prince Leopold? Is he so far beyond the pale that nothing will make him acceptable? Please, Blair, if you feel anything for Marianna, and I know you do, you'll not only stand by your decision to release her from the Handworth match, you'll also give Steven proper consideration." She searched his face in the candlelight. "Or do you mean to make her marry Alex Handworth after all?"

"I said I'd halt the match, and that's what I'll do."

"Have you told her yet?"

"No. The moment hasn't been opportune."

Laura held his gaze. "Tell her, Blair, and mend at least a little of the rift between you. And if you would mend still more, then promise to consider Steven as her husband."

"Steven is unacceptable," he repeated flatly.

"He'd make her happy, doesn't that count at all? You were happy in your marriage," she added.

"Celina was hardly unsuitable."

She remembered what he'd said by the pool. Celina may not have been unsuitable, but on his own admission she was guilty of unspecified misconduct in order to marry him.

He read her thoughts. "Even your silence puts a finger on the pulse, does it not?" he murmured. "Very well, I'll agree to consider Steven for Marianna, but that's *all* I agree to, because in the light of the plan to run away, I fear no amount of eloquent pleading on his behalf can turn him into another Prince Leopold of Coburg!"

"Oh, I do love you so," she murmured, deeply affected by his willingness to listen even now, when those around him had betrayed him.

"Love?" He looked into her eyes. "The trap yawns before me, beguiling in its tenderness, seductive in its promise . . ."

"There's no trap, Blair, just me."

"*Just* you? But you are no ordinary being, Laura Reynolds."

How true that was, for she was a traveler in time, a woman so overwhelmed with love for a man from another century she wanted to spend the rest of her life with him. A woman who was prepared to forsake everything she'd ever known, her very world and culture, just to be near him . . .

He put his hand to her cheek, his fingertips so soft and gentle she could barely feel their touch. "I can't close you out, Laura, you mean too much."

"I—I do?" Tears shone in her eyes, and her voice was so tight with emotion she could barely speak.

"Do you imagine I'd still be here like this if you didn't? I *wanted* you to plead with me, *wanted* you to make me change my mind, but I had to protect myself from you at the same time. My cold words were a defense against a love my heart tells me is too sudden, too intense . . ."

"Is it really love you speak of?" she breathed.

"Can you doubt it?" he replied, moving his hand to her waist, and pulling her close. The candle flames danced in his other hand, their light flickering over them both as he bent his head to kiss her.

Her lips parted yearningly, and she softened against him, her body warm and pliable beneath the muslin of her nightgown. Kisses weren't enough, their reconciliation demanded more. She felt passion carrying her away as her hands moved wantonly over him; her exploring fingers pressed to the arousal that had surged to match her desire.

His breath caught, and he drew back. "I'll have you in a bed this time, Mrs. Reynolds," he said softly, taking her by the hand and leading her across the landing in the direction of his private apartment.

But as they reached the door, there was a sudden rumbling sound in the distance. They both turned in alarm, for the whole house seemed to shake. He caught her close, and she stared fearfully around. An earthquake? *In England?*

They heard the servants' alarmed cries from the floor above, and then the rumbling died away and everything was still again. Blair released her slowly. "Dear God, it's the tunnel," he whispered.

"The tunnel?" Of course, the 1816 roof fall! She looked quickly at him. "Marianna will be frightened!"

He hurried toward his sister's apartment, but as he flung the door open, they saw only darkness beyond. The candles threw an uncertain light over deserted rooms. There was no sign of Marianna, and her bed was still neatly turned back, just as her maid had left it earlier.

Awful realization began to sink through Laura as Blair went into the dressing room. After a moment he returned. "She's gone," he said quietly. "Her portmanteau is missing, and so are her traveling things."

"Are—are you quite certain?"

"Yes." He gave a harsh laugh. "Too late I see the truth about Woodville's visit to Cheltenham. There was no friend; he was simply making arrangements for an elopement!"

Laura stared at him, knowing he was right.

"Damn it, they've run away together after all!" His anger exploded, and he hurled the candelabrum at the fireplace. The flames went out, and the rooms were engulfed in darkness.

She heard the servants on the landing.

No, not servants. Voices outside. And a car. Filled with dismay, she ran to her hotel window, and looked out to see some very late guests arriving. Tears of frustration stung her eyes.

The following morning found Laura still in the future. She felt so helpless. What was happening at Deveril Park? Had Marianna and Steven really eloped? Would Blair go after them? And then there was the tunnel fall . . . She felt like a prisoner, and the future was her cell. Everything that mattered was in 1816, but when she looked in the mirror it was only her modern self that gazed back. She felt so trapped she cried, but after a while pulled herself together. Crying wouldn't do any good, she had to carry on until the past claimed her again, so after breakfast she drove to the Bargee's Arms to meet Ron Sawyer as arranged.

The rain had stopped overnight, and it was sunny as she parked her car. Ron heard her arrive, and came out almost straightaway. He was wearing an oilskin hat and raincoat, and had some oilskins for her to wear too because the tunnel would be very wet after the rain. When she was ready, he helped her into a boat where he'd already put some hurricane lamps, then he rowed strongly toward the tunnel.

She heard the woodpeckers as the canal entered the trees near the portal. Their noise became louder by the ruined cottage, and Laura glanced at the rotting old boat by the gate, remembering how she'd seen it in pristine condition in 1816. The spruce tree cast a long shadow over the water as Ron shipped the oars to glide the final yards to the safety gate just inside the tunnel.

Laura watched him unlock the padlock. "Your great-grandfather lived at that cottage, didn't he?"

"Yes, the old rogue."

"You think he really did visit his mistress that day?"

"There's no doubt. If he was white as a sheet, it was because he was terrified of his fearsome wife." Ron chuckled as he eased the gates open.

Laura turned up her collar, because even just inside the tunnel the air was perceptibly colder. Ron pushed the boat forward, and she looked into the darkness as he paused to light one of the hurricane lamps. The draft she'd heard before still sighed through the tunnel, and spring water splashed somewhere. The atmosphere was creepy, she thought, and although the canal had still been in use in Ron's great-grandfather's time, it can't have been all that different then from now. Someone like the old watchman would have been used to it, and wouldn't get spooked by odd noises. It would take much more to make him row out of here like a bat out of hell, and whatever it was, he'd preferred to run the gauntlet of his wife than be ridiculed for insisting he'd been back in time.

Ron fixed the lamp to the prow, then handed her a torch. "Keep it ready in case the lamp goes out. And don't forget, if you see any roof falls ahead, just give me a yell. We don't want to ram one like old Gulliver."

He began to row, and the light from the portal slid further and further behind. The lamp shone brightly, but all around the darkness was murky and claustrophobic, and there was something eerie about the marks left on the limestone by long-gone bargees who'd legged their vessels through the hill.

Laura glanced up at the roof of the tunnel. It ran with moisture and was spiked with tiny stalactites. Droplets of water pattered constantly on her oilskins, and she could see her breath. The first spring poured through a fissure, splashing noisily as the boat passed.

Ron grinned. "It sounds worse than it is," he shouted.

"I'll take your word for it."

"We'll reach the end of the limestone soon. It's as far as I usually go because the fuller's earth is so unstable. They used to shore it up with brickwork and elm planking, but now it's all badly in need of repair. If it looks okay, I'll risk going a bit further in to see if we can reach the stretch below the cave. From what I remember, it's easy enough to recognize because there's brickwork in the middle of a stretch of limestone." He rowed on.

Suddenly Laura saw a wall of earth directly ahead. It loomed into the arc of lamplight like a dark, soft iceberg, and she cried out in alarm. "Ron, there's a roof fall!"

He hastily rowed backward to slow the boat, and as the prow nudged gently into the earth he shipped the oars to inspect the fall more closely. "I think it's the cave-in that did for poor old Gulliver. Yes, the marks he left behind are still here after all this time. Hand me the torch."

She obeyed, and he shone it at the top of the fall. "See that gap up there? It's where Gulliver tried to get through. You can see where he scrambled up. If he hadn't done that, he'd probably have been all right. Instead, he lost his footing and fell backward, hitting his back on the boat."

Laura stared at him. "But he told me he damaged his spine when the boat actually struck the cave-in."

"Oh, no, it was his infernal curiosity that cost him." Ron drew a long breath. "I'm sorry we can't go any further, miss. I thought this fall came a bit further in than this, but then I haven't been this far for a long time. I'm quite amazed all the marks Gulliver left are still so fresh."

She was puzzled. Why hadn't Gulliver told the truth? What possible reason could he have? Unless . . . She gazed up at the gap. What was on the other side? Had he heard something? Seen something, maybe? "Can I have the torch?" she said, and then flashed it toward the top of the fall.

Beyond the splash of the springs she could hear the draft moaning through the tunnel, and a muffled voice calling from the far side of the fall, *Help us, please . . .*

She gasped. "Did you hear that?"

"Hear what?"

Suddenly the tunnel felt so oppressive she couldn't stay there. "Let's go, please."

He quickly turned the boat and began to row back toward the portal. It seemed an age before they emerged into daylight again, and as she exhaled with relief, Ron grinned at her. "Reckon that's your first and last visit to Deveril Tunnel, eh, miss? "

"You reckon right," she replied, taking off her oilskin hat and shaking her hair loose in the fresh air.

They reached the inn, and Ron helped her out of the boat again. She was just taking off her raincoat when she heard a familiar whirring sound by the inn entrance. She saw Gulliver's wheelchair going in, and her eyes glinted with determination. He might be able to order her out of his cottage, but he couldn't do the same at a public house.

She had questions to which she was sure Gulliver Harcourt had some answers, and this time she wasn't going to take any nonsense.

Sixteen

Gulliver was enjoying a beer by the inglenook, and didn't see Laura until she sat next to him.

"Hi, Gulliver. It's me again, and I'm afraid I'm not going away."

He sighed. "Look, Miss Reynolds, I don't know anything, so you're wasting your time."

"You'd keep it to yourself if aliens landed on Great Deveril church, in case everyone thought you'd gone crazy."

"Well, never having seen aliens, I—"

She interrupted. "No, but you know about time travel, don't you? Oh, come on, Gulliver, I'm going to be on your back until you give in."

He sighed again. "You're a very pushy woman, Miss Reynolds."

"And you're just being plain cussed by refusing to admit that you and I have something very peculiar in common. *Please* talk to me."

He ran a fingertip around his beer glass. "Are you a reporter of some kind?"

"A what? No, I'm not. I'm not in TV, newspapers, or anything, and I'm not writing a book, if that's your next question. I just happen to be here on vacation. That's all, I promise."

"So if I talk to you, it won't go any further?"

Her eyes brightened. "Of course. Does that mean you will?"

He nodded reluctantly. "All right, I admit I know what

you're talking about. Traveling in time isn't a myth, it really can happen, and twenty years ago it happened to me."

She sat back in relief. "I *knew* I wasn't the only one!" Then she looked at him again. "It was in the tunnel, wasn't it? I know you haven't been entirely honest about it so far, because Ron told me you climbed up to try to see past the cave-in, and that *that* was when you hurt your spine, not when your boat actually rammed the fall." Her thoughts raced on. "Something happened to Ron's great-grandfather in the tunnel as well, didn't it?"

"Well, something definitely happened to me, but I can't really comment on Jack Sawyer, except to say I'd guess he experienced it too."

"*Jack* Sawyer?" she repeated, her glance flying to the wall and the picture of the traveling showman.

He knew what she was thinking. "That's right, the same name as his ancestor. Names seem to have something to do with it. I share mine with the butler at Deveril Park, you share yours with the other Laura Reynolds, so I'm pretty sure the same thing applied to Jack Sawyer."

"Does that mean it's happened to Dolly Frampton as well? Sorry, I mean Dolly Renwick."

"No, you see her name isn't really Dolly, it's just a nickname in the Frampton family. She's Irene, but the 1816 Dolly was Dorothy. It seems the names have to be exactly the same. Anyway, you want to know about my brush with time travel. It was the week of the Mercury Fair, and—"

"The fair was still being held twenty years ago?" she interrupted in surprise.

"It's still held now." The interruption exasperated him. "Do you want to hear this tale or not?"

"Yes, of course. I'm sorry."

A little mollified, he continued. "Well, as I told you before, I wanted to examine part of the tunnel, so I rowed in. I didn't see the fall until it was too late, and I rammed right into it, but I didn't hurt myself. I was about to row out again when I heard a strange noise coming from the other side of the cave-in."

Laura sat forward. "Was it someone calling for help?"

He looked quickly at her. "Not at first. The sound I heard was a dull hammering, a thud, thud, thud that seemed to make the whole tunnel shake. I had a torch, and realized it was coming from beyond a gap at the top of the fall, so I scrambled up to look through." He paused to sip his beer, and Laura saw his hand was shaking.

"Go on," she prompted gently.

"Well, I just wasn't expecting what happened next. One moment I was in my own time, the next I was looking on something from the past. I knew without being told that it was 1816, and that the roof fall I'd come upon was a repeat of the one that had happened then, right down to the fact that it was actually two falls, with a fifty-foot stretch of safe rocky tunnel in between. There was a blue rowing boat trapped in the safe part, I could see it plainly because of a lighted lantern on its prow, just like Ron fixes lamps on his boats now. I recognized the boat, because it's been rotting by the old watchman's cottage ever since I can remember. It was found in the tunnel when the 1816 fall was cleared up and made good."

"I know the boat you mean," Laura said.

"Well, it had a young man and woman in it. He was fair-haired and rather frail-looking, and she was a dark little thing, like a young Audrey Hepburn. You know, the movie star?"

Steven and Marianna, Laura thought with a start.

He went on. "Anyway, they were looking up at where the hammering was coming from behind a patch of brick-work set into the tunnel roof. The young woman—Marianna Deveril, I was to find out—was frightened and crying and the young man, her lover, Steven Woodville, was standing up in the boat calling to whoever it was beyond the brickwork. 'Help us, please,' he kept saying."

A cold shiver passed down Laura's spine. She realized

now that it was Steven's voice she'd heard. What were he and Marianna doing in the tunnel? As the question entered her head, the answer came. They'd eloped that way to throw off any pursuit, and no doubt Steven's coachman would have waited at the other portal. Blair had probably been only too right to suspect Steven of never having gone to Cheltenham, but of making arrangements for the elopement instead. Marianna's letter had, after all, merely confirmed her intent to stand by plans already made!

Gulliver continued. "The hammering was almost frantic. I found out later it was mallets and chisels being used to get through from the cave to rescue the two in the tunnel, although how anyone knew they were there I don't know, because to all intents and purposes the roof fall looked like one large cave-in, with no hint of a safe area in the middle. Anyway, the bricks in the roof suddenly gave, knocking Steven into the water. Marianna screamed, and I was so shaken by what I'd seen that I suddenly pulled back sharply. I lost my balance, and rolled back down the fall into my own time again."

She looked anxiously at him. "You say Steven was knocked into the water? Does—does that mean he drowned?"

"No, he didn't, although I didn't find out until the next time I went back." He gave a wry smile. "I'd had the hell frightened out of me the first time, but it didn't stop me wanting to go again the very next day. I rowed to the fall, and saw the past again, only this time I took part in it. There was no one there when I scrambled through into the past, just the barely afloat boat. The lantern had gone out, but I had a good torch, and could see the damage the falling bricks had done to the boat. I also saw a knotted rope dangling down from the hole in the tunnel roof. I tell you, that rope was like a hypnotist's beckoning finger, I *had* to climb up it. So I swam to the boat, and hauled myself into the cave above. The first thing that struck me was the cold that came from the pyramid of ice stored there from the previous winter. It was insulated with straw, but by *God* the air was Arctic!"

Gulliver hesitated. "Up to this point I was having an adventure, but the moment I left the cave and went up into the house above, I changed."

"Changed?"

"Just as you become the other Laura Reynolds, I became my predecessor, the butler."

Predecessor! For the first time Laura wondered if she and her Regency counterpart were related. Why hadn't it occurred to her before? It was so obvious. With a family name like Reynolds, her roots had to be British, so why couldn't the other Laura have been one of her forebears?

Gulliver continued. "It's because I became the butler that I know about the layout of Deveril Park and about the coat-of-arms being an allusion to Sir Blair Deveril and his wife, Celina. I knew all about everyone in the house, including Marianna and Steven Woodville—who, incidentally, was only stunned by the bricks. I also knew that Laura Reynolds and Sir Blair were in love, for nothing abovestairs escapes the servants. I was in love too, with Dolly Frampton, and I was cock-a-hoop because I'd just succeeded in winning her from Ha'penny Jack Sawyer." He smiled a little. "All this knowledge flooded into me in a few seconds as I entered the main part of the house. It felt very strange, as if I were trapped inside this other person."

"I know exactly what you mean," Laura said, recalling the first time it had happened to her.

"If it had just stopped there it would have been wonderful, but the next minutes were so traumatic, I've never wanted to go back again."

She stared at him. "What happened?"

He drew a long breath. "Well, I found myself running toward the staircase. I'd left Dolly in a pony trap outside, and was running because she and I heard pistol shots as we drove back from the fair."

"Pistol shots?" Her eyes widened.

He nodded. "All the servants were at the fair because Sir Blair gave them a day off every year, but Dolly wanted to visit her aunt in Cirencester, and I'd agreed to drive her there. Anything to get her away from the proximity of Ha'penny Jack!" He gave an uneasy chuckle, as if the brief humor felt too out of place in what he had to say. "Well, on hearing the shots we drove more quickly, and I rushed into the house. There was no one around, but I knew Sir Blair, Marianna Deveril, Steven Woodville, and Laura Reynolds were still in the house, so I began to run up the staircase, but as I reached the top I saw a man lying in a pool of blood. He'd been shot through the heart."

Laura's breath caught. Please don't let it have been Blair . . .

"I don't know who he was. His clothes marked him as a gentleman, not a servant, but I didn't see his face. I was so unspeakably shocked by seeing him that I stumbled backward down the stairs. It was a repeat of my fall in the tunnel, but instead of the stairs, I really was falling back in the tunnel. It was a headlong tumble this time, and I landed against my boat with such force I broke my back and passed out. I lay there for hours before Ron Sawyer realized I was missing and raised the alarm. I've been in this wheelchair ever since, and I've closed my mind to everything that happened. I think that's why nothing's happened to me since. One has to *want* to go back, as you do because you love Blair Deveril. You *are* in love with him, aren't you?"

"Yes, I'm in love with him, but from what you've just said, he might be the dead man at the top of the staircase."

"Yes, or it might have been Steven Woodville," he pointed out.

"You really don't know any more?"

"Nothing. I didn't see or hear anyone else; my knowledge ceased at the point I fell back down the stairs. I only know how the situation was until then, just as you only know what's happened up to the last time you were in the past. I've just told you something still to come for you."

She met his eyes. "It will happen soon. You see, it might be January here, but when I go back, it's May, Mercury Fair time, and the servants are about to have their annual day off. So the man, whoever he is, is going to die very soon, if you see what I mean." The imminence shocked her. "Oh, Gulliver, I feel so *trapped* here in the future! I want to go back so badly . . ."

"Take my advice, and hightail it home to the States."

"There's nothing for me there; it's all here now."

"Even if Sir Blair Deveril is killed?"

She closed her eyes. "Yes, even then." She got up slowly. "I—I think I'll return to the hotel now."

"This time I'm the one who must apologize for any upset, but you *did* insist I tell you what I knew."

"I know."

He took her hand and squeezed it. "I hope it goes well for you, my dear, and if you need to talk anymore, you know where I am."

"Thank you, Gulliver," she replied, and impulsively bent to kiss his cheek. Then she hurried to the door, anxious to get out into the fresh air to think a little.

But as she crossed the threshold, she was plunged into the past again, and a grim and frightening figure in black mourning gauze suddenly blocked her path.

"He's mine, not yours, you whore!" Estelle breathed. Her veil was flung back, revealing a haggard face that was twisted with jealousy, and her hatred was so fierce it was tangible.

Seventeen

Laura pressed fearfully back against the door jamb, dismayed to find herself suddenly confronted by the strange woman she believed to be Lady Lowestoft.

Estelle took a step nearer. "He'll never be yours, he's mine in the eyes of God and the world!"

"I—I don't know who you're talking about." Laura glanced around, but there was no one else near; even the barges moored along the canal seemed deserted. Where was everyone? Suddenly she wished she hadn't come out alone while Blair tried to find out where Marianna and Steven had gone. No one yet knew, as she now did, that they were trapped in the tunnel.

Estelle's wild eyes flashed. "Innocence is a grace you haven't known in a very long time, as is conscience, for it constantly slips your mind that Miles is *my* husband, not yours!"

So it *was* Lady Lowestoft! Laura pressed further back against the jamb. "I really don't know what you're talking about," she insisted, glancing desperately around again, for the woman was clearly deranged.

"You know full well, whore."

"Whore?" Laura's eyes cleared. "You—you surely don't believe that Sir Miles and I are . . . ?"

"Lovers? Oh, I *know* you are. He swore you were dead, but I knew I couldn't trust him."

"Dead?" Laura stared at her.

"He claimed you fell from your horse, but here you are,

as brazen and sinful as all your kind, flaunting your body and your red hair like a common harlot!"

Laura was shaken. The woman thought she was Celina, and from what she said, it seemed Miles and Blair's dead wife *must* have been lovers!

The familiar sound of the spaniels interrupted the silence, and Laura turned with relief to see the dogs accompanying Blair as he rode toward the inn. Estelle saw him too, and without another word gathered her gloomy skirts to hurry away. Her carriage must have been drawn up alongside the inn, for a moment later Laura heard the whip crack, then the coachman flung the team forward and the vehicle careened away along the road.

Laura closed her eyes for a moment. She didn't know what Estelle might have done if Blair hadn't appeared, maybe nothing more than curse her with hell and damnation, but at least the woman's constant presence was explained. She thought Miles was seeing Celina again. But one mystery still remained—why had Celina taken Miles as her lover? Unless, of course, she'd been blackmailed . . . Yes, that was always a possibility where Miles was concerned, for it was his stock-in-trade.

The spaniels bounded up to Laura, and after dismounting Blair gazed in astonishment after the dangerously swaying carriage. "Who in God's name was that?"

She faced him. "Lady Lowestoft. She thought I was Celina," she said quietly, wondering what his reaction would be, for it seemed likely that Celina, not the necklace, was the main reason for the dislike between Miles and him.

He met her eyes. "An easy enough mistake to make under the circumstances."

"She made it plain she despises the very sound of Celina's name."

He didn't respond.

"Blair, why does she hate Celina so much?" Laura was consumed with curiosity.

"It's of no consequence now."

"But—"

He broke in. "I'd rather not discuss it, Laura. It's in the past, and I wish it to remain so."

She wanted to ask more, but heeded his wish. Besides, what did Lady Lowestoft's unbalanced suspicions matter when Blair might soon be the man Harcourt would see lying dead at the top of the staircase at Deveril Park?

Blair seemed to have put Miles's wife from his mind. "I can find no trace of Marianna and Steven, they seem to have vanished. By God, if I had him here now, I'd tear his fortune-hunting heart out!"

Laura lowered her eyes. She knew exactly where to find the runaways, but no one could possibly know what she did by any normal means, so how could she say? If only she could think of some way to broach it . . .

Someone shouted across the meadows, and they turned to see Harcourt riding furiously toward them. Blair caught his horse's bridle as he reined in. "What is it? Have you news?"

The butler's face was pale. "Yes, Sir Blair, but I fear it isn't good."

"Tell me, man!"

"Late last night the canal watchman came home the worse for wear, and saw Miss Marianna and Mr. Woodville rowing on the canal close to the tunnel. Someone called him and he turned away, and when he looked again they'd gone. It wasn't long after that that the tunnel caved in."

Blair stared at him. "Are you saying . . . ?" He couldn't finish.

The butler nodded. "I fear so, Sir Blair. I rode over the hill to the other portal, and found Mr. Woodville's carriage still waiting there. I—I'm so sorry, sir, but they must have been caught in the fall."

"Sweet Jesu," Blair breathed.

Laura seized his hands. "You mustn't think the worst!"

He was stricken. "Pray God it was swift," he said softly.

"Blair, maybe they *were* caught in the fall, but that

doesn't mean they were killed," she said quietly. "Think about the tunnel, it isn't all fuller's earth, there's limestone as well. What if they've been trapped between two falls? It's possible, isn't it?"

"*Two* falls?" He shook his head. "That would be too much to hope."

"The alternative is no hope at all, and if fuller's earth is very unstable, maybe one fall could trigger another nearby."

His eyes lightened a little. "You know, it *is* just possible! The fall begins where there's a mixture of earth and stone, and what's more, it's right beneath the cave at Deveril Park. Brickwork is all that separates the cave from the tunnel! Laura, they may be safe, but trapped! There's no time to waste!"

Within seconds they were all three riding back to the house.

Laura's heart pounded as she accompanied Blair, Harcourt, and a rescue party into the cellars, for she alone knew that Marianna and Steven were still alive.

The men carried mallets, chisels, and a sturdily knotted rope to lower into the tunnel when they broke through the brickwork. The silence of the house overhead seemed oppressive, and lanterns sent shadows receding all around as they made their way toward the cave. The door groaned on its hinges, and a draft of frozen air swept out, then the lanterns flared as Blair went first down the steep wooden steps into the darkness, where water dripped from the pyramid of ice that Gulliver had described.

At last they reached the lowermost point of the cave, where the wrongly routed tunnel had come so close that the rock floor had broken away and been replaced. Blair knelt to press his ear to the bricks. He listened but heard nothing, so he nodded at one of the men, who struck a mallet three times against the nearby rock.

Blair listened again, then scrambled to his feet. "They're

there! I can hear them calling! Go to it, lads! We're going to save them!"

Sparks glinted as the chisels were driven into the mortar between the bricks, and he came quickly over to hug Laura in front of everyone. "I don't know how to thank you for this, Laura. If it weren't for you, they wouldn't have been found until too late."

Feeling guilty because she had so many secrets, she circled her arms tightly around him. She wanted to be honest about everything, but confession wouldn't be good for either of their souls. She couldn't expect him to understand about the time travel, nor could she hope he'd forgive her involvement in Miles's plot. So she had to keep her own counsel, but right now it was very hard indeed . . .

He released her, and returned to help the men, taking a mallet and swinging it mightily. The sound joined with the others, and as a small hole was at last driven through, Steven's cries drifted up to the rescuers. "Help us, please! Help us!" With his voice came the dim glow of the lantern fixed to the rowing boat's prow.

The men redoubled their efforts, until Blair suddenly realized a large portion of brickwood was about to give way. "Watch out below!" he shouted, as everyone in the cave drew hastily aside to solid rock.

The bricks fell with a rushing sound, and Marianna screamed. "Steven!" Laura closed her eyes, for this was the moment Gulliver's first brush with time travel had ended.

Blair looked anxiously down. As the dust settled, he saw the boat on the dark water. The falling bricks had damaged it and struck Steven, who was lying unconscious in Marianna's arms.

The men quickly lowered Blair into the tunnel, and Marianna sobbed distractedly as he examined Steven. Then he put a reassuring hand on her arm. "He's all right, sweetheart, it's just a glancing blow. Now let's get you both out of here. You first."

Marianna was pulled up. She was very distressed and

covered in dust, and her wet skirts clung to her ankles. As soon as Steven was hauled safely onto the cave floor, she knelt to cradle his head on her lap. "Steven? Oh, Steven, please open your eyes, for I love you with all my heart!" she begged, ignoring the blood that trickled over her clothes from his forehead.

The men glanced at each other, and Harcourt frowned at them. "Your task's not done yet, lads; we've Sir Blair to get out now!"

They tossed the rope down again and as Blair caught it, Laura saw debris splashing into the dust-covered canal water. The boat was awash, but she knew it wouldn't sink just yet, for Gulliver would climb up from it to become Harcourt for a few fateful minutes. She glanced at the butler, and saw how like his namesake from the future he was. When he was older, if he were to wear a beard, he'd be the Gulliver Harcourt she knew . . .

The boat wallowed as Blair swung his weight onto the rope, and as he began to climb, the lantern on the prow suddenly went out, plunging the tunnel into darkness. When he reached the cave again, Blair went to Marianna, and put a gentle hand to her dirty, tear-stained cheek. "Are you all right now, sweeting?"

"I am, but Steven—"

"I'm certain he's only suffered a grazing, but I'll have the doctor brought as quickly as possible, just to be certain."

"Are—are you very angry with me?"

"Right now I'm too relieved you're safe, but I have no doubt my anger will return. You've been very foolish, Marianna, but it's Steven I really blame."

"Please don't say that! It was all my fault, Blair, *I* was the one who wanted to run away."

"And he's the one who's old enough to know better," was the terse reply.

Marianna stroked Steven's hair. "You just don't understand how much I love him."

Belatedly conscious of the listening men, Blair straightened. "I think we've said enough for the moment, Marianna," he warned, thinking of what was left of her reputation. He turned to Harcourt. "I wish to thank everyone for their help. I know the servants have tomorrow off for the fair, but they may take the rest of today as well."

There was a delighted stir, and the butler bowed. "Thank you, sir."

"And now please see Mr. Woodville is carried up to the house. Put him in the suite in the north wing, and then send someone for the doctor."

"Sir." Harcourt bowed again. As the men picked Steven up, Marianna got to her feet and looked accusingly at her brother. "The north wing? There's no need to separate us so obviously!"

He waited until the servants had gone, then faced her. "No need to separate you? Marianna, your behavior has been appalling, and Steven's has been worse, so I don't intend to encourage further transgressions. Like it or not, Lord Sivintree and his son will soon be here for your betrothal, and although I—"

Before he could tell her of his decision not to proceed with the match, Marianna's resentment erupted in a blaze of continuing defiance. "I *won't* marry Alex Handworth, and nothing you can say will change my mind!"

"Marianna—"

"I hate you!" she cried, and with a sob fled from the cave.

A nerve fluttered at his temple, and as his lips pressed angrily together, Laura went to him. "Don't think too badly of her, she's suffered a terrible ordeal."

"We all have, but Marianna thinks only of herself and Woodville; no one else matters," he said bitterly.

She cajoled a little. "Come, sir, you were once eighteen, and you'll always be a loving and understanding brother."

"Indeed? Well it may interest you to know that right now

I feel like throttling my little sister," he replied, but with a smile.

She linked his arm. "I love you," she whispered, her eyes shining in the light from the lantern the rescue party had left behind.

He drew a fingertip over her lips. "Even now, when everything else is so chaotic, you have the power to soothe and arouse me. I've lost my heart to you, Laura."

"Do—do you really mean that?" she whispered.

"Mean that I love you? Yes, completely."

The air sang around her. He loved her. Blair loved her!

Eighteen

Later that afternoon, as the servants enjoyed their unexpected holiday, and Marianna sat crying relievedly in the drawing room after learning that the doctor was sure Steven would soon be quite well again, in Blair's private apartment the only sounds were soft kisses and sighs as he and Laura made love.

The cool silk sheets were fragrant with lavender, and their bodies were warm and damp. She was lost in the ecstasy of a fulfillment that drove all else into oblivion. She gasped as she felt him between her thighs. He lingered before penetration, teasing, promising, enticing, and then he slowly slid inside. Shudders of intense delight passed through them both as he entered completely, and began the long, easy strokes that would soon carry them both to the peak of ecstasy.

She felt as if her flesh were melting. She was no longer a living creature, but something ethereal, lacking all substance, ruled by pure sensation. He slowed his movements to prolong the pleasure, from time to time becoming totally still in defiance of final release. She could feel him throbbing deep within her, joining him to her in a way that meant everything, and she knew that when next he moved neither of them would be able to prevent the climax.

Their eyes met for those final seconds, and they continued to gaze at each other as he slowly eased out a little before sinking voluptuously in one last time. Her whole body shuddered as it was invaded by a maelstrom of joy she wished would last forever.

But the chaos of pleasure began to subside, and she heard

him sigh as he gathered her close to savor the fading moments. His lips found hers in a long, adoring kiss that put another seal upon her fate. She couldn't exist without him, he was the destiny she'd been created for. She didn't want the whole universe, just this small but exquisite existence in his arms.

She wrapped her legs wantonly around him, and pressed her lips to his shoulder, tasting the salt of his skin. What was going to happen tomorrow? Who was going to lie dead at the top of the staircase? She silently beseeched fate to show compassion. Don't take him from me, please . . .

She closed her eyes then, for if Blair didn't die, who did? She didn't want it to be Steven either.

They were discreet, leaving the apartment separately when there was no one to see. She left first, wearing the blue and white floral gown she'd changed into a little earlier, but as she passed the drawing room door, she heard Marianna still sobbing softly inside.

Blair's sister was sitting on one of the deep window ledges, with her knees drawn up and her head bowed. The sun shone on her short dark hair and mauve lawn gown, and the spaniels were on the floor beside her. She didn't know Laura was there until the dogs whined, then she looked up swiftly. "Oh, it's only you, Laura, I thought . . ."

"It was Blair?"

Marianna nodded, her chin setting with familiar mutinousness, but then she noticed the glow on Laura's cheeks. "What have you been doing?" she asked.

Laura colored. "Me? Nothing."

"Fibber." Marianna smiled a little. "You're much more to Blair than the chaperone he engaged for me, aren't you?" she observed shrewdly.

"Do—do you mind?" Laura feared Marianna might resent that someone who was little more than a glorified servant should presume to love her brother.

But Marianna smiled and shook her head. "I'm in love, so

why should I mind if Blair is too? I only wish Steven and I could just be allowed to be happy. Oh, Laura, I'm so afraid there'll be a duel. Steven's no match for my brother."

Footsteps approached, and Blair himself came in. Marianna got up from the window sill and faced him defiantly. "Are you going to call Steven out?" she demanded.

Her tone rankled. "He's seduced you, persuaded you to elope, and endangered your life, good reasons to bring him to account, don't you think?"

"You should blame me for everything, not him. *I* set my cap at *him*, not the other way around."

He drew a long breath. "Yes, I'm quite prepared to believe you did," he murmured, "but he didn't put up much resistance."

"Please don't call him out, Blair," she begged.

"It so happens that I don't intend to. There's scandal enough attaching to all this already, without the additional infamy of a duel."

Tears of relief sprang from Marianna's dark eyes. "Do—do you really mean that?"

"Of course I do. I'm not going to proceed with the Handworth match either. I've been, er, persuaded that forcing you to marry Alex would be a monumental error." He glanced at Laura.

Marianna's joy bubbled over, and she ran to fling herself into his arms. "Oh, thank you! Thank you!" Then she smiled at Laura. "Thank you too, for I know I have you to thank."

Blair held Marianna away for a moment. "Don't read too much into my decision, for it doesn't mean I accept Steven."

But nothing could dampen Marianna's happiness. "You will in the end, I know you will, because no matter what, he's still your good friend."

Blair released her. "He *was* my friend," he corrected. "Marianna, I can never countenance a match between you and Steven, is that clear?" Before she could say anything more, he turned on his heel and walked from the room.

Marianna remained motionless, then whirled about to

Laura. "Why can't he understand how much Steven and I love each other?" she cried.

"Marianna—"

"Why must he be so unkind?"

"Please try to see it from his point of view—"

"He doesn't try to see it from mine!" Marianna sobbed, then gathered her skirts to hurry out.

Laura didn't know what to say. In years to come, Blair wouldn't have the power to overrule his sister's wishes, but here in the nineteenth century, female rights and freedom were still a long way off. He *had* to protect Marianna according to the rules of his time, and there was no denying that Steven hadn't shown himself to be a shining example of moral or financial rectitude.

After a moment she left the room too, but as she reached the landing she saw Marianna looking cautiously over the balustrade into the hall, where male voices could be heard. Laura joined her, and saw Blair talking to two men who'd just arrived. One was Alex Handworth, whom Laura had seen at the ball; the other she supposed was his father.

Alex looked singularly unattractive in a brick-colored coat that emphasized his sallow complexion, and Lord Sivintree was stout and sour-faced in brown. Harcourt lingered nearby with their hats and gloves, waiting to see if anything more was required of him, and the spaniels sat at Blair's feet, growling now and then at the newcomers, whom they clearly didn't like.

Marianna's knuckles were white as she gripped the balustrade. Before Laura realized what was happening, she suddenly called down, her voice echoing with awful clarity, "I can't marry you, Alex, nor do I wish to! I'm scandalous, you see, I've tried to elope with Steven Woodville, so I'll have to marry *him* if my reputation is to be saved!"

Lord Sivintree and his son gaped, and Blair's face was furious as he looked up at her. "Go to your rooms, Marianna!"

With a toss of her head she obeyed.

Lord Sivintree's face was thunderous. "What's the meaning of this, Deveril?"

"I apologize for my sister's outburst, sir."

"Is there any truth in her claims?"

"I fear so," Blair had to admit.

Lord Sivintree suddenly noticed Laura, and his jaw dropped. "Well, I'll be damned . . ." he breathed, then turned to Blair. "So you're still clinging to the past, eh, Deveril? Still falling for beautiful redheads!"

Blair flushed. "Have a care what you say, sir," he warned.

"Why should I? I know your wife is dead, but lo and behold, here she is again. Except we both know this strumpet isn't sweet Celina!"

Blair's eyes darkened. "I'd advise you not to speak of Mrs. Reynolds in such a derogatory fashion, sir, for she is a lady and must be treated as such."

"A *lady?*" Lord Sivintree gave an unpleasant throaty laugh. "My dear fellow, you surely don't expect me to treat a tawdry figurante as anything *but* a tawdry figurante!"

Laura's heart sank like a stone as she realized he must have seen her at the Hannover.

Lord Sivintree gave Blair a cold smile. "Well, I suppose I can understand your interest, for the creature's a very tasty morsel, as I'm sure Lowestoft will confirm."

Laura went unutterably cold inside.

Blair became still. "Lowestoft? I trust you mean to explain, my lord?" he said controlledly.

"Explain? By all means. I saw your redheaded actress on the stage at the opening night of the Hannover theater. I noticed her because of her remarkable resemblance to Celina, and it seems I wasn't the only one who took note, for as I left, I saw her with Miles Lowestoft. It was a very tender scene, I promise. Now I find her here with you. My, my, how you and Lowestoft must both miss your dear departed wife if you're prepared to share a cheap actress who resembles her!"

A nerve flickered at Blair's temple. "Get out, before I throw you out, Sivintree," he breathed.

"By all means. But before I do, let me warn you I intend to spread your sister's name further than Gloucestershire!" Lord Sivintree snapped his fingers for Harcourt to bring their things, then looked at Blair again. "I believe you intended to foist a soiled bride upon my son, and that warrants revenge."

Blair's jaw set, as he didn't trust himself to respond.

Followed by Alex, who looked too bemused to say or do anything, Lord Sivintree turned to leave, but then paused again. "Oh, and Deveril, you'd better know I also intend to let the *monde* know you're laying ghosts here! Laying ghosts! Ha!" With another unpleasant laugh, he strode away, his son at his heels like an obedient dog.

Blair's gaze immediately swung to Laura. "I trust Sivintree was lying, because if not, you and I have nothing more to say to each other."

But his voice died away on a strange note that seemed to move all around her. She couldn't see him anymore, for Deveril Park had disappeared and she was once again surrounded by the impersonal modern furnishings of her hotel suite.

A torrent of disbelief thundered sickeningly through her. She *couldn't* be here in the future again, not at such a crucial moment! She hid her face in her hands to try to shut out the clamoring emotions that beat at her from all sides. She could still hear Blair's voice. *I trust Sivintree was lying, because if not, you and I have nothing more to say to each other.* Lord Sivintree *wasn't* lying, he had indeed seen what he claimed, but it wasn't what it appeared to be. Why, of *all* moments, had he witnessed Miles's cruel mock gallantry outside the theater? Sir Miles Lowestoft was her tormentor, not her lover, but how could she explain that to Blair when he was in 1816 and she was here?

Slowly she lowered her hands. What if this really was the end of it, and she didn't go back at all? What if Blair was to be shot tomorrow, and she'd never see him again? Tears of anguish stung her eyes as she gazed toward the window. The May afternoon she'd left behind had been bright with sunshine, but here the January light had almost gone. The shadows were almost comforting, for they came between her and harsh reality.

The phone rang suddenly, and with a start she answered it. "Yes?"

It was Mrs. Fitzgerald. "Laura? It's me. I'm sorry to call instead of popping up, but things are a bit busy down here. I just wanted to let you know Kieran's back from Dijon, and we'd like you to have dinner with us tonight to hear all about Jenny and Alun. They'll soon be home too."

Laura tried to sound as natural as possible. "Alun's better?"

Mrs. Fitzgerald chuckled. "Oh, yes, and beginning to grumble, which is always a good sign."

"That's true."

"Anyway, I'll be relieved when Jenny's here again, for I've had a conscience about you, my dear."

"Me? There's no need."

"No matter what you say, you must have been bored witless on your own."

Laura could have laughed out loud. Bored witless? Oh, if only Jenny's mother knew the truth!

Mrs. Fitzgerald spoke again. "You *will* dine with us, won't you?"

"Yes, of course. Thank you for inviting me."

"It's a pleasure." There was a pause. "You didn't change your mind about the audition, then?"

"No."

"Are you quite sure you're doing the right thing?"

"Quite sure, but thanks for trying, I appreciate it."

There was another chuckle at the other end of the line. "Busybodies like me can't keep their noses out, I'm afraid. Oh, I'm needed, so I'll go now. See you later, my dear. Bye."

"Bye."

Laura replaced the receiver, then glanced around at the dim rooms. Defiance stirred through her suddenly. This was crazy. What good did moping in the dark do? She needed some light on the subject, and with a determined breath, she went to flick a few switches. Soon the rooms were brightly lit, the TV was on, and she'd made herself some coffee. She sat in a comfortable chair, dodging from channel to channel until she found something she liked the look of, then she leaned her head back. She wouldn't give in to despair, she *wouldn't!* Instinct told her that sooner or later she'd go back to 1816 again, and when she did, she'd be ready to plead her cause with Blair. She closed her eyes, feeling very tired. The coffee went cold, the TV droned on, and she fell asleep.

Several hours passed, and she was suddenly awakened by a noisy game show that was shrill with sound effects and canned laughter. Something made her turn to look at the watercolor above the mantelpiece. She got up, for the painted scene seemed oddly real. It must be a trick of the eyes, she decided, but then realized it was no illusion. The brushstrokes had taken on a new vitality. The trees actually stirred in a summer breeze, the carpet of bluebells nodded gently, and the leafy shadows of a May morning moved delicately over the track by the blasted oak tree in the center of the scene!

Shaken, she crossed the room, and the closer she got, the less like a painting the picture seemed. It was no longer an artist's handiwork, but a window into the woods. She put a trembling hand to the frame, and then, very tentatively, to the glass. It was cold and firm to the touch, but beyond it, the woods were in motion, and now she could actually smell the flowers and hear the birds singing!

She swallowed. Something was about to happen, she could sense it as surely as if someone had whispered a warning. She waited, her eyes searching the trees and undergrowth for . . . for what? She didn't know. Suddenly she heard someone riding swiftly along the track! Instinctively, she drew back a little, for fear whoever it was might see her, even though she knew that was impossible. The rider came nearer, and then her breath caught as she saw it was Miles. He wore a royal blue coat and white breeches, and as he reined in by the oak tree she knew he was waiting for her. It was ten o'clock in the morning, and he hoped she'd be there with news of the necklace!

She gazed at him with unutterable loathing. This man was living, breathing malevolence. Jealous spite was his creed, and vengeance his sole reason for existence. How *could* Celina have taken him as her lover? It could only be because he was blackmailing her; there simply wasn't any other explanation. As she watched, he suddenly whirled about to look directly toward her. She was so certain he could see her that she expected him to speak, but then someone else stepped into view in front of her. It was Estelle, her skirt and veil fluttering the breeze as she seemed to glide toward him through the drifts of bluebells.

She halted by his horse, and gave a laugh that came from the edge of madness. "You thought me still in Scotland, Miles?"

"Scotland is where you should be, and where I'll be returning you directly!" he snapped.

"Is she to meet you here, your redheaded whore?"

He became very still. "I don't know what you're talking about."

"Oh, don't deny her existence, for I've seen her. I saw you lying together here among the flowers."

He began to understand, and his lips curled into a sneer. "You're a fool, Estelle, and even if you *had* seen what you think, it has nothing to do with you. Who I see and what I do is my business."

"I'm your wife!" she cried in a rising voice.

"A fact I bitterly regret," he said coldly.

"We made vows before God, Miles."

"And He's been in bed with us ever since!"

"It's a sin to blaspheme, but you know all about sin, don't

you, Miles? I married you because you *swore* she'd gone forever, but she's here, and you've come to be with her again, haven't you? Haven't you!" She caught his reins, and his horse moved uneasily.

He remained calm. "Your mind's playing more tricks on you, my dear. I'm on my own here."

"Don't lie, Miles! I've spoken to your precious Celina!" Her voice became shrill, and his horse tossed its head.

"What did you say to her?" Miles demanded, his hand clenching on his riding crop as if he'd like to strike her.

Estelle gave a gurgle of uneven laughter. "Wouldn't you like to know!" she taunted. "If you think I'll relinquish you without a battle, you're sadly mistaken. You're mine before God, and I intend to keep you!"

"Damn you!" Miles breathed, raising the riding crop and hitting her savagely across the face.

It was such a vicious blow that Laura flinched. Estelle fell to her knees on the track, and the frightened horse reared, its hooves cutting down within inches of her face. Miles looked down hatefully. "Stay away from everyone at Deveril Park, is that clear? If I find out you've uttered so much as one more word, I'll thrash you to within an inch of your pious life!"

"If it weren't for her, you and I would have been happy!" Estelle cried.

"Don't delude yourself, my dear, for you and I could never have been, and will never be, happy. I despise the very sight of your sanctimonious face, and I abhor your martyr's body! Now, if you know what's good for you, you'll get back to Scotland without delay."

Estelle scrambled up to seize one of his stirrups. "I'm your wife, Miles! I'm faithful and true, and I adore you with all my heart!"

"Don't touch me!" he cried, trying to kick her away.

She clung on. "Please, Miles! For pity's sake be kind to me!"

Miles's revulsion and rage boiled over, and he struck her again, this time so brutally that she fell like a bundle of black rags among the bluebells. He began to ride away, and she hauled herself up on her elbows to scream after him. "I won't let her have you, Miles! You're mine, and you'll remain mine forever!"

He didn't look around, and as he rode out of view the scene became a painting again. Estelle's black-swathed figure disappeared, and the trees became still.

Laura backed away from the painting. Her mouth was dry, and her heart was pounding like a tom-tom. Then she heard a sound in the bedroom behind her, and turned fearfully. "Who's there?" There was no response, but she knew she'd definitely heard something, so she went warily toward the door.

As she stepped over the threshold she saw the ballroom doors swing open in the wall opposite! She was seized by a powerful blend of trepidation and joy, and her steps didn't falter as she crossed through into the past.

Her hair had been pinned up hurriedly, and felt loose in its pins. She was flustered and uncertain, and for a moment hesitated, her nervous fingers creeping to the rich lace trimming at the low neckline of her white muslin gown. She clutched her reticule tightly in her other hand, and as she went further into the ballroom, her skirts clung sensuously to her legs.

The ballroom seemed deserted, with the fading rays of a dying sunset lying in bars across the gleaming floor, and the droplets of the chandeliers shone like rubies as they moved in a draft. Then she saw Blair looking out of one of the windows. He'd discarded his coat, and his frilled white shirt was bright in the crimson light. Tight gray breeches clung to his hips and thighs, and there was a full neckcloth at his throat. He didn't yet know she was there, but when he did, she knew he'd be bitterly angry. She was supposed to be dressed for traveling, and a carriage was waiting right now to convey her from Deveril Park forever, but instead she'd come to try to speak to him one last time.

Nineteen

Blair heard Laura's step, and turned. His eyes were bleak, his voice even bleaker. "Get out of my sight," he breathed.

She managed to stand her ground. She'd already tried to make him listen to what she had to say, but he'd refused. She had to try one last time. She *had* to! He'd guessed Miles was behind her presence at Deveril Park, and now could hardly bear to even look at her. "Please hear me out," she begged.

"You're here under false colors, Mrs. Reynolds, and now I wish to be rid of you."

"The false colors were not of my seeking."

"Are you suggesting they were mine?"

A draft stole through the ballroom, jostling the chandeliers and swinging the doors to behind her. She halted a few steps from him. "No, they were Sir Miles Lowestoft's doing."

"You didn't seem to be acting under duress."

"But I was, I swear!"

"Indeed? Forgive me if I find that impossible to believe. You came here pretending to be a respectable widow who was suitable as Marianna's chaperone, but you're really Lowestoft's *belle de nuit*. And I'd guess your resemblance to Celina is his prime concern, for when he lies with you, he lies with her! Oh, don't pretend it's news to you, for if you're Lowestoft's paramour, you know all about it!"

"I don't know anything, and I'm *not* his paramour!"

"Butter wouldn't melt in your mouth, would it? No wonder Lowestoft took you up, and no wonder his wretched wife is here in Gloucestershire. I'll warrant she's following him, just to torture herself still more with his infidelities. And with Celina!" He held her eyes. "Just tell me one thing, is Steven party to this miserable charade?"

The question caught her off-guard, and her split second of hesitation told him what he wished to know. "So he is!"

"Blair, neither of us was willing, we had to be forced! Miles threatened to call all Steven's IOU's in at once, which would have meant jail, and in his state of health—"

"Oh, poor Steven, so deep in debt and unwell he had to do something he didn't want to? Don't play me for a fool, Laura! He chose to assist Lowestoft because it would bring him closer to my sister's inheritance!"

"You're wrong. He truly loves Marianna."

He corrected her. "He loves himself and he's after her fortune. Well, I may have decided not to call him out before, but I can't stand by now he's not only seduced Marianna, but been party to Lowestoft's schemes as well. And once I've faced him, I'll face Lowestoft himself!"

"Blair—"

"Be warned, madam, if you were a man, I'd call you out too for what you've done."

"Your hatred is punishment enough," she whispered.

"If only it were, but I fear you're made of far sterner stuff than you'd have me believe. You've offered nothing in your defense, except to insist you were forced, and unless you're gone from this house within five minutes, I'll have you forcibly removed. Do I make myself clear?"

He walked toward the doors, and in desperation she took the paste necklace from her reticule and tossed it after him. The fake diamonds sparkled in the dying sunlight as they slithered across the floor at his feet. Slowly he picked them up, and the stone spilled over his fingers as the real necklace had done that night in the library. "Is *this* why you're here? To steal my property as well as my heart?" he breathed incredulously, not realizing he held a fake.

"The necklace in your hand isn't yours."

He turned. "Dear God, does Lowestoft *still* cling to the mistaken belief that my father cheated his?"

"The necklace in your hand is a paste forgery I was supposed to substitute for the real one," she said quietly.

He searched her face for a moment, and then studied the necklace more closely. "Yes, I can see now that it's a copy, although I fail to see how you can submit it in your defense. Surely it merely serves to prove your guilt still more?"

She took out the letter Miles had given to her in the woods. "This is how I was forced," she said, holding it out to him. "I was not only supposed to come here and exchange the necklaces, but to break your heart as well by being Celina all over again. Only it didn't quite work out like that, because although I may have won your heart, I also lost mine. Read it, Blair, and maybe you'll understand why I had to do what he demanded."

He unfolded the letter, and the fake diamonds continued to shimmer over his fingers as he read. "And this is supposed to convince me?" he said when he'd finished.

Dismay swept through her. "Yes! Yes, of course!"

"But anyone could have written this missive, even you."

"I didn't."

"So you say."

"It's the truth!" she cried.

"Truth is something with which you have little acquaintance." He tossed the necklace and letter back to her.

She made no move to catch them. "If I'd really come here as Miles's eager accomplice, I'd have done all I possibly could to hurt you."

"Well, didn't you?" He gave a cold laugh.

"*No!* Blair, if that was my motive, I wouldn't have said anything to you about there maybe being two falls in the tunnel, and Marianna and Steven would have remained trapped."

"Maybe even your conscience balked at that!"

"Is that what you really think of me?"

"Why not? What have you done to warrant more?"

"I've shown you how much I love you."

He faced her squarely. "So you love me, do you?"

"Yes."

"And if Sivintree hadn't exposed you, you'd have confessed all anyway?"

"I—I don't know whether or not I'd have told you, but I do know I'd decided not to do Miles's work any longer. I could have stolen the necklace in the library the other night, but I didn't. I told him Steven and I couldn't find it anywhere, and that you weren't interested in me."

"How smoothly you lie, but then you *are* an actress," he murmured.

It was too much, and the reticule slipped from her fingers as she sank to her knees before him. "*Please* believe in me again, Blair," she implored, her voice breaking with emotion. "I meant every kiss and caress we've shared, and I'd give myself to you here and now if it would prove—"

He reached down to seize her chin in viselike fingers. "All it would prove is that you're an accomplished whore!" he breathed.

"No!"

"A whore to the very tips of your skillful fingers," he said, releasing her contemptuously.

"If I've failed you, please forgive me," she whispered, reaching up tentatively to touch him.

"You've failed me in every way," he replied, but he didn't pull away from her.

She knelt up to put her trembling arms around his thighs and press her face against the rich stuff of his breeches. "Forgive me, forgive me, I beg of you. Let me love you again . . ."

"Have you any notion how meaningless it would be if I

took you now, Laura? I could use you and then fling you aside without a second's guilt. I owe you nothing, *nothing*, least of all forgiveness."

She raised her face to look up at him. "Then use me," she invited. "Take me here on this floor, and then discard me. Do it, Blair, treat me with all the cruelty and contempt you think I deserve."

"Don't provoke me, Laura," he warned.

"Why? Because you're afraid I may mean something to you after all? Is that it, Blair? You fear to be close to me because you can't hate me?"

"Oh, I can hate you," he breathed, reaching down to push her away, but the knot in her hair undid, and the warm chestnut curls spilled down over his fingers. He seemed unable to draw away, as if the soft tresses cast a spell over him.

She slid her hands luxuriously up the back of his thighs toward his buttocks. "Walk away now if you despise me as much as you say," she said softly as she looked up into his eyes.

"Damn you, Laura," he whispered.

"Oh, I'm damned indeed, Blair, damned to love you until eternity."

She slid her questing fingers to the front of his breeches, and at last he overcame the spell to put his hand firmly over hers. "No!"

"Let me love you, Blair," she whispered enticingly. "Let me. Please—"

"I don't want this, Laura."

"I don't believe you," she breathed, and slowly his fingers relaxed over hers. It was consent, unspoken but as clear as any words. Her pulse quickened as a breathlessly erotic excitement filled her. She was unable to resist the exquisite sexual temptation that enriched her very blood as she undid the first button. And then the next.

Her fingers stole gently into the forest of dark hair at his groin, and her body quivered with anticipation as she saw he couldn't deny his own arousal. There was nothing half-hearted about his erection, it was strong and imperative, springing eagerly into her hand.

She breathed out with slow delight as her fingers encased him. The images from the mirror trembled in the air before her, luring her toward the sort of intimacy she'd never wanted with Kyle. A different kind of desire ached through her, a voluptuous desire that made her raise her mouth longingly to take him in her lips.

She heard him gasp, and felt his fingers curl in her hair. She was lost in a pleasure so exquisite she felt weak. She took him deep into her mouth, exploring him with her tongue, and savoring sensations that were bewildering in their intensity. It was a craving, a torment of desire that made her whole body feel as if it were on fire. Her lips were relentless, and her abandon complete.

He drew back, his eyes dark as he looked at her, then he pulled her to her feet and led her to a window embrasure, where the last light of the sun fell fully upon her flushed face as he pressed her back against the unclosed shutter. He undid the bodice of her gown, and put his lips to her breasts, making her cry out with sheer joy, then he raised her gown to put his hand between her thighs. He stroked and aroused her, sliding his fingers knowingly.

When she was almost weeping with pleasure, he lifted her gently from her feet to gain entry with a shaft that was now raging with excitement. A sob escaped her as she felt him push deep inside her, and she wrapped her legs needfully around him as he began to thrust.

She knew no shame or pride, just complete enslavement, heart, body, and soul, and as the final moment could no longer be denied, she knew he was hers again. She could taste it in his lips, and feel it as his body shuddered against hers. She clung to him, her arms entwined around his neck, and her lips seared to his in a kiss that seemed without end, but gradually and gently he lowered her to the floor again.

She looked anxiously up into his eyes. "I *do* love you, Blair," she said softly.

"I know," he replied, straightening his clothes and then gently doing up her bodice.

"Tell me you still love me too," she begged.

He put his hands to her cheek, stroking her warm skin with his thumb. "You know I love you, Laura," he breathed, kissing her again.

She clung to him, yearning to finally cleanse her soul by telling him she was from the future, but she knew she must remain Regency Laura, the actress whose family resided in Norwich. Confessing anything else was unthinkable because he was bound by the narrow horizons of his century. Even with her modern outlook she'd found time travel hard enough to accept; he'd find it impossible. And besides, risking the complete truth now might be to ruin what little time they had left together, for she still didn't know who was to die when all the servants were at the fair.

Remembering this was like an icy douche, and she circled her arms more tightly around him, hiding her face against his shoulder. Let it be neither Steven nor him, but a stranger, someone who didn't matter . . .

His fingers curled lovingly in her hair. "It seems so unfair that you and I should be happy again, but that Marianna . . ." He didn't finish.

Determined to pretend the future was going to be good for them *and* for Marianna and Steven, she looked up at him. "Let them marry. Steven isn't a fortune hunter, you know."

"Do you really believe that?"

"Yes," she answered truthfully. "Marianna was right in what she shouted down to Lord Sivintree; letting her marry Steven, especially with your apparent approval, *will* limit the damage to her reputation."

"I know, but I should extinguish him at dawn, not hand over the prize he's schemed for."

"Call him out and you'll not only wreck what's left of

Marianna's good name, you'll also make her despise you. It's not worth it, Blair. Life's too short." And the minutes were even now ticking away for someone . . .

"But should gross misconduct be rewarded? Oh, I don't know *what* to do." He sighed and ran his fingers through his hair, then he smiled at her again, bending his head to kiss her tenderly on the lips. "I'll try to do the right thing by them, truly I will, but first there is Lowestoft to deal with. He's been a canker in my side for too long, and it's time to apply the scalpel."

She drew away. "Your quarrel with him is about Celina, not the necklace, isn't it?"

"Yes."

"I know you don't want to speak of it, but—"

He interrupted. "I'm ready to tell you now. You see, she left Lowestoft at the altar in order to marry me."

Laura stared. "At the altar?" she repeated.

He turned away to gaze out at the remnants of the sunset. "When I met her I didn't know she was betrothed to him; they'd known each other since childhood because their family's estates adjoined in Scotland. I lost my heart completely and proposed to her within three weeks of meeting her in London. She was residing with an elderly aunt who, it later seemed knew very little of Celina's activities while under her roof. Anyway, Celina accepted me, and then went home to Scotland to tell her family. At least, that was what she said to me. The truth was that her wedding to Lowestoft was due to take place, and I fear that, rather reprehensibly to say the least, she permitted arrangements to proceed right up to an hour before the ceremony. Only then did she tell him about me. Needless to say, he was devastated, but although he implored her to still marry him, she left for London that very day. He continued to regard her as his, and became my implacable enemy from that moment on."

He faced her again. "Celina's conduct was indefensible, so I can't blame him for his antagonism. She should have told him the truth long before she did, but he was as obsessive about her then as he is now, and she was simply afraid of his reaction. Only when it was the eleventh hour and she really couldn't delay any longer, did she find the courage to speak out. I thought his interest might wane when I heard he'd married at last, but his poor, unstable wife is more suited to a convent than the marriage bed, and it was soon clear he chose her for her dowry, not herself. Celina was still his ruling passion, and that, incidentally, is the only reason he feels so intensely about the necklace. He knows it was won fairly in a game of cards, but because it was her favorite piece of jewelry, he wants it. He lives and breathes for her, even to the extent of commissioning Lawrence to paint a duplicate of the portrait in the library here." He gave a weary sigh. "Oh, how tired I am of him and his fixation. No matter how culpable Celina was, he's been the bane of my life for too long now, and this business with you is the last straw. It's time to confront him. Do you know where he is?"

"No, just that he must be staying somewhere in the neighborhood. If I wish to see him, I'm supposed to wait by the old oak tree in the woods at ten in the morning. He says he rides that way each day." She explained about the encounter she'd had.

Blair thought for a moment. "When the Mercury Fair opens tomorrow, the woods become too public for the sort of confrontation I have in mind. The track through them is a short cut from the other villages along the valley, so better he's lured here to Deveril Park." He smiled. "Nothing could be more private, for all the servants will be at the fair."

Her heart went cold.

Twenty

Laura's pulse quickened. If Miles was to be lured to the house, maybe *he* would be the one to die! A fresh draft suddenly crept though the ballroom from the doors, and she turned to see Marianna and Steven coming in.

Embarrassed color immediately suffused her cheeks as she thought of what had taken place only a few short minutes ago. If that were to have been witnessed . . . ! But the new arrivals had only entered in time to hear Blair's last words, and in spite of her quarrel with her brother, Marianna was anxious for him.

"Please be careful, Blair, Sir Miles is a very unpleasant man," she begged. Her eyes were red from crying, and she held on tightly to Steven's hand as she looked at her brother. "Blair, Steven's told me everything about Sir Miles's horrid plot, so if you believe Laura and he were willing participants in it all, you couldn't be more wrong."

Blair smiled a little. "I think I know that now," he said, glancing at Steven, who had a bandage around his head and definitely looked as if he shouldn't have left his bed yet.

Steven met his eyes. "I know you won't be able to forgive me, but I entreat you to at least try to understand."

"I do, and I've forgiven Laura, so I forgive you."

Steven smiled relievedly. "Thank you, Blair. I'm not proud of myself for any of this. I was afraid to stand up to Miles, and I've been guilty of shabby behavior toward Marianna."

"Well, you'll pay the price for the latter, because I intend to let you marry her, since that appears to be the only way to salvage her good name," Blair replied.

Marianna flung herself into her brother's arms, and he rested his cheek fondly against her hair. "Marianna Deveril, you've been a sore trial to me, do you know that? First you elope, then you make a shockingly public declaration intended to force me into doing as you wish! I've spoilt you all your life, but at least if you marry Steven, *he'll* have to endure the consequences."

Steven smiled a little as he came toward them. "It's a responsibility I gladly accept, Blair, and I *will* look after her and love her, that I swear to you." He extended a hand.

"You'd better," Blair murmured, accepting the olive branch.

Laura had to blink tears away. Let nothing stand in the way of happiness, for *all* of them . . .

Steven grinned relievedly at Blair. "I trust you regard me as your friend again?"

"I suppose I must."

Marianna linked Steven's arm happily, and then glanced around the ballroom. "Suddenly Deveril Park isn't important anymore," she declared. "I don't mind that it's been sold, or that we don't know who the new owner is."

Blair raised an eyebrow. "So much for your wailing and gnashing of teeth," he murmured dryly.

She was penitent. "I know, but it came as such a shock. One minute I had no idea you planned anything, then it was suddenly all signed and sealed."

"I shouldn't have done it without consulting you, for it's your home as much as mine, but I *had* to sell. You do understand now, don't you?"

"Yes."

"Good, because nothing's going to prevent me from starting anew at Castle Liscoole."

"Is the new owner's identity really unknown to you?"

"He's a complete mystery, but although I was curious

first, now I really couldn't care. I just want to settle everything here, and leave."

Marianna looked at him. "Blair, about what you were saying when Steven and I came in a short while ago. What *are* you going to do about Sir Miles Lowestoft?"

"Deal with him once and for all," Blair replied firmly. "There'll be no peace for any of us until that happens."

Steven looked at him. "You have something in mind?"

Blair nodded. "It shouldn't be too difficult to get him here to Deveril Park if he thinks it's safe."

Laura swallowed. Let this house be safe for everyone *except* Sir Miles Lowestoft . . .

Blair went on. "Once he's in my grasp, I see no reason why I can't use a little of the coercion of which he's so very fond. A few hours in the cave should make him malleable, don't you think? After that I'm sure he'll not only agree to hand over the IOU's and the deeds to certain properties in Norwich, but also write a full confession of his sins. He'll be warned that any dark deeds in the future will mean the letter's being made horribly public, which will lead to society's shunning him and the authorities' becoming exceeding interested in his blackmailing activities."

Steven nodded approvingly. "I like it, Blair, but have one small complaint."

"Which is?"

"That my name has been omitted from the proceedings. I can't let you take this on alone."

Blair smiled. "I'll be glad of your assistance."

But Marianna had misgivings about the whole thing. "What if Sir Miles refuses your demands?"

Blair laughed. "He won't. I know his type, only brave when *he's* in command. Take that command away, and you're left with a craven coward."

Steven sighed. "I wish to God I'd never even heard his name."

As he spoke, he swayed a little, and Marianna immediately put a steadying arm around his waist. "Steven, don't you think you should lie down again?" she asked anxiously.

He nodded, then gave Blair a contrite smile. "I swear I'll be in finer fettle when you need me," he promised as Marianna ushered him away.

Blair immediately turned to Laura. "You had very little to say. Don't you approve of my plan?"

"Of course I do, it's just that I'm afraid." Other unspoken words screamed through her. Something dreadful happens here tomorrow, so take care, my darling, take care!

He cupped her chin in his hand, tilting her face to his. "All this has made me realize how very little I know of you. I thought you were a Northumberland widow, instead you're Miss Reynolds of the Hannover."

What was he thinking? That her obvious experience in lovemaking revealed her morals to be those of only too many minor actresses in this Regency age? She couldn't explain that her knowledge came from the future, when women were liberated and informed. What could she say?

He read her thoughts, and put a gentle finger to her lips. "Don't think you have to say anything, my love, for there is no need. What happened before you came to me is of no consequence. I love and trust you, that's all that counts." He took the finger away and kissed her.

She returned the kiss gladly, for she knew he meant what he said.

He pulled her into his arms, and rested his forehead against hers. "Laura, about this business with Lowestoft . . ."

Somehow she managed to keep a grip on herself. "Yes?"

"It necessarily involves you, you realize that, don't you?"

"Yes. I—I'll have to meet him by the oak tree."

He looked into her eyes. "If it frightens you in any way—"

She interrupted. "Just tell me what you wish me to do."

"Well, the diamonds must be the lure." He rescued the

paste necklace and letter from the floor, gave them to her, then held out his hand. "Come with me."

"Where are we going?"

"To the library." His fingers closed warmly over hers, and he led her from the ballroom.

It was dark now, so he lit a candle from the table on the landing, then held it aloft as they entered the gloomy library. The dust sheets seemed to tower for a moment as the light fell upon them, and the air was heavy with the smell of paint and varnish. Neither of them glanced toward Celina's portrait as he led Laura to one of the tall bookcases, and moved some volumes aside to reveal a tiny safe set into the wall.

He unlocked it with a key from his pocket, then turned to her. "See if you can open it."

She tried hard, but the little door remained tightly closed.

Blair smiled. "There's an art to it. Look." He pushed the top left-hand corner, and suddenly the door swung open, revealing documents in the compartment beyond. On top of the documents was the leather case containing the real necklace. "If you give Lowestoft the key and tell him you know where the diamonds are but can't open the safe because it needs a man's strength, I think he'll take the bait. The safe manufacturer's name on the key will make your story seem all the more believable, and if he's staying in the immediate area, by now he may have heard about the rescue in the tunnel, so if you tell him Steven's too unwell to help you, he'll probably believe that as well. Urge him to come to the house when everyone's at the fair; tell him you'll cry off with a headache and then show him to the safe. Once he's here, Steven and I will deal with him. Do you think you can convince him?"

"Yes," she whispered.

He searched her face. "What is it? Is there something wrong?"

She forced a smile. "Nothing at all. I'll convince him; I'm an actress, remember?"

"So you are," he murmured, pulling her close.

But as their lips met again, a needle of fear pricked her. She was keeping the future from him. Tomorrow wasn't going to go the way it was planned, but there was nothing she could do about it. All she could pray was that cruel, blackmailing Sir Miles Lowestoft would be the one to die, for he didn't deserve any other fate!

She was a little early the next morning when she set off on horseback to meet Miles, so to keep herself as calm as possible she rode the long way, through the village.

The weather was fine and clear. Deveril Park was already deserted because the fair had been in full swing since dawn, and the servants were making good use of every minute of their time off. Hurdy-gurdies, drums, shouts, and squeals of excitement were audible long before she reached the green, where she found so many people she thought the whole county must have come to enjoy the fun.

Ha'penny Jack seemed to be doing particularly well, for there was a long queue waiting to view his little theater, but his scowl didn't reflect the briskness of trade; he was in a black mood because he knew he'd lost Dolly to Harcourt.

The church clock struck the half hour, and Laura rode determinedly on to the rendezvous with Miles. She had to have faith that before this day was over, justice would well and truly be done and the right man would suffer.

She reached the track into the valley woods, and soon found Blair had been right about the number of people using it to get to the fair. She rode past many groups of villagers, some on foot, some in carts, and even one or two private carriages, although not, she was relieved to note, the one belonging to Lady Lowestoft.

The breeze rustled through the branches of the blasted oak tree as she reined in to wait, but almost immediately she saw Miles riding toward her, his peacock coat standing out even against the vivid greens and blues of the May woodland.

He didn't waste time in idle pleasantry. "You have the necklace?"

"No."

His amber eyes flickered. "Then why have you come?"

"Because I know where it is, but can't get at it." She held up the key to the safe.

He took it, and then searched her eyes. "If you have the key, why can't you open the safe?" he asked softly.

"It's stuck fast, and needs a man's strength."

"You have Steven."

"I don't. He's been injured, didn't you know? I—I thought you'd have heard about the roof fall in the canal tunnel."

Miles flicked his horse's mane with a gloved hand. "Yes, but I didn't know he'd been injured."

"He's bedridden."

"Poor fellow," Miles murmured insincerely.

Laura hid her loathing. "Steven can't open the safe, but you can."

"Go to Deveril Park? Are you mad?" he replied incredulously.

"You don't understand. Steven and I will be the only ones there. Everyone else, servants included, will be at the fair."

He didn't reply, for some people from the next village approached along the track. Laura found her glance moving unwillingly toward the bushes from where she knew Estelle had come when the painting came to life. For a moment there seemed to be the flutter of a black veil, then it was gone.

"What is it?" Miles demanded, seeing the start she gave.

"I—I thought I saw someone over there by those bushes. A woman in black. Your wife," she added, remembering the unpleasant confrontation she'd witnessed when the watercolor came to life.

The villagers were passing as his eyes flew in the direction she looked, but there was nothing to see, and after a moment he turned back to her. "You imagined it, madam, because I promise you my wife will not approach you again; indeed, she is at this moment on her way back to Scotland." He waited until the villagers were out of earshot, then spoke again. "Are you sure we'd be alone at Deveril Park this afternoon?"

He was taking the bait! "Yes. The servants have been at the fair since it started at dawn, and Sir Blair and his sister will leave at about three. I am to go with them, but could plead a headache and stay to show you the safe. Unless, of course, you'd prefer to wait until Steven has recovered?"

"I want the necklace as quickly as possible."

"Then today is the ideal opportunity."

He thought for a moment, then nodded. "Very well, I'll come to the house. What time do you suggest?"

"It will be completely safe at four."

He leaned across suddenly to clamp steely fingers over her wrist. "You'd better be genuine in this, my dear, because if you aren't . . ." He allowed his voice to trail away warningly.

Somehow she managed to meet his eyes. "Why would I lie to you? I wish to get away from this place, so believe me I'm telling the truth. Sir Blair still shows no interest in me, and all I want now is to go home to my family. I—I trust that when you have your necklace, you'll honor your word? I know I haven't succeeded with Sir Blair, but it isn't because I haven't tried, truly it isn't." Again her glance flew toward the bushes. She couldn't see anything, but she could *feel* Estelle's presence.

"I always honor my word," he replied softly, releasing her wrist to suddenly put his fingers to her cheek. "You're so like Celina, so very like her . . ."

"But I'm *not* her," she reminded him a little uneasily.

"True. Nevertheless, you'd make a satisfactory substitute."

She stiffened. "What do you mean?"

"That once I have the necklace, I'm of a mind to enjoy you a little before letting you go to your family."

It was all she could do not to show her revulsion.

He took his hand away, "I see no point in prolonging this meeting now. I'll come to the house at four."

He urged his horse away, and she exhaled with slow relief. As he disappeared, her gaze returned to the bushes, and on impulse she rode toward them. There was no one there, but she saw a fragment of black gauze caught on a freshly broken twig. She glanced quickly around again, but the undergrowth was so dense Estelle could have been within a few feet of her and yet remain hidden. One thing was certain, Miles was wrong to think his wife was on her way back to Scotland! Shivering a little, she rode quickly away along the track.

She returned by way of the canal. The Bargee's Arms was quiet, and there wasn't anyone to be seen on the vessels moored along the canal. The breeze rippled the surface of the water as she followed the towpath, but as she entered the trees near the culvert, the air became perceptibly cooler, and there were fewer leafy shadows across the path.

Suddenly she saw the spruce fir, tall and startling by the cottage ruins. The spruce fir? But it shouldn't be here yet, it hadn't been planted! Nor should the rowing boat be lying rotting by the wall, or the cottage itself be ruined! She was in the future again!

As a dismayed sob leapt to her lips, she began to fall from the saddle into an impenetrable darkness. She thought she heard Gulliver's voice, but then pain swept sickeningly over her, and she lost consciousness.

Twenty-one

Laura felt as if she were floating in a warm sea. It was a pleasant feeling, and her thoughts were muddled. Was she in the past, or the future? She was afraid to open her eyes, because she didn't want to see her hotel suite.

She heard the chink of a cup and saucer, a sound as familiar in 1816 as in modern times. Whose cup was it? She had to know. She looked, and could have wept with disappointment when she saw Jenny's mother by her bed.

Mrs. Fitzgerald gave a relieved smile, and put her cup down. "At last! How are you feeling, my dear?"

"What—what happened?"

"Don't you remember? Gulliver found you down by the tunnel."

Laura remembered hearing Gulliver's voice before she lost consciousness. But what was he doing on the towpath? Had he decided to go to the portal again?

Jenny's mother continued. "He saw you walk along the path and then slip. You shook yourself up quite badly, so he made you sit quietly while he went back to the Bargee's Arms for help. Ron Sawyer brought you back here in his car and we sent for the doctor, who wanted you to go to the hospital to be on the safe side, but you got yourself in such a state about it that he decided not to upset you even more. He said that as you hadn't knocked your head or broken anything, he wouldn't insist, so he just gave you something to make you sleep, and said he'd pop back this evening."

"I'm sorry to cause such a fuss."

"Oh, don't apologize, my dear." Mrs. Fitzgerald got up to tidy the bedclothes. "It's strange how things happen. Gulliver only occasionally decides to make himself use his walking sticks, and today he felt a sudden urge to leave his wheelchair and walk to the portal again. He's so worried about you, he followed Ron's car here in his wheelchair, and has refused to go home until he's absolutely certain you're all right."

"He's here now?"

"Yes."

"Can I see him please?"

"Of course. I'll get him now." Mrs. Fitzgerald went to the door, then paused to smile back. "Jenny's going to have two invalids to take care of when she gets here, isn't she?"

"Two?"

"Well, you're one as well for the time being."

Laura returned the smile, but knew quite suddenly that by the time Jenny and Alun returned from Dijon, she'd be in the past forever! Her heartbeats quickened. How did she know? It was like gaining second sight, or looking into a crystal ball. Outwardly there'd still be a Laura Reynolds here in the future, but her twin would be permanently in the England of the past. Facing what, though? A life of happiness with Blair? Or a barren existence mourning his death? She wished she could be as certain of that as she was of being about to leave this modern world forever.

Mrs. Fitzgerald hurried away, and after what seemed an age Gulliver hobbled in on his walking sticks. He made his way clumsily to the bedside chair, and sank down thankfully, propping his sticks. Then he smiled at her. "How are you now, my dear?"

"Frustrated. I'm in the wrong century."

"I know."

She held his eyes. "Gulliver, when I go back next, I'll never return here again," she said quietly.

He was silent for a moment, then said, "You seem very sure."

"I am. Don't ask me how, because I can't answer but there's no doubt in my mind. I know it as certainly as I know night will follow day."

He nodded. "I believe you."

She looked at him. "Why did you want to see the portal again?" she asked then.

"Because I wondered if anything would happen."

"If you went back again, you mean?"

"Yes."

"So you've changed your mind, and *want* to go back again?"

He took a long breath. "I don't know what I want, Laura. Since my accident I've been doing my damnedest to forget it, but you've made that impossible. Since we last spoke, I've done nothing but examine my feelings toward it all."

"I guess you're mad at me for dragging it all up again?"

"Not really." He smiled.

"I'm glad. Gulliver, I've been thinking too. We know going back has something to do with sharing names with ancestors, but it's like we suddenly became two people at once. Twins if you like, except our consciousness only remains with one."

He smiled. "We fly in the face of reason," he murmured.

"Just think, Gulliver, if you went back again now, you'd be able to walk again, and you'd be with Dolly."

"Not the Dolly who's here in the future, just an ancestor," he reminded her.

"Whoever she is, in your previous life you loved her, and won her from Ha'penny Jack Sawyer."

He didn't say anything.

"Maybe you could come with me when I go back," she said suddenly.

"Maybe, maybe not. We know *one* person can go, but as to whether *two* could . . ." He shrugged.

"Well, you want to, don't you? You must have already decided that much or you wouldn't have tried to get to the tunnel," she said shrewdly.

"I admit it, but the truth has to be faced. What happened twenty years ago may be all I'll ever experience."

"Or it may not. I kept thinking I'd had my allotted number of adventures, but it always happened again. Now I know I'm going back for good." She smiled. "It's written in tablets of stone."

"Thou shalt return forever to Regency England?"

"Something like that." She glanced toward the window, and for the first time realized the January afternoon had drawn in. Just how long had she been lying in this darned bed? What had been happening back in 1816 while she slept? She sat up quickly. "What time is it, Gulliver?"

"Twenty to four. Why?"

"Four is when Sir Miles Lowestoft is to come to the house! I need to be back there now!"

"My dear—"

"It's important I return, I—" Her voice died away as a strange feeling crept slowly over her. Something was about to happen. Instinctively she turned to look at the bedroom wall, and a glad smile leapt to her lips, for the ballroom doors were there.

"Look, Gulliver!" she breathed.

He went a little pale.

She turned shining eyes toward him. "You can see them, so surely that means you can go through them? We *can* go together, I know we can!" She eased herself from the bed and stood very carefully, because she was still shaken from the fall, then she held her hand out to him. "Come with me, Gulliver, *please*."

He hesitated. "Laura, what if Blair Deveril is the man I saw dead? What's there for you then?"

"Five minutes with him is worth a lifetime on my own."

"You say that with such fervor, but when those five minutes are over . . ."

"That's a chance I'm prepared to take." Still she held out her hand. "Are you coming?"

Suddenly he reached for his walking sticks and rose unsteadily to his feet. "Take my arm, my dear, and let's go before I turn chicken," he muttered.

Together they approached the entrance to the past, and the doors swung open on the sunlit ballroom, but as they stepped through, Gulliver disappeared. She turned in confusion, for she'd expected him to stay with her, but then she remembered. Harcourt and all the servants were at the fair. She wasn't alone, though, for Marianna and Steven were with her, Steven still looking pale, but much better than he had. They were all three waiting at the ballroom doors for Blair, and as she heard his familiar step across the landing, the clock in the hall below began to strike a quarter to four.

Blair wore a dark gray coat and cream breeches, and the diamond pin in his neckcloth flashed as he reached them. Laura pressed her hands nervously into the folds of her blue floral gown, praying that all was going to end well, and that this new life would be one with him safe at her side. Tears stung her eyes, for until Blair Deveril she'd never realized how deep and fierce love could be.

His eyes were only for her, and he said nothing to the others as he took her hands. "If you wish to back out of this, you only have to say," he said gently.

"I don't want to back out."

"Are you sure?"

"Absolutely."

He turned to the others. "Are we all quite clear upon the plan?"

Steven nodded. He looked tired but determined, his pallor disguised a little by the rich clover color of his coat, and Marianna clung to his arm, her yellow lawn gown too cheerful for such a moment.

Blair saw how tense she was, and looked at Steven. "Take her to her rooms, and make sure she stays there. Lowestoft mustn't realize anyone else is in the house."

Steven began to obey, but then paused. "Just remember, I'll be within hearing." He patted his pocket, where one of

Blair's dueling pistols was primed and ready. Blair had the other.

When they'd gone, Blair took Laura in his arms and kissed her tenderly on the lips. It was a slow kiss, gentle, loving, and complete. The house was very quiet. Outside, she could hear the cries of the peacocks and the barking of the spaniels in the kitchen garden, but here, in Blair's arms, there was only the beating of their hearts.

After a long moment, he rested his cheek against her hair. "When you've brought Lowestoft to the library, just remember to stand well away from him; I don't want you within his reach. If he poses any threat to you, no matter how small, I'll stay my hand. I'll be in the room waiting, though, you may be sure of that." He held her even closer. "I don't like involving you any more than you already have been, but I know him, he'll be too much on his guard to be surprised before the library. Only when his attention is on the safe will he be fully exposed."

"I'll do everything you ask."

"Just take care, my darling."

She closed her eyes. And you, my love. And you . . .

He glanced around. "I'm so glad I've sold this house, soon the past will be behind forever," he said softly.

She kept her head bowed to hide the anguish that suddenly choked her.

They both heard a horse coming down the drive, and her heart missed a beat. Blair turned. "That must be Lowestoft!"

"I—I'm ready."

Their eyes met, but before he could say anything more she turned to a nearby console table to pick up the reticule containing the fake necklace, then hurried across the landing and down the staircase.

Blair watched as she crossed toward the main hall. Suddenly he wanted to call her back. A sixth sense told him something was wrong. "Laura!" The name echoed after her, but she didn't look back.

The horse had halted outside, so he went quickly to the library, where the airing fire had burned so low it was almost out. A few embers glowed in the draft from the open window, and the smell of paint and varnish was still strong, but didn't overpower the lingering headiness of damp plaster.

Suddenly there was a soft step behind him. He whirled about, and his face changed. "*You!* What in God's name—"

He was silenced by a savage blow with a candlestick, and he knew a sickening moment's pain before he pitched forward into unconsciousness.

The candlestick was tossed aside as his assailant quickly dragged a chair forward, concealed him with the dust sheet draped over it, then slipped silently out again.

Twenty-two

Laura led Miles up the staircase, and paused at the top. "You see? The house is completely deserted. Steven's in his bed on the next floor, and there's absolutely no one else here."

The black unicorn ring was very plain as Miles's hand rested on the polished rail. "I'd be a fool to take your word."

"Don't you trust me?"

"No, my dear. I don't doubt you'd trick me if you could."

"There is no trick."

"You'd better mean it," he replied coolly, taking out a pistol and leveling it at her. "Just to make sure you know I mean business, my dear," he said, but then thought he heard something. "What was that?"

"I—I didn't hear anything!"

"If there's someone else here . . ." His fingers dug in cruelly, and he pressed the pistol to her temple.

"I swear there isn't! Just Steven, and he can't leave his room."

To her relief he slowly lowered the gun, but he remained as taut as a bowstring. "Very well, let's get on with it in case someone *does* choose to return. You have the paste necklace with you?"

"In my reticule."

He continued to grip her arm as they crossed the landing to the library. There he hesitated in the doorway, glancing suspiciously at the ghostly dust sheets and clutter of decorators' trappings. Celina's portrait was in shadow, and he didn't notice it as he pushed Laura over the threshold into the room.

"You—you're hurting me!" she cried, wanting him to release her so that Blair could make a move, but he took no notice. Then she noticed one of the chairs had been moved. Blair must have done it, but why? Her thoughts were snapped off as Miles shook her a little.

"Show me the safe."

"Over there, behind that shelf of books."

He propelled her across the room. "Where, exactly?"

"Let me go, *please!* You're hurting me!"

"Oh, no, my dear, I feel more secure with you in my grasp! Now, the safe, if you please!"

It was almost as if he knew the plan, she thought as with trembling hands she pushed the books aside. Without relaxing his hold for a moment, he took out the key. "Unlock it."

She obeyed, and then showed him how it wouldn't open.

"Try a little harder."

Still the door refused to budge, and at last he seemed convinced she was telling the truth. To her relief he released her and put the pistol down in order to try the safe himself. She moved aside, expecting Blair to step out of hiding, but there was no sign of him. Dismayed, she looked around. The seconds ticked by, and a finger of alarm began to creep down her spine. Where was he? Why didn't he make his move?"

The safe door suddenly opened, and Miles gave a triumphant cry as he took out the necklace. The diamonds flashed as he thrust them into his pocket, then held his hand out for the paste copy.

Not knowing what else to do, she took them from her reticule. He arranged them in the case, then locked the door. As he turned to face her again, he saw the disquiet in her eyes. "What's wrong?" he demanded, suspicion descending over him like a cloak.

"Nothing."

"This is a trick after all, isn't it?" he breathed, seizing her wrist and twisting it agonizingly behind her back. His lips were only inches from hers as he hissed a warning. "Just be warned, sweetheart, I'm not only stronger than you, I'm armed as well, and if you think I wouldn't use it, you're very much mistaken." He thrust her roughly against the shelves, and the jolt sent the pistol scudding along the polished wooden shelf, but he didn't seem to notice as he pressed his body to hers.

"There's nothing going on! We're alone in the house except for Steven."

Suddenly he noticed Celina's portrait, and a strange look entered his eyes. He still held Laura too tightly for her to escape, but his attention was solely upon the portrait. "Oh, Celina, you were meant to be mine," he breathed, for all the world as if the painting could hear.

Laura was frightened. "Please let me go," she begged.

He didn't hear, for he was alone with Celina.

Laura cast desperately around for Blair. Where was he? Why didn't he come out?

Miles's glazed eyes swung from the portrait to her. "You're mine, Celina, not Deveril's."

He'd called her Celina! Laura suddenly realized he'd slipped as much into delusion as his poor tortured wife. Her mouth ran dry, and she felt cold in spite of the warmth of the May afternoon.

"You shouldn't have left me at the altar, Celina."

"I—I'm not Celina," she whispered.

"You can't fool me, my darling," he breathed, pressing to her.

It was Celina's body he felt, Celina's warmth that aroused him. He bent his head and forced his lips over hers. Laura froze with fear and loathing. Miles's breath was hot on her face as his tongue forced itself between her lips, but as his hand slid to enclose one of her breasts, Estelle's trembling voice interrupted him.

"Forget her, Miles, for *I'm* the one who wears your ring!"

A curse jerked from him as he whirled about to face the black figure in the doorway, and his face turned to wax as he saw the little pistol she directed at his heart. "Sweet God above, Estelle," he whispered, and then remembered his own pistol. His hand darted to where he'd left it, but it wasn't there. His gaze flew back to Estelle. "How did you know I was here?" he asked, trying to divert her attention.

She gave a brittle laugh. "I was in the woods yesterday; I heard you make this assignation with your whore!" The pistol moved toward Laura for a moment, and then back to him.

He strove to placate her. "This isn't an assignation, Estelle. I'm getting the diamond necklace for you, see?" He took the necklace from his pocket. "It's yours now, my love, and should have been since the moment you became my bride."

"Since I became your victim," she corrected. "Sir Blair Deveril has suffered as I suffered, because he's the whore's deceived husband, but I've made sure he doesn't see her with you right here in his own house." She pointed the pistol toward the shape beneath the dust sheet, and the bloodstained candlestick nearby.

Miles's fingers clenched over the diamonds as he realized there'd been a trap after all. She didn't even notice, she was too distraught about Blair. "What have you done to him? Is he dead?" she cried.

The reply was full of scorn. "Don't pretend you care, whore! Your husband doesn't matter to you, you're only interested in mine!" Estelle turned accusingly to Miles. "Why have you always betrayed me so cruelly? You break your vows every day with your lust, but God will punish you through me."

"Estelle—"

"*I'm* the one you should have loved, not her. You lied when you said she was dead, but you won't lie again.

Ever." She cocked the pistol, and the sinister clicking sound fell into a sudden silence.

Miles was terrified. "Estelle, I was only trifling with her a moment ago! I wouldn't have gone further because you're right, she *is* a whore!"

"You'd have taken her against the bookcase!" Her finger began to tighten on the trigger.

"No!" he screamed, then ducked with his arms over his head to run from the library, but she calmly leveled the pistol at his back, and shot him as he fled to the top of the staircase.

Laura screamed as he staggered to a halt. Blood stained his shoulder, and there was puzzlement on his face as he turned to stare at his wife. "Estelle?"

She showed no mercy, but calmly reloaded the pistol and squeezed the trigger again. The shot found its mark in his heart. He tottered for a moment, the necklace fell from his hand, then he collapsed by the topmost step.

The ensuing silence seemed to echo. Laura could hear the distant clamor of the spaniels in the kitchen garden, excited by the shots, but here in the house it was absolutely still.

She stared at Miles. His was the body Gulliver had seen! But were there two dead men? Was Blair dead too? Her wretched gaze was glued to the still shape beneath the dust-sheet shroud.

The dread thoughts broke off as suddenly Estelle put a third ball into the pistol, then whirled about to face her. "It's your turn now, Celina," she breathed, bringing the weapon swiftly to bear.

But before she could fire, another report rang out from somewhere on the landing. Her eyes started, and the pistol slipped from her fingers as she turned to see who'd fired, but then her knees sagged and she crumpled to the floor. Black gauze fluttered and settled around her until she resembled little more than a heap of mourning cloth.

Steven dropped his weapon and ran to Laura. "Are you all right?"

Too shocked to speak, she managed to nod.

"I came as soon as I heard the first shot. Where's Blair?" he demanded.

The question brought her to her wits, and she hurried to drag the dust sheet away. Blair lay like a corpse. His face was ashen and there was blood from the wound on his temple. She sank to her knees, too afraid to touch him in case his skin was cold.

Marianna had crept past Miles's body to the library door. She glanced at Estelle's body for a moment, but then saw Blair and gave a cry of dismay. Her big brown eyes filled with frightened tears as Steven went to her.

Laura at last stretched a hand to Blair's cheek. Her fingertips brushed softly against him. His flesh was warm, and he stirred a little. Her breath caught on a sob as she lovingly smoothed the blood from his face, then looked at the others. "He's alive!"

His eyes opened and he looked up at her. Realization swept over him, and he tried to struggle up, but she wouldn't let him. "No, it's all right, there's no danger. I'm all right, so are Marianna and Steven. It's over, Blair. Miles is dead."

His lips parted. "Dead?" he repeated dully.

"His wife did it." She drew aside so he could see Estelle's body. "She struck you with a candlestick, and then waited for him. She shot him when he tried to run away, and then Steven shot her as she turned the pistol on me."

He stared at her, trying to assimilate all she said, then Steven came over. "It really is all right," he said reassuringly.

Blair insisted on getting up; then he looked at Estelle's body again. "I remember turning and seeing her, then there was a blinding pain and I can't recall anything more." He turned to Steven. "You saved Laura, and for that I gladly forgive everything else."

Laura gazed at Estelle's body. "She really thought I was

Celina, and in the end, Miles thought so too," she said, remembering.

Steven looked curiously at her. "Are you saying he was as mad as his wife?"

"I think he must have been."

Marianna shuddered. "I—I'm frightened . . ."

Steven pulled her close, then glanced at Blair. "What shall we do about the, er . . . ?" He nodded toward the bodies.

Blair thought for a moment. "It won't do for you to be implicated in any way. Where's your pistol?"

"I dropped it on the landing."

Blair went to place it in Miles's hand. "There, now we can say he shot his wife. Poetic justice, don't you think?" As an afterthought, he bent to make certain Miles was dead. "Better to be safe than sorry. Yes, he's quite dead."

Steven checked one of Estelle's thin wrists, and then looked at Blair. "So is she."

Suddenly Laura remembered the necklace. "Blair, the diamonds are on the floor by Miles, and his pistol is in here on the shelf."

He took the necklace, and then returned to the library. "I'll put the pistol with my collection in the billiard room," he said, then smiled at them. "Now, I think we'll give ourselves a little time to recover, then we'll have to notify the authorities in Cirencester."

"What, exactly, are we going to report? Our stories must match," Steven said.

"Simply that we four were about to leave for the fair when Miles and his wife arrived demanding the return of the necklace. There was an argument between them over his infatuation for Celina, and when I tried to mediate, I was knocked on the head. The argument got out of hand completely, and ended with them both lying dead at each other's hand. We should be able to limit any questions to you and me, and keep Laura and Marianna out of it by saying they were waiting in the drawing room and knew nothing until it was too late. You and I can agree on the finer details in a short while, but for the moment my head's thumping like an anvil, and—"

Blair broke off as they all suddenly heard a man shouting from the bottom of the staircase. "Is anyone here? Sir Blair? Miss Marianna?"

It was Harcourt. Laura remembered Gulliver had told her how the butler returned from the fair with Dolly Frampton, and they'd heard pistol shots from the house. In a second or so he'd come up and see Miles's dead body!

Steven gave a nervous laugh. "It seems we weren't a moment too soon with our evidence-tampering," he murmured.

Harcourt ascended the staircase. "Is anyone here?" he called again, and then suddenly saw Miles. He was so shocked he stumbled backward a few steps, but managed to grab the handrail.

Laura conquered an overwhelming sense of *déjà vu*. This was the moment that terrified Gulliver so much he found himself falling back in the tunnel to injure himself so badly he'd never walk properly again. . . . She gazed at the butler. Was he Gulliver now? Surely he must be.

Blair went out to him. "I'm afraid we've had some trouble here, Harcourt. Unwelcome visitors."

Relieved to see his master, and the other three behind him, the butler recovered a little, but his face remained white as he came up the final steps. "We heard shots, Sir Blair. I—I have Mrs. Frampton outside in the pony trap," he explained.

Blair told him the story they'd agreed upon, and his eyes widened. "There—there's another body in the library?"

"Yes, I fear so."

Harcourt swallowed. "Lord above. I, er, suppose the authorities in Cirencester should be told? I was about to drive Mrs. Frampton to see her sick aunt, so maybe I could still do that, and make the report for you at the same time?"

"Please do that."

"Very well, sir." But before hurrying back downstairs,

Harcourt glanced directly at Laura, and in that split second she knew he was Gulliver. He went quickly down the stairs again, and a moment later they heard a whip crack, then the rattle of the pony trap.

Steven went to drape a dust sheet over Estelle, but as he brought one to cover Miles as well, Marianna turned anxiously to Blair. "We haven't achieved what we wanted, have we? We still don't have Steven's IOU's, and Laura's family are still—"

Blair interrupted her. "All threat was removed the moment Miles expired," he said quietly. "If the IOU's come to light now, I'll settle them for Steven. As for Laura's family, I'll approach the Lowestoft estate and offer to defray the Reynolds's debts and purchase their property. I'm sure no difficulty will arise."

Marianna stared. "Is it really that simple?"

"Why not? IOU's need only be met in full to eliminate them, and why should Lowestoft's heir wish to hold on to debts and property instead of accepting a generous offer? But for the moment, *mes enfants,* I don't know about you, but I'm gravely in need of a drink, and I don't mean tea. Besides, this has all served to concentrate my mind. Everything's perfectly clear to me now, and there are propositions I wish to put to you and Steven concerning the future."

"Propositions?"

"I thought that maybe when you and Steven are married, you'd like to come to live at Castle Liscoole." Smiling, he put his arm around his sister, and ushered her away toward the drawing room.

He glanced back at Laura, but didn't say anything, and suddenly she felt excluded. She remained where she was as Steven went out too, and as they entered the drawing room she felt more shut out than ever. Blair hadn't even said her name when he looked back. It was as if he didn't want her to go with them, because there was no place for her in the future he spoke of; that future concerned only him, Marianna, and Steven . . .

Oh, surely she was imagining it? She took a hesitant step after them, then halted. He *had* excluded her. Why else had he looked back like that and said nothing? Tears sprang to her eyes. She was already overwrought, and now this. Upset and bewildered, she gathered her skirts and fled up to her room on the floor above. There she flung herself on the bed and sobbed her heartbreak into her pillow.

But in the library, things were not quite as they seemed. Steven's examination of Estelle had been too cursory, for there was a slight movement beneath the dust sheet, and her thin hand crept out to claw the carpet for a moment.

She wasn't quite conscious, but soon she would be. And she had just enough strength left to take Celina and Deveril Park itself into the hereafter with her.

Twenty-three

It seemed to Laura she'd lain there weeping for a long time, but in reality only a few minutes had passed. Desolation gripped her as she tried to understand the change in Blair, who seemed to have abruptly consigned her to the past as much as Celina and Deveril Park.

Too late she realized her modern ideals simply couldn't be applied to the Regency world. Maybe Blair *had* loved her for a while, but Lord Sivintree's open contempt was a sharp reminder that a respectable widow was one thing, a member of the chorus at the Hannover quite another. It *did* matter what she'd been before meeting him, and he'd hidden his true feelings until Miles had been dealt with. Now he was showing his hand. Restoring her family's property and defraying their debts was nothing more than payment for services rendered. The proverbial money on the dressing table!

This was an outcome she hadn't foreseen. She'd naively pictured either an idyllic existence at Blair's side, or dreadful loneliness because of his death, but not the possibility of rejection.

"Laura?"

She gave a start, for he was outside the door.

"Laura? Why don't you answer me?"

She sat up. "I—I have a headache, and need to rest a while, that's all," she replied, but couldn't hide the break in her voice.

He detected it, and came in immediately. "What is it, Laura?"

She gazed tearfully at him, taking in the dressing on the wound on his forehead.

He came concernedly to her bedside. "You've been crying! What's wrong?" he asked, stretching out a hand to touch her cheek.

She pulled back. "Just a headache," she said again, avoiding his eyes.

"I don't believe you. Is it the strain of today? It can't have been easy for you, and for it to have ended with two deaths—"

"It's the truth, I do have a headache." She hesitated then. "No, the truth is, I realize my presence is no longer required. I'll leave as soon as the authorities are satisfied about today's events."

There was a pause, but she couldn't tell if it was one of startlement or relief. "If you wish to leave, there's nothing I can do to prevent you," he said then.

"Nor anything you'd *wish* to do," she murmured, unable to keep the bitterness from her voice.

He exhaled slowly, and ran his hand through his hair. "Laura, I don't profess to understand why you've changed, but I'll respect your wish."

There seemed genuine bewilderment in his voice, but she remembered the backward glance in the library. He wasn't bewildered at all; he knew *exactly* why she was going to leave. She got up from the bed. "Credit me with at least some intelligence, Blair. I know I've been gullible, but I understand fully now."

"Understand what? Please tell me."

She went to the window and looked out at the stables and kitchen gardens to hide the fresh tears welling in her eyes. The sunlight shone on the wing opposite, where one day the Fitzgeralds would have their private apartment. The spaniels had been lying quietly beneath a walnut tree, but suddenly got up eagerly as Marianna and Steven emerged to take them for a walk. Marianna's head was bowed, and Laura could see she'd been crying. But she gave a brave smile as Steven drew her hand over his sleeve. With the dogs at their heels they went through into the stableyard, then down the hillside.

Blair was disconcerted by the long silence. "Laura, why are you being like this?" he asked. "You say you understand something, but I swear that's more than I do! Please do me the courtesy of explaining."

She rounded on him. "*I* do *you* the courtesy?" she cried incredulously.

His anger stirred. "Yes, dammit. One moment things are good between us, the next you're coldly informing me you intend to leave. I believe I have the right to an explanation."

She struggled not to give in to the torrent of heartbreak pounding through her. "I'd have thought you'd hope a common actress would go quietly, especially when you so graciously intend to pay for her past favors by settling all her family's debts and restoring their home. In your eyes she should know you've been more than generous, and certainly shouldn't be so presumptuous as to hope to join everyone in the drawing room!"

His eyes flashed. "Is *that* what you think? Well, you couldn't be more wrong! I expected you to accompany us to the drawing room, but instead you came up here."

"You spoke of a future that clearly didn't include me; in fact, it couldn't have been made more plain you wished to sever all dealings with someone you now know is nothing more than a common actress!"

He stared at her. "That's nonsense."

"Is it? Steven is suddenly acceptable, yet it isn't that long since his faults were so legion you intended to call him out. Now he's not only welcome to marry Marianna, but to live at Castle Liscoole! There's only one reason for that, Blair—he's a gentleman. Whatever his shortcomings, his breeding makes him suitable. But I'm only an actress, a demirep whose morals don't bear close inspection!"

"Laura, this is arrant nonsense."

"No, you've been thinking about it since Lord Sivintree exposed me. Well, please don't fear I'll make a fuss, for even actresses have dignity."

"Laura, I don't look down on you, nor have I excluded you."

"You didn't *include* me," she pointed out quietly.

"Because I didn't think it had to be put into words. Laura, I thought we were now sufficiently close for you to just know you were included. Clearly, I was wrong."

"You spoke of a future that made no mention of me, then you left the room and glanced back in a way only a fool could misinterpret. Well, I may have been a fool until now, but not anymore." Her voice was shaking so much she found it hard to speak, and she stared out of the window again.

"You've misinterpreted my motives, Laura," he said levelly.

She didn't reply, for her voice wouldn't obey her.

He came a little closer. "I looked back at you because there was so much I wished to say, but couldn't. Good things, Laura, private things that should not be aired in front of anyone else. Far from wishing to *exclude* you from my future, I want you to be part of it. Not as my mistress, or a doxy with whom to amuse myself from time to time, but as my wife."

Her heart stopped, and she turned. "As your wife?" she breathed.

"I can't believe you ever imagined I'd want anything less."

"Oh, Blair . . ."

"You misunderstood completely, didn't you?" he said quietly.

"Yes," she said in a small voice.

He held her gaze. "And what is your answer now things have been explained?"

"Do you still want me after I've been so foolish?" she whispered.

He teased her gently. "Well, although I know you're only a very common actress—indeed, little better than a Seven Dials strumpet who charges a farthing for her dubious favors—you're also the most precious thing in my world, and I want you to live with me in Castle Liscoole as Lady Deveril."

She hardly knew she'd run to him, only that she was in his arms. "Oh, forgive me, Blair, forgive me . . ."

He held her tightly. "Do I take it I'm accepted?"

"Yes! Oh, yes!"

He smiled into her tear-filled but suddenly joyous eyes. "I adore you, Laura Reynolds, and I need you with me night and day. I need you now," he added softly, bending his head to kiss the soft white skin at the base of her throat.

"I need you too," she whispered, taking his hand and leading him to the bed.

Their lovemaking was tender and fulfilling, and when they lay in each other's arms afterward, there were no words, just an adoring embrace. The warmth and quiet of the early evening drifted over them, their eyes closed, and they fell asleep.

In the library, full consciousness at last returned to Estelle. Gasping with pain and weakness, she crawled from beneath the sheet, then dragged herself to her feet. Pain touched the swaying room with scarlet, and she could feel her life blood ebbing away as her tormented glance fell upon Celina's picture. Hatred renewed her strength. She saw the buckets of paint and varnish, the faintly glowing embers in the hearth, and the little jar of wooden spills on the mantelshelf.

She gazed at the portrait again, and an uneven laugh rose through her. "Miles is mine forever, and so is this house!

You didn't know that, did you? *I'm* mistress of Deveril Park now! I bought your domain so I could destroy it, and now you're going to die in the flames with me, Celina. You made my life a hell; now I'll make a hell of your death . . ."

Summoning all her strength, she seized a bucket of varnish in both hands and flung it over the portrait. Then her skeletal fingers closed over the slender spills, and she sank exhaustedly to her knees in the pools of varnish in the hearth to hold the wands of wood to the embers.

They burst into flames that reflected in her eyes as she sat back on her heels. Varnish soaked into her flowing black clothes, but she didn't care as she tossed the lighted spills up at the portrait, which burst into immediate flame.

Content that at last her hated rival was perishing in eternal damnation, Estelle clasped her hands joyfully. "Burn, whore, burn!" she breathed as the flames blistered the face on the portrait.

After that she didn't move as the fire licked around her, nor did she feel as her black gauze clothing ignited. She knew nothing, for her life had expired as she knelt there.

After consuming the portrait, the hungry flames moved on to the bookshelves, then the curtains and the furniture. In minutes, the whole library was a furnace that could never be extinguished, and Deveril Park was consigned to its fate.

Smoke stole out onto the landing, inching toward Miles's body as it lay awaiting examination by the authorities, but on the floor above, Laura and Blair slept on in each other's arms, oblivious to the fact that soon the staircases would be an impassable inferno.

Marianna and Steven were walking back up toward the house with the spaniels. Marianna was a little happier now, although anxious about whether the Cirencester authorities would believe their version of how Miles and his wife had died. Steven would also be glad when that part of it was over, but didn't doubt the outcome would be as they wished.

The May evening was tranquil, and the calls of the peacocks drifted over the park. The Mercury Fair had been audible too, though they hadn't heard it for nearly a quarter of an hour now. It was early for the merrymaking to finish, Steven thought, but only with passing curiosity because he preferred to think of the wonderful future that now stretched ahead for Marianna and him, provided the deaths of Miles and Estelle could be satisfactorily dealt with. He knew that Blair's offer of a home at Castle Liscoole was the perfect thing, and hoped his own private guess—that Blair intended to propose to Laura, and she'd accept—was correct. The four of them could exist very companionably together, and if, after the nuptials, their numbers increased, well, so much the better.

He wished he could contribute more to his marriage than gambling debts, poor health, and an overwhelming love for the young woman at his side. He prayed the latter would be sufficient to eliminate the former, because there was nothing he wouldn't do for Marianna, and if it were in his power to make her happy, then he'd do it gladly to the end of his days.

The spaniels suddenly came to an uneasy standstill, stared up the hill and began to whine. Marianna halted too. "What it it?" she said, her yellow skirts whispering as she bent to them.

Steven gazed up at the house and saw smoke billowing from several open windows on the second floor. "Dear God, there's a fire!" Blair and Laura! Seizing one of Marianna's hands, he began to run up the hillside. The spaniels dashed ahead, barking loudly.

There was a reason why Steven hadn't heard the fair for a while now. The smoke had been seen from the village green, and people came running down the drive as he and Marianna reached the front of the house. There was no sign of Blair or Laura, and Steven ran to the main entrance, accompanied by Ha'penny Jack, but then there was an explosion of glass overhead as several landing windows burst. The two men ducked and shielded their heads as shining splinters cascaded around them. The onlookers gasped as the ferocity of the newly liberated flames told of the fire's extent. Everyone knew Deveril Park couldn't be saved.

Steven and the showman pressed bravely on, but found the entrance hall full of choking smoke, and as they reached the staircase one of the landing chandeliers fell with a crash as the flames devoured the ceiling. The fire was beginning to creep down the staircase handrail, but Steven ran forward again. He had to get to Blair and Laura! The heat singed his hair and eyebrows, and he stumbled back, coughing and retching from the smoke. Ha'penny Jack dragged him away, and they staggered outside again.

No one in the crowd spoke, for words couldn't express the way they felt as the great house went to its doom.

In Laura's third-floor room, there was little sign yet of the conflagration below, but the falling chandelier disturbed Blair's sleep. His eyes opened, and he became aware that the hair on the back of his neck was stirring unpleasantly. Something was wrong he sat up.

Laura awoke too. "What is it?" she whispered, seeing the unease on his face.

He drew her hand briefly to his lips. "Wait here," he said, then slipped from the bed and went to the door. He saw the first tendrils of smoke creeping along the passage.

"Sweet God above," he breathed, and hurried toward the staircase. He heard the crackle of flames, and looked down at the inferno. Thick acrid smoke choked the air, and the heat was unendurable.

He ran back to Laura, and closed the door. She was sitting up nervously, her eyes wide and apprehensive. "Is—is that smoke I can smell?"

"Yes. The house is on fire."

Her heart lurched, and she got up slowly from the bed.

How could she have forgotten that fire would destroy most of Deveril Park?

Blair went to the window. The kitchen garden and stables were deserted, and so far the windows directly below were intact, although one or two further along had burst and flames were licking out. Returning to the bed, he dragged the sheets off and began to tie them together.

Laura's lips parted. "We're going to climb down?" she gasped.

"We have no choice."

"But we're on the third floor!"

"We'll manage somehow, but we must be quick. If the windows of the room below us should blow, we won't be able to get past."

He attached a blanket to the sheets, and when he'd used all the bedding, he tied one end of the makeshift rope to the bed. More windows shattered on the floor below, and he looked out hurriedly to see if their escape route was still safe. All seemed well, so he lowered the rope, then held his hand out to her.

She hesitated. "I—I don't think I can do it!"

He pulled her briefly into his arms. "We'll go down together," he said softly, brushing his lips over hers. "Now, sit on the window ledge, with your legs on the outside."

She did as he said, trying not to look down as he joined her. Then he turned away from her. "Hold me, and I'll carry you."

She circled her shaking arms around his shoulders, and closed her eyes. There was a loud splintering of glass, and then the roar of flames as another nearby window burst from the heat. Then she felt Blair slip from the ledge onto the rope, and take both their weights.

Suddenly there were shouts from the stableyard as people came from the front of the house and saw them escaping, but Laura kept her eyes tightly closed. She heard Marianna and Steven calling out, and the spaniels barking, but nothing would induce her to look.

Blair lowered them both very slowly toward the next window. He knew it wouldn't be long before the heat proved too much. When that happened, and the flames licked out, the rope would soon catch fire . . . His arms shook with the effort as he continued toward the ground as quickly as he could, and at last helping hands reached out to take Laura almost fainting from his back.

The window above exploded, and everyone dashed back to safety as hot glass scattered like hail.

Blair caught Laura close again, his smoke-marked lips moving tenderly against her forehead as he watched Deveril Park burn. A thick column of smoke stained the summer sky, and the roar seemed to shake the hillside.

The fire didn't raze Deveril Park entirely to the ground, but left the L-shape that would one day become the hotel, and no one would ever know exactly how the house came to burn down, though it was suspected a spark from the library hearth had somehow ignited paint and varnish left too close.

The authorities accepted the story of how Miles and Estelle died. Miles's obsession with Celina was well known, so it wasn't doubted that Estelle killed her husband out of jealousy, or that he'd managed to fire back and take her with him.

As far as ownership of Deveril Park was concerned, Estelle's wish for anonymity endured after her death, and this together with a dispute among her and Miles's prospective heirs, preserved the mystery for twenty-five years, until the courts eventually settled the inheritance upon one of her distant cousins. In the meantime, the once magnificent house had lain in ruins in its overgrown park, a neglected corner of the Cotswolds that in 1850 was at last sold to a Victorian gentleman who turned it into a farm.

But the house kept its secrets, and over the years the mystery began. The fire and the deaths were reported in the local press, but then the newspaper's own premises were burned to the ground, and the records destroyed. The Deveril Park fire was forgotten, and people started to wonder how and why such a magnificent property had become a farmhouse only a third its size. The enigma of the lost mansion became another local puzzle, like the skeleton in the secret vault at Minster Lovell, the ghosts at Littledean Hall, and the similar disappearance of another great Cotswold house, Cassey Compton.

At the beginning of 1817, after spending the intervening months at their London residence in Berkeley Square, Sir Blair and the second Lady Deveril moved across the Irish Sea to Castle Liscoole. With them went Mr. and Mrs. Steven Woodville.

Many of the servants from Deveril Park also chose to start anew in Ireland, including Mr. and Mrs. Harcourt. Gulliver was happy with Dolly, and, like Laura, didn't regret exchanging the future for the past. For a while he was afraid that he'd be whisked away again to the confines of his hated wheelchair, but it didn't happen. For both Laura and him the travels in time ended with the fire, as if the destruction of Deveril Park brought everything to a close.

But before leaving for Ireland, Laura was to experience one more fleeting brush with time, not a journey to the future, but a close encounter that somehow served only to confirm that the astonishing adventures were over.

It happened in Blair's Berkeley Square townhouse, on the eve of their departure. Blair had already gone up to their bedroom, while she lingered downstairs to finish a letter to her "parents" in Norwich. An hour passed before she went up to join him. It was a hot August night, and the windows stood open to the square, where the leaves of the famous plane trees were motionless beneath the starry sky. Blair had fallen asleep naked on the bed, his body pale against the embroidered satin.

She paused in the entrance of what would one day be the Art Deco living room of an apartment occupied by four actresses. Instead of hooves and carriage wheels outside, there would be traffic noise of a very different kind. She drew a thoughtful breath. Her life in the future seldom crossed her mind, but tonight for some reason it felt near.

For a moment a finger of alarm touched her. Was she going to go back again? No, please . . . She closed her eyes, fearing to hear the sound of the square change, but nothing happened, there were still just hooves and carriage wheels on cobbles.

She looked again, and something drew her attention to the mirror above the fireplace. With a start she saw her future self looking at her. It was the moment after the gala fund-raising night at the Hannover, when modern Laura had looked into the mirror and seen her Regency counterpart, except now it was the other way around, and she *was* her Regency counterpart! She remembered what happened next too! Smiling at herself in the mirror, she slipped out of her clothes and lay down next to Blair.

He didn't stir as she bent over to kiss his thigh. Her yearning fingers moved gently between his legs, sliding richly into the moist forest of hair that grew there. Desire kindled irresistibly through her as she kissed his thigh again. Still he did not stir. Her hand crept to touch his dormant maleness. How soft and quiescent it was, how immeasurably inviting . . .

She kissed it, then moved her lips gently to the tip, toying with it with her tongue before taking it fully into her mouth. She trembled with excitement and desire as she stole an intimacy of which he knew nothing.

But he soon awoke as arousal began to flood into him, and he arched with pleasure as her tongue and lips made free with his willing body.

"You take shameless liberties, madam," he whispered, "but tonight *I* intend to be the master."

Before she knew it, he'd rolled her quickly onto her back, and was straddling her, pinning her arms back as he smiled down into her eyes. "You're a very forward hussy, Lady Deveril," he murmured.

"Fie, sir, for I am but an innocent," she whispered seductively.

"Are you, indeed? Then I must teach you how to be a little wicked," he breathed, bending his head to kiss her parted lips.

For a fleeting moment she glanced toward the mirror, but when she saw her future self had gone, she gave herself up to his lovemaking.